The Amish Doll

AMISH KNITTING NOVEL

Karen Anna Vogel

Lamb Books

He restores my soul

The Amish Doll: Amish Knitting Novel

© 2012 by Karen Anna Vogel
Second Edition 2013 by Lamb Books
ISBN-13:978-0615930640
ISBN-10: 0615930646

Contact the author on Facebook at: www.facebook.com/VogelReaders
Learn more the author at: www.karenannavogel.com
Visit her blog, Amish Crossings, at
www.karenannavogel.blogspot.com

DEDICATION
This book dedicated is Marilyn and Jim Rowland, my neighbors in Ellington, New York, who reached out to all the kids who piled on their porch to sip lemonade, talk, and feel loved.

OTHER BOOKS BY KAREN ANNA VOGEL

Continuing Serials:
Amish Knitting Circle: Smicksburg Tales 1
Amish Knitting Circle: Smicksburg Tales 2
Amish Knit Lit Circle: Smicksburg Tales 3
Amish Knit & Stitch Circle: Smicksburg Tales 4 coming 2014
Novels:
Knit Together: Amish Knitting Novel
The Amish Doll: Amish Knitting Novel
Novellas:
Amish Knitting Circle Christmas: Granny & Jeb's Love Story
Amish Pen Pals: Rachael's Confession
Christmas Union: Quaker Abolitionist of Chester County, PA

"Author Karen Vogel has approached the often misunderstood beliefs or the Amish with tact and tenderness, and I highly recommend this heart-stirring story."

Kathi Macias award-winning author of 35 novels, including *Deliver Me from Evil* and *A Christmas Journey Home*

"Karen writes with heart-touching insight and her characters are gripping. Highly recommended."

Jennifer Hudson Taylor, author of *Highland Blessings & Highland Sanctuary*

AMISH – ENGLISH DICTIONARY

Pennsylvania Dutch dialect is used throughout this book, common to the Amish of Western Pennsylvania. You may want to refer to this little dictionary from time to time.

ach – oh
Ausbund – Amish hymn book
boppli – baby
brieder - brothers
bruder - brother
daed - dad
danki – thank you
dawdyhaus – grandfather house
Die Botschaft – An Amish weekly newspaper
dochder – daughter
Gmay - community
Guder mariye. Good morning.
goot - good
jah - yes
kapp- cap; Amish women's head covering
kinner - children
maedel - maid
mamm – mom
oma – grandma
opa - grandfather
Ordnung – order; set of unwritten rules
rumspringa – running around years, starting at sixteen, when Amish youth experience the Outsiders' way of life before joining the church.
wunderbar – wonderful
yinz – plural for you, common among Western Pennsylvania Amish and English. A *Pittsburghese* word.
Anabaptist – "Radical Reformers" in the 16th century who were baptized again as believing adults. Contemporary denominations include Amish, Hutterites, Mennonites and Brethren.
Dordrecht Confession of Faith – Amish and Mennonite doctrinal beliefs, also called the "Eighteen Articles"

TABLE OF CONTENTS

The Amish Doll

Chapter 1

Joshua Yoder yanked at the hand crank water pump and filled the pan with water. Then he sat it on the woodstove to heat. He stared out the kitchen window at the barn swallows and sighed. They were free to come and go as they pleased. As soon as the thought entered his mind he felt selfish. His *mamm* was ill and it was a blessing to care for her. But he just couldn't believe she wanted to take in foster kids. The article she read in the *Die Botschaft* about Amish families taking in foster children had touched her heart…but now? When she was so ill?

Joshua stirred the soup he was preparing. In the last stage of kidney failure her diet was so restricted; he had a hard time coming up with something she was allowed to eat. Joshua took a wooden spoon and tasted it. Too bland. He walked over to the blue pantry that extended from the ceiling to the floor. He grabbed dried sage, parsley, and thyme all in pint size mason jars, and stood a second to take inventory. He counted the beans, peas, jams, pears, and apples he'd already put up. Then he thought of all the other fruits and vegetables that needed harvested, and his heart sank.

How he wished he had a wife to help shoulder this burden. Joshua thought of Lottie Miller as he sprinkled the herbs in the soup. It was probably a good thing she called off their courtship last year. A girl who felt neglected because he was caring for his *mamm* was not the girl for him. He ladled the soup in a bowl to take upstairs to his *mamm* and noticed, as he ascended, the white paint was chipping on the wall. He'd have to wait until after harvest to make repairs.

When he entered his *mamm's* room he saw she was asleep, so he placed the soup on the ornately carved wood tray his *daed* had made for her, and then sat in the chair near her bed. She didn't have her prayer *kapp* on and he noticed her blond hair was more heavily speckled with gray every day, but she was still such a beautiful woman. *Daed* had always said her big light blue eyes first drew him, but it was her kindness and strength that made him pursue. He knew she was born with only one-half of a kidney functioning; the other one was shriveled up and dead. They might never have their own children, but it didn't matter to him. He loved her. She ended up having two children, risking her life, as gifts to her husband. Joshua's sister's offer to have their parents live in Ohio with her so he would have more time to find the right girl and settle down ran through his mind. You're twenty-four and need to find a wife, she harped. But he objected. His *mamm* deserved to be in her home, in a familiar setting.

He saw his *mamm* open her heavy eyes to look warmly at him then shut them again. He knew it took strength for her to wake up. Joshua put his hand on hers and prayed the Lord would help. That by some chance they'd hear that a match came in and she could get a transplant. Susanna opened her eyes again and smiled at him. "*Danki* for the soup. Smells like chicken," she said, her voice faint.

"When you get better, I want you to make sage chicken again. I crave it at times."

"Lord willing, Joshua, Lord willing. No kidney matches yet..."

"But I hear several more people are getting tested this week. Let's hope someone's a match."

She slowly sat up and took the tray. "How do you feel about the foster boys?"

"Couldn't we get a girl who can cook?"

Susanna bit her lower lip. "Why don't you admit you like to cook?"

Joshua looked at her loving eyes. Any boy who got to have a *mamm* like his for even a little while would be blessed. "I'm ready to take one boy if you are..."

~*~

Raven looked intently on the new red sweater she was knitting for her ragdoll. Her stomach turned. At twenty-four, she was still trying to find where home was. When would she knit the last sweater for her ragdoll?

Some of her long hair fell on the knitting and she pushed it away, but then took a piece of it. She needed to get mahogany highlights again? The black of her hair always took over. But what did she care? She no longer had a boyfriend who cared about her looking Native American. Brandon told people she was French. How did she date him, even consider marriage, for so long?

Her grandparents were Native American, and she was now living back in the area she vowed never to return, Western New York. But her ethnic group was well represented, and respected. She'd keep her hair black. Her mind turned to her grandmother, who'd twisted her hair into two braids every morning before school. Raven knew she'd been a burden to raise and it shortened her grandmother's life. Her grandfather died of grief soon after.

Yes, her black hair brought back many memories, some not so good. Little Half-Breed, her cousins called her, half Seneca Indian and half white. She was fair skinned, compared to other Native Americans and her grandmother assumed she got it from her father...her green eyes too.

Raven cast off the yarn and put the sweater on her doll and placed it right on her bed. No more hiding it, afraid Brandon would make some demeaning joke. No, she was in the land of snow, and he was in the land of sun, Florida, and for that, she was glad.

But Raven had to sigh inwardly. She couldn't believe she accepted this job as a social worker in the very place she vowed never to return. She'd spent so many years in foster homes scattered across Cattaraugus and Chautauqua counties for nine years, until she was eighteen and on her own. Maybe she was rash in accepting the first offer. But she could no longer tolerate Brandon and his temper.

She got up and went to her new dresser, parted her hair down the middle and picked her favorite bronze antique barrette, pulled her hair in a bunch at the nape of her neck, and clipped it on. She turned to take a second look at her new room. Light mint walls with a red floral border all around the top. Cherry woodwork around all the windows and doors. Living in a Victorian mansion wasn't something on her bucket list. She preferred a log cabin in the woods, not a small town, picture perfect out of a Thomas Kinkade painting.

She heard Mrs. Rowe calling from downstairs that breakfast was ready. She looked again at her room. Boxes that needed unpacked stared her down. After meeting the boys and taking a short jog, she'd start unpacking. Work didn't start until tomorrow, but she didn't want to appear lazy and that she wasn't earning her keep.

She opened her door and looked down at the ornate red carpet in the hallway. She hadn't noticed it when she came in last night. Why not brown carpet, the same color as dirt, with boys running all over it? Walking down the long hallway, she ran her fingers along the fancy red and green wallpaper, as smooth as satin. How could the state afford something so grand? As she reached the beautifully carved staircase, she saw an elderly gentleman standing at the bottom of the steps, smiling up at her.

"I was going to come up to see if you escaped using the emergency fire ladders. Having second thoughts about being here?"

His smile was more in his eyes than anywhere and it captured her gaze as she descended the stairs. "I'm not having second thoughts. Sorry I'm late for work." She extended her hand. "I'm Raven Meadow. Do you work for the state too?"

He took her hand and cupped it with his other. "I work in a state of chaos a lot but no, not for the state of New York. I'm Jim Rowe. I'm married to Marilyn."

Raven still was transfixed with Mr. Rowe's twinkling hazel eyes. "You own this house? I thought it was owned by the state."

"No, it's a privately run non-profit home. We've been housing boys here for years. We try to keep a low profile but the boys seem to make the house scream for attention from the neighbors. Always testing the boundaries."

Raven clasped her hands in front of her. "So, Mr. Rowe, I'm working for you? Are you the man who interviewed me over the phone?"

"The very one and I liked you right off the bat. I knew you could empathize with hurting children after you told me you'd been in foster homes. You've had a good education, too, Masters in Social Work."

Mrs. Rowe opened the kitchen door with a huff. "Doesn't anyone take me seriously? I yelled breakfast was ready fifteen minutes ago."

"I'm sorry Mrs. Rowe. I got down as soon as I could," Raven said.

Mrs. Rowe looked at her puzzled. "I'm not talking to you, dear; I'm talking about those boys most likely still sleeping upstairs. They need to eat before the bus comes." She paused to take a breath. "I am so glad you're here." She winked at Raven. "Call me Marilyn."

"Okay. I'm more than willing to help. Do you want me to go upstairs and get the boys?"

Jim put up his hand in protest. "They're not babies. The youngest is ten and able to set an alarm clock. When I was their age I was up at the crack of dawn selling apples. Kids are pampered too much today."

"You and your Great Depression stories. I bet you were late a day or two," Marilyn said.

"And I learned by the age of ten there were consequences to my behavior."

"Ten? I thought it was twelve. Next time you tell that story you'll be selling apples in the dead of winter in your diapers. Exaggeration is the same as a white lie and you know what the Good Book says about that." She pinched his cheek in a playful way, and then cupped her hands around her mouth and aimed upstairs. "Boys, get up. The bus is here!" she yelled.

"It never amazes me that for a little thing, you can yell so loud," Jim said leaning over to pat her curly silver hair. She pushed his arm away, hiding a smile. The sound of doors slamming echoed through the downstairs entry way. The boys came running down the stairs, tripping over each other.

"You boys walk. We don't want an avalanche on our hands," Jim said firmly.

The boys slowed down and walked out the front door, books in tow. Then in unison they all turned around and tried to hide their laughter. "She did it again! Blast it," one of the boys yelled. "The bus isn't here."

"Ha, I got you up, though," Marilyn said, very happy with herself. "Now you boys sit down in the kitchen and eat your breakfast - cold."

A round of complaints circled the room. "This is not a hotel boys; how many times do I have to say it? I am not Paula Deen with her southern hospitality. Now go sit down, say grace, and eat."

The boys walked forlornly into the kitchen and closed the door. "I'll heat your eggs up, Raven. Don't worry. I'm trying to teach them a lesson."

Raven crossed her arms. "How can you make a child pray if he doesn't want to?"

"Excuse me, dear. I don't understand your meaning."

"You told the boys to say grace. Isn't that an infringement on their rights?"

"Saying grace before a meal never hurt anyone," Jim said. "We're Christians and own and run this house like we see fit."

Raven narrowed her gaze. "Why didn't you tell me when I interviewed?"

"I didn't think you'd have any objections. Our other workers never have." He scratched the back of his neck. "You don't have to pray or read a Bible to work here."

Raven didn't know what to do or say, but she knew she wanted to run. After breakfast she'd run her jog and try to figure out why she was so irritated at the Rowes this very moment.

~*~

Joshua scattered cracked corn to the chickens in the henhouse. He could just dump the whole bag in the feeder, but he relished the time in the barn. He heard footsteps and turned to see his *daed*, pulling his long beard.

"Son, are you sure you can handle foster kids? Sometimes I think we're being selfish, asking you to take on more responsibility." He leaned up against the cow stall.

"You know what the doc said. Her will to live is important. I haven't seen her so excited about anything in years."

"Do you think it's all the medicine though? Maybe she's not thinking right."

Joshua threw the rest of the corn at the chickens and picked up the metal bucket and walked into the cow stall. After wiping down the udder and smoothing down the cow's side, he started to squirt milk into the bucket.

He saw his *daed* look over into the stall. "I think you need to be the one who goes to Appleton. Jim Rowe will give you an honest opinion about what you're getting into. We can always get girls, too; we don't have to limit ourselves to Appleton."

Joshua leaned against the cow for support. "*Jah*, a girl would be *goot*, but *mamm* wants an Appleton boy since Jim and Marilyn run it. They'll make sure a well behaved boy will come live here."

"You mean boys. Your *mamm* thinks one would feel too lonely. Ask about two or three boys."

Joshua closed his eyes and said a prayer.

~*~

Raven smelt the crisp autumn air as she ran down Main Street. She didn't need to wear a scarf, but she'd made this one on the plane coming up, and couldn't wait. The multicolored yarn was on sale, but she marveled at what a nice speckled-like pattern it turned into. I wish my life could form a nice pattern. She pulled the scarf tighter around her neck; she always felt like Granny Nora, one of the few people she bonded with in foster care, was hugging her. She'd taught Raven to knit when she was eleven.

Raven saw pumpkins displayed on the grand front porches of the Victorian homes. She remembered the pumpkins she used to carve with her grandmother. The roasted seeds were always eaten at the Harvest Festival, a time to celebrate the protection the Great Spirit had given over their small farms. She sighed and tried not to think too unkindly of Mr. Rowe when he said the house was a Christian house, but Christianity was what divided people, not brought them together. Didn't religion cause most wars?

She soon saw the town square Mrs. Rowe had told her about. It was a grassy square in the center of town with a gazebo in the middle. A white banner hung in between two large oak trees, *Annual Fall Festival, October 24-26.* Well, she had two weeks to come up with an excuse not to go, even though the Rowe's said they haven't missed it in forty years.

She ran past three antique shops, a craft store, book store, library, and convenience store, but stopped when she saw the Ellington Congregational Church. The white clapboard church with a soaring steeple with a cross on the top, caught her eye. When she looked down, she saw a man come out of the church. He was tall and lanky, walking so fast he was soon to the sidewalk where she stood. He had a Bible tucked under his arm with several notebooks. "Hello there. Can I help you?" he asked.

"Oh, no, I'm just jogging and stopped to admire the steeple. Sure is tall," Raven said.

He extended his hand. "I'm Lawrence Turner, pastor of this church, and your name is?"

She shook his large hand. "I'm Raven Meadows. I just moved here to work at Appleton Children's Home."

"So, you're the new social worker then?" he asked, his dark brown eyes inquiring to know more.

"Well, yes. I came last night. I thought I'd jog around town to see what it looks like."

"And what do you think?"

"It's very quaint. Charming," she said.

"I was smitten by the town when I moved here to be pastor of this church," he said. "Folks are friendly to a young pastor and have me over for dinner most Sundays."

"Well, I better get going. Don't want to keep you," she said.

"So I'll be seeing you at Bible Study with the boys?"

"No, I'm not religious," she said, nervously twisting her hair between her fingers.

"Well, the boys from Appleton come here every Wednesday night and they need a chaperon. The other social workers always came."

Raven felt heat rise to her cheeks. "It's not in my job description," she said evenly. "If you don't mind, I need to get going."

Lawrence smiled. "Well, it was nice to meet you, Raven. Hope to see you again soon."

She nodded and continued to jog past a large hardware store. She could hear her heart pound in her ears and when orange and yellow leaves swirled up at her she swatted them with her hand. I will not attend this local Christian church.

As she turned the corner to head back to Appleton, Raven thought she saw a black van, but on closer inspection, it was an Amish buggy. When she reached the house she saw a handsome Amish man with blue eyes peeping through long blonde bangs. "Hello, can I help you?"

"*Jah*, I suppose. I'm Joshua Yoder." He took off his straw hat and shook her hand. "We'd like to apply to be foster parents."

She felt light headed. Not only was she working in a Christian home, but now the Amish wanted to be foster parents. She motioned for him to walk up and have a seat on the front porch. "Let me get this straight. You're Amish and want to be considered for foster care?" She collapsed on one of the white wicker chairs. "Need help on the farm?"

Joshua nodded. "A child raised on a farm learns a lot about life. It's *goot* for them."

Jim came out of the house, and put his hand up. "Hello Joshua, how's your mom?"

"She needs that miracle we talked about."

Jim nodded. "We're praying hard." He turned toward her. "Raven, I've known this Amish family for years. They're not asking for a boy to work to death, but honestly believe hard work and being close to God and nature is good. I tend to agree."

She glared at Mr. Rowe, then looked politely at Joshua. "I'll get you the application." She went inside and got some paperwork from the box labeled "desk stuff". When she went back out on the porch she heard Joshua talking to Mr. Rowe.

"Here's a couple dozen ears of corn. I figured the boys would enjoy it." Joshua turned to look at her and their eyes locked. His eyes seemed to want to reach out and help her, for some reason. But why? She lowered her gaze and handed him the paperwork. "Well, we'll get this paperwork done and returned in no time," Joshua said.

"The background criminal check will take a while," Raven said. "Get that done first."

"But that can be faxed and the whole process expedited. I'll pay the expense," Jim said.

"*Danki*," Joshua nodded. "I'd best be going. Have more corn to pick. I'll bring more over in a few days."

Jim waved at Joshua as he left. "You were awfully rude to my friend, Raven. Why? The Amish are wonderful people."

Raven took her hair out of a ponytail and shook it free. She remembered some Amish men coming to the reservation. Her grandfather didn't like them. They were cowards and wouldn't fight the men, instead standing silent as they were slapped around. She didn't think they'd make good role models for the boys at Appleton. "I've never cared for them. They're strange, still living in the Dark Ages."

"When you get to know them, your opinion will change. They're good Christian people."

Raven felt fury heavy on her cheeks. "I met Lawrence, your pastor. He asked me if I'd chaperone the boys on Wednesday and I said no. I'm not religious and if I'd know this was a Christian home…"

Jim's eyebrows shot up. "You'd what?"

"Maybe have turned down the job…"

"I see…are you of a different religion?" he asked.

"If I had to pick one, it would be the one of my ancestors: the Longhouse religion I grew up with. I'm half Native American. I'd deny my roots by being a Christian." Fatigue ran through her from head to toe and she excused herself, wanting to lie down in her room

Chapter 2

Joshua drove down Main Street and thought of Raven. Was she prejudiced against the Amish, or was she just cold toward everyone? He prayed that she didn't treat the boys like she'd treated him. Certainly Jim wouldn't hire someone who was unkind. Maybe she was having a rough time adjusting to her new job. He silently prayed for her, and then he prayed for a kidney match for his *mamm*.

Soon he passed Eb's house. When would he come to his senses and repent before the People? He missed talking to him, but Eb was under the ban. No amount of persuading could convince Eb that God hadn't forgotten him. Yes, he'd suffered great loss, but to go down the road of sin wasn't right under any circumstances.

He saw Eb on the front porch and couldn't help but wave, but he soon saw he was drinking again. Didn't he realize that he could ruin his liver with all this alcohol? Joshua felt like stopping and having words with him, to talk sense into him. His *mamm* secretly tried. She saw life as a gift and hated to see people abusing their bodies. Eb never listened to anyone.

To his surprise, Eb walked toward the road, waving for him to stop. He looked straight ahead until Eb ran up by his horse. "Do you have any money I can borrow?"

Joshua wished he could talk to him but didn't look his way, until the buggy stopped. Eb had taken the horse by the bridle.

"I'm flat broke," Eb said. "Need to go get some pills from Doc Mast, but don't have the money."

Joshua glanced over at him. He knew he shouldn't but Eb always grabbed his heart. When he was a kid, Eb played marbles with him. He was the one who helped him get over his fear of plowing behind a draft horse. "How much?"

"Twenty dollars," Eb said, green eyes filled with shame.

"This is for medicine and not alcohol, right?" Joshua knew from his *rumspringa* years this amount of money was more than enough to make a man drunk.

"Absolutely. I've never lied to you Joshua, you know that."

Joshua knew exactly what Eb meant. He'd lied to Eb several times growing up. Being neighbors, he helped with chores since Eb only had a daughter. How many times had he cut corners to make his work faster? How many times had Eb sat him down, like a father, and read him an Amish parable about honesty? His teaching had set him straight. How could he do the same for him now? "I don't have twenty dollars on me, but I'll put it in the hiding place, alright?"

He saw Eb look up at him with warm misty eyes. "I miss you, Son."

Joshua wanted to get down off the buggy and embrace this dear man, even give him a holy kiss on the cheek, but how could he? Eb wasn't leading a holy life. He looked at the car that pulled into Eb's driveway. He saw it was Lawrence Turner. Maybe the English pastor could help him.

~*~

Raven shook each boy's hand and told them to take a seat in the large living room. She looked at the overstuffed chairs and felt they were calling her to lie down and take a nap. "I want you boys to know that all the rules I've written down are fixed and not changeable. But if you ever need to talk to me, just let me know. I grew up in several foster homes and understand your feelings of being invisible. I want you to know that I see you." She turned to Jim and waited for him to comment, but he didn't. "Mr. Rowe has provided you with a wonderful home but you all want to be placed in foster homes, is that correct?" She saw all six heads nod in agreement. "Can I ask one of you to share why you don't want to live here until you're eighteen? It's a beautiful place."

She saw a small framed boy with mousy, straight brown hair in his eyes raise his hand. "You're Timmy, right?"

"Yes. Ma'am," he said.

She looked at her chart. "At twelve, what makes you want to be put in another home?"

He looked puzzled. "Everybody wants a real family. A place to belong, right? We hear some foster kids get adopted."

17

Raven's breath caught in a gasp. He said out loud something she was never able to say...a place to belong. She willed back tears. No foster parent ever wanted to adopt her. She asked if anyone else had a reason they wanted to be adopted. Another hand went up. "Yes?"

"I'm Chad, but everyone calls me Bud. I'm eleven." He looked over at Mr. Rowe and his chubby cheeks swelled up as he smiled. "It's nothing against Mr. Rowe and he knows it. We all like it here, but we agree with what Timmy said. We want a permanent mom and dad."

Another boy raised his hand. "*Ya*, one that will be with you after you turn eighteen," he said.

Barely able to speak, Raven asked him his name. "Charles, but everyone calls me Chuckey. Oh, and I'm twelve."

Raven straightened herself in her chair. "I have another question. Do you boys know we can take you to Jamestown on Wednesday night for activities? You don't have to do something here in Ellington."

Bud's eyes grew round. "That's Bible Club Night. We love it. Pastor Turner's cool."

"But I see they have karate at the YMCA that night. Wouldn't you boys like to do that?"

A boy shook his white hair so fast she thought he looked like a bobble head doll. "No way. I'm beating everyone in Bible Trivia," he blurted. "Oh, my name is Paul, and everyone calls me Paul, too. I'm eleven."

"How about the rest of you? Doesn't Karate sound like a guy thing to do?" Raven asked.

Bud raised his hand. "We like Bible Club. Jesus was a guy. We think it's a guy thing to do, right Mr. Rowe?"

Jim nodded in agreement, but Raven saw him hide a snicker. She observed the boys, her eyes narrowed. "How is it that all six boys want the same thing? Do they give you candy at Bible Club?"

"No," Bud said. "Pastor Turner gets us some but..." he turned to Jim, "we aren't allowed to take any."

Jim clapped his knee and roared. "Bud, you will not get me to change my mind. You can feel sorry for yourself all you want." He patted his lean stomach. "Some of us are watching our weight, remember?"

Bud glared at Jim, but then laughed. "I know, I know."

Raven wasn't convinced all six boys wanted to go and knew they were being bribed somehow. She'd go to Bible Club and find out for herself. "Okay, so it's Bible Club on Wednesday and the activity for the month is what?"

A short thin boy with a large black afro that matched the color of his skin raised his hand. "The Fall Festival, Ma'am. I'm Toby, and I'm eleven."

"Once again, boys," Raven said. "We have a van and you're not limited to Ellington. We could go to Cockaigne Fall Festival and ride the ski lifts. How about that?"

The boys all shook their heads in disagreement. "We're helping in the festival here," Chuckey said. "We're doing the dunking booth." The boys got up and gave each other high fives. "We're going to dunk Mr. Rowe good," he said with a vengeance, then high fived the boy next to him again.

Raven looked at the boy laughing with Chuckey. He hadn't said a word. "You're Cliff, right?" she asked him.

Cliff's face matched his red-colored hair. He pushed up his wire-rimmed glasses and nodded.

"And how old are you?" Raven asked, empathizing with the boy's shyness.

"Ten," Cliff said.

"Everyone calls him Cliffy, not Cliff though," Chuckey interjected.

Raven hid her grin by putting the pencil to her lips. She remembered her childhood friend, Jody, who she hid behind. Jody always told her Raven would take her "funny bone" if she'd take her "shy bone".

Mr. Rowe looked at his watch and popped out of his chair. "The bus will be here any minute. We need to join hands and pray."

Raven couldn't believe what she'd just heard, but two hands took hers and she heard them take turns praying out loud.

~*~

Raven rubbed her eyes, dreading this day; the Yoder's home visit, and at 6:30 a.m. of all things. She was invited over for breakfast. Jim sure must want them to be foster parents, since he expedited the paperwork so quickly, but why?

She started combing her hair, and thought of Joshua. Yes, he seemed sweet, but why did he seem familiar to her? She'd never been to Cherry Creek or Ellington, thinking both towns were small, so why bother? She spent most of her growing up years in Salamanca or Jamestown.

When her hair was detangled enough, she clipped it back and dressed quickly. Raven looked in her closet and grinned to think the boys wanted to help unpack her things, even women's clothing. She was fond of them already, but of course children were easy to get close to. She scanned her wardrobe and grabbed black pants and a blue blouse, Amish colors. Why did they so freely wear black? She was always told as a child it was a color of magical power and to be feared if misused.

Raven tip-toed down the hallway and steps, not to disturb the boys, and was soon driving down Main Street out toward Cherry Creek. She looked at her GPS. It was only five miles away. She turned on the radio to light jazz and soon started to see some Amish houses. They were all white with navy blue curtains peeping out. Large red barns were built close to the houses. The morning sun shot beams through the thick clouds. Was it a good sign?

She pulled into the Yoder's driveway that was to the right of their house. She saw a man staggering to a large maple tree behind the barn. Was this Mr. Yoder and was he drunk? She saw him reach up into a birdhouse to pull something out. He smiled as he counted money. What on earth? She opened her car door and he turned to look at her, and tears filled his eyes. She heard him call out to her with outstretched arms, "My love." He looked at her as if something from a vision. She ran up the steps onto the Yoder front porch and knocked hard on the door.

Joshua opened the door. "Are you alright, Raven?"

She didn't know what to say, but blurted out, "Is that man out there in the yard your dad?"

"My *Daed's* washing up for breakfast in the utility room." Joshua stepped out on the porch to look across the yard. "I don't see anyone."

"Maybe he was a helper, then," she gasped, her heart in her throat. Her eyes met Joshua's and she felt everything come into focus again and then felt oddly at ease. Stepping inside the house, she looked over the large living room. It was so sparse. No stuffed chairs or couch, only two wooden benches with spindled backs faced each other, separated by a chest-type coffee table. Two Amish rockers were placed in the corners of the room. Oil lamps hung from oak sconces. She found the simplicity charming.

Joshua led her into the kitchen, but when her eyes met Susanna's, she was not prepared. The woman sat in an Amish rocker in the corner next to the wood burning stove. Her light hair was the color of her skin. Her eyelids looked like window shades, half down, but no doubt, the light in her eyes shone through. She went over to shake her hand. "Hello, Mrs. Yoder. My name is Raven Meadows."

"Call me Susanna. We Amish aren't real proper, going by Mr. and Mrs." She shook her hand warmly.

"I love your shawl." Raven noticed the blue yarn looked homespun.

Susanna pulled the shawl closer around her. "It's called a prayer shawl. A friend in Pennsylvania made it. Said that with each stitch, a prayer was said for me. It makes me feel like someone's hugging me all the time."

Raven had seen books in craft stores for prayer shawls, but didn't realize they really helped anyone. But Susanna seemed to feel special; remembered in her illness. "I knit. Do you?"

"Jah, on my knitting loom. Some days I get one row done, and feel like it's an accomplishment. Would love to learn to knit with needles, though. Something different."

"I've taught others to knit. It's so easy. Maybe I can teach you."

"I'd like that."

Raven saw a man come in from a room off the kitchen. He came over and shook her hand, green eyes twinkling. "I'm Rueben, Susanna's husband. Nice to meet you."

She smiled at the man, but couldn't help gawk at his long black beard; it needed trimmed. "Shall we start the interview?"

"Not until we eat," Rueben chuckled. "I've been out choring since four this morning and I'm famished." He looked at Joshua. "I smell pancakes. What else you got?"

"Plenty of eggs and sausage. Toast, too, and left over apple pie from last night."

Rueben licked his lips and rubbed his hands together. "I'll take the pie first."

Joshua cleared his throat. "Raven, what would you like?"

"Pie for breakfast? I'll take that." She didn't add that the stress she felt called for a comfort food. Joshua hurried around the kitchen like a master chef. He soon had all the plates on the table and she eyed her pie. It wasn't a piece; it was a quarter of a pie. Oh well, she must need it. "Is it okay if I ask questions while we eat?"

"*Jah*, go ahead," Rueben said.

She saw Joshua tenderly help his mother move close to the table and sit in a chair with a pillow up against the back. "Now we're ready," he said.

"Well, it appears no one here is a criminal," she grinned. "Your background checks came back clear. Now I have to interview you to see why it is you want a foster child."

All eyes looked at Susanna. "I'm sick, as you can see. I have the blessed hope of seeing my Redeemer, so I'm not sad. But I want to leave this world with all the love I can give. What better way than to share my home and love with children who have neither?"

Raven looked at Susanna tenderly. "That is a very special thought, but you're so ill."

"I have more than thoughts; I have a plan. We have a wonderful *goot* church district that wants to pitch in and help. So, you see, I won't be doing this alone."

Raven looked at Joshua. He already looked overworked. "Who will coordinate all the help?"

"Well, our *Gmay* meets every other week and needs are brought up and made known. We'll have plenty of help."

"What's a *Gmay*?" Raven asked.

"It's German for community. It's what *Englishers*, like you, call church."

Raven thought of the clans in the Seneca Nation. She remembered the community they shared and how they worked together. They shared things in common. If someone had a good sewing machine all the women in the clan used it. The rules for the community were made by the wise elderly women. She looked over at Susanna and knew she'd be considered a wise mother to a clan.

She didn't want to ask the next question, but she knew she had to. "I don't mean any disrespect, but what are your motives for wanting foster children? Are they to help you on the farm?"

"A few boys can learn a lot on a farm, so yes, I'd be willing to teach them," Rueben chimed in.

Raven's head spun. "A few boys? You want more than one? And for farm work?"

"It's *goot* for them. Makes them learn what real work is. It's a gift to teach a child hard work."

Raven shifted on the hard wooden bench. "We can't have children being exploited, made to work for your profit."

Susanna leaned forward and clenched her hands in her lap. "We don't think ten year olds are wee ones. We let the little ones play all they want, but when they're old enough to do a chore, we let them. It makes them feel important to the family."

Raven thought back to some classes she took on child development. The Montessori Method believed the same thing. When a child was old enough to do simple tasks, they were encouraged. "What type of work would you expect a ten year old boy to do?"

"I milked the cow when I was ten," Joshua said. "I fed chickens, collected eggs, cleaned the horse stalls, and fed the cattle. At harvest time there's lots of wheat to stack and dry. "

Raven let out a sigh. "So you decided to get some boys during the harvest season for help, right?"

"It's not a bad thing to work," Joshua said. "I feel blessed to be healthy enough to toil in the fields." He looked over at his mother. "I even put up fruits and vegetables, which is women's work, but it's the least I can do."

Raven was taken aback by the love in Joshua's eyes when he looked at his mother. She pursed her lips together so she wouldn't tear up. She'd never know what it was like to have a bond with her mother. Raven pushed the thought out of her mind, and continued with her questions. "Susanna, can you tell me what your health status is?"

"I'm in kidney failure and am praying a kidney will come in. I've been on the list for three years."

Susanna had no fear or sadness in her voice. She simply stated facts. She wasn't in denial at all. Raven looked into Susanna's serene eyes. What was this woman's trick? She was dying, yet so calm. Again, she willed back tears.

"And if you were denied being a foster parent, how would you feel?"

"Real sad," Susanna said. "The Good Lord put love in my heart for these children I hear have no parents. It's a sad thing. I can help."

"I understand these children. I was raised in foster homes since I was nine and they need love…" Raven said.

"Did your parents die, dear one," Susanna asked.

"I never knew my parents. I was raised by my grandparents… until they died."

Susanna got up out of her chair and walked to Raven and embraced her. "I'm sorry child. I didn't know. So sorry."

Raven felt the warmth of the prayer shawl around her and something deep inside began to melt. No one hugged her like this woman she hardly knew. She tried to hold back her emotions, but the more Susanna just stood there and embraced her, she felt the avalanche of hurt and rejection start to topple, and tears escaped and ran down her face. Susanna walked over to the big blue pantry and got out a handkerchief. "Here child, take this. I embroidered the flowers. Whenever you cry, think of me. I'm here for you."

Raven eyed the white cloth with embroidered purple flowers. "Thank you, Susanna." She looked over at Joshua for that comforting look he always gave. He smiled at her, and she regained her composure. "I have more forms for you to fill out. They're mostly yes or no questions. I'll leave them here and pick them up in a few days.

"I hope to see you soon," Susanna said.

She got up to go, but hesitated, and looked at Susanna. "Is there anything I can do?"

"Well, we know Appleton's number by heart. The Rowes' are our trusted English friends and drivers for us, but if you'd like to take a turn, that would be nice. I have to get blood work taken once a week."

Chapter 3

*J*oshua hooked his thumbs around his suspenders near his chest and looked at Raven as she ate her pie. She tugged at his heart. He was right. It was pain he saw in her eyes. To think she went to school to help foster children, but she needed help herself. He looked at the way she melted in his *mamm's* arms and cried. How could he cheer her up before she left?

"Raven, would you like to take a buggy ride?"

She looked at him and smiled. "I'd love to."

They went out to the barn where two wagons were housed. He helped her into the open buggy and they were on the road in no time. They passed Eb's house and he saw Raven gasp. "That's the man I saw."

Joshua groaned. "Eb's our neighbor. He was most likely drunk when you saw him and probably still is." He hoped Eb wouldn't come out to meet them on the road, but he did.

"*Danki* for the money, Joshua. I'll pay you back."

Joshua saw Eb was tipsy and tried to ignore him. "That's fine, but can you let the horse go?"

"Hey, is that you?" he said as he noticed Raven. "I've always loved you and still do…"

Joshua looked at Raven in disbelief. "Do you know him?"

Raven's eyes were round as buttons. "No, but he said the same thing to me this morning. What's wrong with him? Does he have a mental disorder?"

"Alcohol, if you call that a disorder." Joshua looked at Eb evenly. "Let go of the horse." He could see Eb was transfixed on Raven and didn't move, and she felt uncomfortable. "Eb, this is Raven, and you don't know her."

"Pretty face," he said, not taking his eyes off of her.

Joshua clicked his mouth for the horse to go and it did, and Eb let go of the bit, trying to run alongside the buggy. He soon had the horse trotting and Eb couldn't keep up. He looked at Raven. "Are you alright?"

"I'm fine, "she said.

"Well, *goot*. No man should talk to a woman like that." He looked at her and grinned. "Would you like to try some pumpkin ice cream? I've been craving some all week."

"I just had pie! Being around the Amish will make me gain weight," she said with a crooked grin. "Well, okay, as long as I can get back to the car in half an hour. I have other home visits to make, now that it's eight o'clock, when most people are up for business." She elbowed Joshua in a playful way.

"My aunt makes the best ice cream and she doesn't live far. Only a mile away."

They went past the Cockaigne Ski Resort. "Do the Amish ski?" she asked.

"*Jah*, but we don't pay for it like the English, and we have a different way of doing it."

"There's more than one way?"

"*Jah*, there is. When it snows in a few weeks, I'll show you how."

"I know, the annual foot of snow on Halloween," she moaned. "I don't care for the snow too much. "

They soon reached his aunt's and after pulling in, he jumped out of the buggy to Raven's side to help her out. When he touched her soft hand, his heart beat faster. He couldn't be attracted to an English woman, for sure and for certain. He'd have to do some talking to his Heavenly Father tonight.

When they entered the large Amish house, he noticed it wasn't a good time. Several women were around a quilting frame, having a frolic. His Aunt Hannah came over to greet them and said she'd make them two pumpkin ice cream cones in a jiffy. Joshua looked across the room and met Lottie's dark brown eyes. She nodded and smiled at him, keeping his gaze. Soon his aunt handed him two cones and told them to stop back again. When they walked to the buggy, he was surprised by Raven.

"Is that girl with the red hair and freckles your girlfriend?"

He helped her in the buggy. "Why do you ask?"

"I do have eyes and I've been in love before, for a short time…sort of."

"Well, we courted for a long while, but she just felt neglected with me helping my *mamm* and doing all my chores."

He heard Raven huff. "How selfish. Why didn't she help you instead of complaining?"

A grin spread out across Joshua's face. She was so frank and said out loud what he wished he could admit. Lottie was selfish, not common for an Amish girl who was taught to sacrifice for family. Here was Raven, not Amish and tossed around in foster homes, and she had better sense...she had more of a heart.

~*~

Raven sat between Toby and Ethan on the oak pew in the church. She had pen in hand to take down notes of anything peculiar. The other boys, who sat in the pew in front of her, were so excited. Why? She'd find out who was bribing them to come here.

The boys were being bribed at Appleton too, she was certain. They hardly watched TV, and sat around the table like old men, playing Five-Hundred- Rummy with Marilyn and Jim. But she couldn't deny that there was a lot of roaring and laughter coming from the kitchen.

Soon Lawrence ran into the church. "Sorry I'm late, everyone. I got behind an Amish buggy coming back from Randolph and couldn't find a place to pass for miles. OK, I see we have a full house of twenty some kids. How are you all doing this week? Any prayer requests?"

A girl who appeared to be ten raised her hand. "My grandma's back in the hospital and I'm scared. My parents aren't telling me what's really wrong."

Lawrence, who was now sitting on a chair in the front, leaned forward. "Well, God knows and we'll just ask Him to help her where she needs it. Any other prayer requests?"

Bud shot his arm up. "Sometimes Mr. Rowe looks tired and I don't know why. Maybe he needs God's strength. He's old."

"God gives strength to the weary," Lawrence said. "We'll pray."

She looked at the concern on Bud's face. Jim had a special bond with him, and was the anchor in his life. She remembered the bond she had with Granny Nora. Raven wished she could stay in that foster home forever. Granny taught her how to knit and she remembered it calmed her down. She remembered when Granny passed on. Raven was told one day she had to move on, too. Not enough adult-to-child ratio in the home. Her throat tightened.

Raven heard another child ask that prayer be given for her dog. When Lawrence said he'd pray for her dog, she felt indignant. Didn't God have more important things to do, like running the universe, to care about a dog? How silly.

All the children bowed their heads and one after another, a child prayed out loud about one of the prayer requests. She looked around the room at their serious expressions. Were they being sincere or was this just another childhood game? Did they really believe that God was listening? How ridiculous. They didn't even know for sure there was a God. No one knew.

After the prayer time, Lawrence asked them to open their Bibles. They were going to pick up where they left off last week. They were studying a book called John. When a volunteer was needed to read, Toby stood up and read:

"John 14: 16-18, I will ask the Father, and he will give you another Advocate, who will never leave you. He is the Holy Spirit, who leads into all truth. The world cannot receive him, because it isn't looking for him and doesn't recognize him. But you know him, because he lives with you now and later will be in you. No, I will not abandon you as orphans—I will come to you."

Raven felt her mouth grow dry. An advocate who will never leave you? How many social workers, who were called her advocates, left her for a better job? She remembered Mrs. Pfeiffer. She thought she was the apple of this woman's eye, but she left her. Lawrence's voice interrupted her thoughts.

"An advocate is someone who pleads your case or speaks up for you. I'm an advocate for Compassion International, and I speak up for the poor. But Jesus is saying something powerful here; the Holy Spirit will live in you and never leave you, like orphans are left with no care."

Raven glanced at the boys. So this was it. They were being told they weren't really orphans. No foster child liked that label. This religion offered a way to be adopted. She was told this same story as a child. The Great Spirit will be with you always. Why did she feel like an orphan deep down then? Religion never answered her questions, but why did the boys find such comfort in what the Bible said?

Soon all the boys got on one side of the church and the girls on the other. Now she would find out why they really came. She was shocked when it was time for a Bible Bee. Whoever memorized the most scriptures won? That was it? No sweets or prizes? Why would the boys do this week after week? What was in the Bible that made them want to read it? She noticed a stack of paperback Bibles in the church entry that were free for the taking. She'd take one and find out.

~*~

Raven sat up in bed and flipped the paperback Bible to John 14 and read it over and over. The Bible didn't make her mad, like she supposed, but was comforting. She reread the first few lines:

"Do not let your hearts be troubled. You believe in God; believe also in me. My Father's house has many rooms; if that were not so, would I have told you that I am going there to prepare a place for you? And if I go and prepare a place for you, I will come back and take you to be with me that you also may be where I am. You know the way to the place where I am going."

God was preparing a permanent home? She read down further. Thomas asked where he was going to make this home, but Jesus never answered but only said, "I am the way and the truth and the life. No one comes to the Father except through me." Comfort stirred in her, but she did think Jesus seemed a little arrogant. How could he say he was the only way to God? Raven read the whole chapter again, and a gentle peace waved over her heart. What was wrong with her? She felt like crying again, but why? She never cried… She thought of Susanna who was dying unless she got a kidney. The hug she gave her made her feel like God was wrapping his arms around her.

~*~

Joshua sat at his *mamm's* side. She complained of pain and had a fever of 102. He took more ice and placed it on her forehead; she looked up at him with thankful eyes, though her teeth were gritting. He hoped his *daed* would come back from the phone shanty soon to let them know the Rowes' could drive. The sound of charging feet came up the steps. "Raven will drive and she said she'll be her soon. I'll bundle your *mamm* up and you watch for her car."

Joshua did as he was told. He grabbed his black wool coat and hat and waited on the porch. Raven was driving? Why not the Rowes'? Were they sick? He always felt bad calling people in the middle of the night, but this could not be avoided. He looked up into the inky black sky. The stars looked like sparkling diamonds. Christ's light shines brightest when all is dark around us. He bowed and prayed his *mamm* would make it through the night. Soon he saw headlights pull into the driveway, and Raven darted out of the car. "Is she alright?" she yelled as she slid on the ice. Soon she was lying flat on the drive way.

He ran to her and helped her up. "Are you okay?" He scooped her up and helped her into the house. "Are you hurt? "

"I'm fine, really," she said, her face beet red. "I was so afraid for your mother; I sped over here as fast as I could."

Joshua looked at her massive curls falling over the sides of her face and down onto her white coat. But such fear in her eyes. "God won't take *Mamm* one minute before her time."

"You really believe that?"

"Well, we've had three years to meditate on it…"

Joshua heard one set of loud footsteps coming down the steps and knew his *daed* was carrying his *mamm*. This wasn't good. He went to the bottom of the steps and gathered his *mamm* into his arms, as he watched his *daed* gasp for air. He looked down at his *mamm* to see her eyes were closed. Dear Lord, not tonight!

~*~

When they were told to take Susanna back to one of the rooms, they asked Raven to come. She protested, but they treated her like she was part of the family. Did they treat all drivers like this? She sat in a chair next to Joshua while Rueben took a seat on the other side of the exam table where Susanna lay sleeping. She saw their faces were twisted in grief yet their hands where folded in prayer. Soon a nurse came in to take Susanna's vitals and draw vials of blood. Rueben followed the nurse out of the room as he asked questions.

Joshua looked at her and tried to smile, but his eyes were full of grief. Moved with compassion, she took his hand and held it. When she realized what she did, she squeezed his hand and smiled at him, and then nervously put her hands in her lap.

"*Danki*, Raven, for everything. You have a caring heart."

She grinned. "Most people don't thank me for driving them anywhere; usually they complain that I drive too fast," she said, heat rising in her cheeks. "A caring heart, though? No one's told me that in a long time."

"Maybe they don't see the real you. When I first met you a few weeks ago, you seemed, well, mean, but then I realized you were in pain."

She tried to compose herself. Why did she feel like she could talk to Joshua? Why did she feel like crying? Raven felt him take her hand. "Was the English world hard for you?"

"English world?"

"Non-Amish," he said.

She pursed her lips. "Yes, it was hard." Her breath caught in her throat, and a sensation she hadn't felt since she was a little girl welled up in her. It was like coming up for air after being submerged in water. She thought of her grandma holding her hand in a tender way, and now she found it in Joshua's. "I'm s-sorry. This is a hard time for you. I'm so selfish."

Joshua squeezed her hand tighter, as if trying to give her strength. "You're not selfish…"

The door opened and Rueben came in with a team of nurses, his face solemn. "They're taking her to surgery. She needs emergency dialysis."

Raven watched as Joshua got up and embraced his father and both sobbed. Soon they took Susanna out and Rueben sat down, putting his handkerchief in his pocket. He looked over at her. "Susanna's more afraid of dialysis than the transplant. We were hoping to avoid it."

"She'll be okay, though, right? I mean, lots of people are on dialysis," Raven said, leaning forward.

Rueben forced a smile. "*Jah*, it will keep her alive, until we find a live donor or a cadaver comes in. Many of the people are getting tested, and it's a comfort." Tears welled in his eyes and he cleared his throat. "Raven, I'll be staying the night here. You and Joshua can go home."

"I'm staying too," Joshua said. "We can get someone to do the chores in the morning."

"How will we get word to them?"

Joshua turned to Raven. "Do you remember where my Aunt Hannah lives? The one who gave us ice cream? Can you tell her we need help?"

"I can do it," she said. "I've done chores on a farm before."

Joshua's jaw dropped. "Are you sure? You've hand-milked a cow?"

"We had a cow on my grandparents' little farm. Is your cow friendly to strangers, though?"

"*Jah*, just pet her first and talk to her a little. Then pet her sides so the cow's milk let's down."

She knew exactly what to do and put up her hand. "I can manage."

Chapter 4

$\mathscr{R}$aven lit the lantern and headed out to the barn. The lantern let out more light than she thought imaginable. She saw the black and white cow, and hanging up the lantern, she pet her nose and talked to her. "I feel like Anne of Green Gables today. She was an orphan and didn't have any love, but I think I'm starting to feel loved again."

When she knew the cow was calm, she took the three legged stool that sat next to her. Taking the wet cloth she'd brought, Raven wiped down the cows udder and then pet down her side so the milk would release. She soon heard the squirting of liquid on the bottom of the tin pail. Memories of her childhood flooded her mind, her Aunt Brook. She favored her children and never expected them to milk the cow they shared on the farm. Her grandmother told the other grandkids to take a turn and be fair, but somehow Raven always milked the cow, even in the dead of winter. Her grandfather took the days it was below zero. Sometimes he'd slip her a dollar for her milking efforts, if she promised not to tell anyone. Why did Aunt Brook rule the roost?

When her grandparents died, the chores became harder and she remembered feeling hungry, but she wasn't to tell anyone. Her Uncle Ram secretly gave her peanut butter and jelly sandwiches. She remembered sitting in the attic eating sandwiches while she heard her cousins laugh around the dinner table. Soon memories overwhelmed her. The guidance counselor didn't let her go home after school because there were bruises on her arms. A knot twisted deep in her stomach. How could she forget? She was taken from the home because of abuse.

Deep within her, where pain had been rooted for years, it rushed up and she doubled over and screamed. "How could she?" Raven felt the hot tears on her cheeks. Shaking uncontrollably, she wailed as she held her stomach. "Why God?" she screamed. "Why?" She went to the stack of hay and buried her face in it, trying to stifle the screams, to no avail. Her Uncle Ram was not kind to bring her peanut butter sandwiches. He was cruel. He allowed her to be locked in the attic, hours upon lonely hours. She could taste the stale bread and old crystalized peanut butter sandwiches he brought, and screamed all the more.

She felt like jumping out of her skin when she felt a hand on her shoulder. She turned to see an Amish man. His eyes held such sorrow. "Is Susanna gone?" he asked.

Raven swiped at tears running down her cheeks, and willed herself to calm down. "Susanna's alive. She's in the hospital."

He looked at her with penetrating green eyes. "I'm a neighbor. I heard the screaming and thought that…"

"Oh, I'm so sorry. I took Susanna to the hospital and she'll need dialysis. She's in surgery now to get her ready for it," she said, as another sob caught in her throat. Embarrassed, Raven looked sheepishly into the Amish man's eyes. He took off his black wool hat and she realized it was Eb. He was so kind and empathetic when he wasn't drunk.

"Would you like me to finish milking the cow? I know how to do everything in this barn."

She looked at him and nodded. "Thank you."

~*~

Raven stood while looking across the living room at Marilyn. "The boys missed me for morning prayers?" she asked. "I'm surprised." Collapsing into one of the overstuffed chairs in the living room, she rubbed her temples. "Any word about Susanna?"

Marilyn sat in the chair next to her. "Jim left for the hospital this morning. I've been pacing the floor all morning, but still no word."

"But I thought Jim was sick."

Concern etched Marilyn's face. "Can't hold the old fool down. He'll catch his death yet."

"At least the boys won't be able to dunk him at the Fall Festival this weekend."

"Ha," Marilyn said. "He'll do it anyhow. He feels he needs to always keep his word to the boys."

"He's really dedicated to them; that's for sure."

"Well, he didn't really have parents. He really did sell apples on the streets of Jamestown. The Great Depression robbed him of dreams." She sat in the chair opposite Raven. "I tease him about selling apples, but he knows I'm only trying to change the subject to these happier days." She sighed. "He had a full scholarship to college, but couldn't take it since he had to work. When he talks of apples, I start talking about Appleton."

"Is there a connection?" Raven asked.

Marilyn grinned. "I came up with the name. After hearing Jim moan about selling tons of apples, I came up with Appleton. Get it? Apple? Ton? Life can give us lemons, like they say, but we need to make lemonade, right? So Jim started this place to help boys get what he never had: a stable home and a chance at their dreams."

Raven was flabbergasted. Jim had a hard life, but he seemed so happy. Someone in his shoes might be bitter. "How about you Marilyn? How did the Depression affect you?"

Marilyn's eyes grew misty. "Well, I worked hard, too. Farm work. Never liked it, but we lived off the land. Some days we just had thick broth to eat. We didn't have electricity or indoor plumbing. We were almost Amish," she mused.

"What did you want to do instead?" Raven leaned forward in curiosity.

"Be a seamstress, like my mom," she quipped. "I was a little girl when the Depression started, and Mom made extra money by making clothes. She was so good; women came to the little shop she made in our living room."

"So what kept you from learning to sew?"

"Knitting," Marilyn snarled. "The circular needles just came out and Mom taught me at six how to make a sock." She sighed. "The government promoted knitting as a way to boost morale. So knitting magazines with patterns in them were cheap. My sisters and I had to knit if we weren't doing school work. "

"What did you make?"

"Winter things living here. Lots of sweaters, scarves, gloves. But I also crocheted, and learned to make lace that Mom put on dresses. Then when World War II started, I knit for the troops. After the war, I threw my needles out and have never knitted since."

"But it's so calming."

"Not when you have to do it. Oh, it was fun knitting in a group, gossiping though."

Raven leaned closer. "I see the craft store in town has a knitting circle. Want to go?"

Marilyn put both hands up. "No thank you. My knitting days are over." She turned to Raven. "I'm sorry. You're new here in town. Do you want someone to go with?"

"No, I don't mind going alone. But, I have so much to do to settle in. Maybe I'll try it when the weather gets really bad."

Marilyn pat Raven's knee and said she needed to stir the pot of soup she had on the stove. Raven thought of what comfort knitting was to her, but it seemed like a curse to Marilyn. All a matter of perspective, she'd learned in counseling, sure was true in this case. Knitting had kept her sane.

~*~

She went to her bedroom, exhausted, but her mind raced. She hadn't thought of her Aunt Brook and some of the foster homes she'd been in for years. She hadn't remembered being taken from her home and put in a strange place. Raven thought of her Amish doll her grandmother gave her. The only thing she took along with her small wardrobe.

She picked up her knitting needles, working on another scarf. The boys would all have scarves for Christmas. But she felt like crying again, so she did. It was part exhaustion. Sleeping on the wooden bench in the Yoder's living room kept her up half the night. How kind Eb was to come and check on her. She'd have to thank him for all he did, not only milking the cow, but collecting eggs and tending to the other animals. How could such a nice man be shunned?

Raven looked at the rich brown tones of the yarn, and decided right there that the scarf belonged to Eb. She had to be careful, though. Knitting was at times too calming, and she might fall asleep. *I need to greet the boys when they get home and help them with homework.*

~*~

Raven opened her eyes with a start; someone was pounding on her bedroom door. "Yes?"

"It's me, Jim. Sorry if I woke you but you have a visitor."

Raven looked out the window and saw twilight. She spun her head around to look at the clock, 6:16. She missed greeting the boys when they got home. *I fell asleep knitting again!* "I'll be out in a minute," she said. She took her comb and ran it through the thick mass of curls, put on a sweater, and went out to see who had come to visit.

When she got to the bottom of the steps the boys gathered around her, asking her if she was okay. They said they had prayed for her in case she was sick. How they warmed her heart. She looked over at the front door and saw Joshua leaning against the wall with one arm. He looked kind as usual, but concern was on his face. His mom must be gravely ill. "How are you Joshua? How's your mom?"

"Ach, she's fine. Will come home tomorrow." His brows furrowed. "There's something I need to talk to you about. Want to go on a buggy ride?"

She felt famished, but maybe he needed to tell her they were pulling out of the foster program. "I'd love to."

"Better take a coat," Bud said. "It gets chilly when it's dark."

"*Ya*, it'll snow soon," Timmy said. "We always get a foot of snow on Halloween."

They were so concerned for her, and she was here to care for them. "Thank you for reminding me. I'll get my jacket."

Raven retrieved her jean jacket from her bedroom and then ran downstairs once more. She felt Joshua's eyes heavy on her, and shyness flooded her. He led her out to the buggy and took her hand as she stepped inside. It was a closed buggy that was charming. Raven heard him make a clicking noise and the horse was off. They headed down Main Street and passed the Town Square before he spoke.

"Eb told me what happened last night."

She looked down. "Told you what?"

"You were crying so hard you couldn't milk the cow. He came over because he heard screaming. Are you okay?"

A familiar sense of shame swept over her, making her speechless. Why would he care?

He slowed the buggy to a stop on the side of the road and jumped down and went behind the buggy. She looked behind to see he was turning on battery operated lights. Then he turned the set on in the front of the buggy. He had a handsome profile, a strong jawline like his father and with a small turned up nose like his mom. He looked at her thoughtfully when he got into the buggy but she still couldn't talk. "God could save us from trauma, but instead he sends us a Comforter." That's my favorite Amish proverb. It's helped me get through my mom's illness. God can comfort like no other human can, but I'd like to help you."

There it was again. Talk about God and his comfort. It was in the chapter she was reading in the Bible: She was well acquainted with the wall she was about to put up, but for some reason, she found it harder to do with Joshua. Raven looked forward, trying to ignore him. She wanted to tell him a lie, like the cow kicked her and she screamed. That she'd never really milked a cow and was afraid, but instead she felt her chin quiver. She quickly put her hand to her mouth to hide it, and she felt tears as she gasped for air. She felt Joshua's arm around her. "It'll be okay," he said. "I'm here to listen if you want to talk."

Her throat hurt, trying to swallow her pain. She felt Joshua's arm withdraw from her and she soon heard the clip clop of the horse's hoofs and the rhythm calmed her. Raven looked out of the buggy at the fields full of wheat. Some of it was drying in piles stacked like tee pees. She felt rude being so silent, and tried to find her voice. She heard an owl hoot. Surely she could speak up, too. "I was raised on a farm on the Indian Reservation in Salamanca. When I milked the cow, it brought back bad memories."

Joshua didn't say anything, just nodded his head for her to go on. She wasn't used to sharing her feelings, but for some reason she felt safe. "The reason I was put in a foster home was abuse. My Aunt Brook never liked me, and after my grandparents died, there was no one to protect me from her."

Joshua took her hand. "I'm sorry, Raven," he said. "Foster children are blessed to have you work with them. You weren't protected and now you're making sure other children are."

She looked into his blue eyes, and found she could see herself more clearly in them. They were like deep pools of water that brought refreshment. She felt accepted by him … unconditionally. And he knew her; deep down she wanted to make sure other children would be protected. She couldn't look away from him and wanted to tell him more, but he turned his head and let go of her hand. "I better get you back to Appleton."

~*~

A few days later, Raven had another home visit to make at Joshua's Aunt Hannah's house. Susanna had told her of the burden she had for the boys and now she and her husband wanted to be foster parents as well. Then

49

she would interview the Millers, Lottie's parents. If they were anything like her, they wouldn't qualify. If she stopped dating Joshua because his time was spent taking care of Susanna, then they didn't have the hearts to be foster parents.

Raven thought of all the foster families she'd had. Lucky to never suffer abuse in a foster home and maybe there was a God who had been looking out for her. The more she read the Bible, she felt like Jesus cared. She'd been in so many Sunday Schools, but the song, "Jesus Loves Me" was sung in them all. Jesus loves me this I know, for the Bible tells me so…Maybe it was true?

As she pulled up to Hannah's house, she remembered Joshua taking her here for ice cream, and warmth filled her heart. Raven went up the front steps and knocked. The blue curtains in the two large windows on either side of the door shook and swayed. Soon several small children were smiling at her and waving. The door opened and Hannah smiled. "The children aren't used to anyone knocking on the front door. We Amish use the backdoor." She motioned for Raven to come in. "Would you like some coffee to warm you up? The juncos have their feathers fluffed out, so the temperature's going down."

Raven knew a junco was also called a snowbird. She noticed how the Amish were so connected to nature, as were Native Americans. "I'd love some coffee. Thank you." She looked at the sparsely furnished living room, so similar to the Yoder's. When they went into the kitchen, she was surprised to see the long table with matching china closet. It was just like Susanna's. She mentioned the similarity to Hannah.

"Oh, the same man made them," she said.

"He's a good craftsman. What's his name?"

Hannah's eyes darkened. "He lives next to Susanna. Eb. Made the furniture ages ago." She put a cup of coffee on the table and motioned for Raven to sit down. "My husband will be in shortly. Harvest time is so busy."

Raven ran her fingers over the fine oak grain of the table. Eb was a master carpenter. He was a shunned man, and from what she'd been reading about the Amish, he was not to be spoken to, so he'd repent. But she could talk about him, she supposed. "Eb helped me milk the cow the other night. He's very nice."

"He was at my sister's house?" Hannah's eyes were round as saucers.

"I drove your sister to the hospital and told Joshua I'd milk the cow, but I had a problem. Eb helped me."

Hannah nodded. "Would you like some doughnuts? I made them this morning."

She put her hand up. "I stopped by to visit Susanna yesterday and had some oatmeal cookies Joshua made. I need to watch my figure."

"My sister is blessed to have such a son. I do worry, though. He's twenty-four and not married."

Raven gasped. "I'm twenty-four and not married, too. The Amish get married young compared to the English, as you call us. Joshua's young."

"Lottie Miller's the one for him," she said. "When my sister's better, I'm sure they'll court again." Hannah's eyes mellowed. "Lottie's a dear girl."

"Self-absorbed, I'd say," Raven said without thinking. She cupped her mouth with her hand. "I'm sorry. I should keep my opinions to myself. "

Hannah tilted her head to one side. "You don't know Lottie. What makes you say such a thing?"

"She stopped dating Joshua because he didn't give her enough attention. Doesn't she realize how ill Susanna is?"

"My nephew told you something so personal? Was it part of his interview for the foster program?"

"He told me when we came over for ice cream, when I first met you."

Raven saw coldness in Hannah's eyes. "Amish men aren't supposed to share such things with..."

"...Outsiders?" Raven finished. "We 'Outsiders' can learn a lot from you Amish. I know I have. Joshua's been a great friend to me in a difficult time." She was glad when a tall, lanky man with a black beard came into the kitchen.

"Hello there, I'm Hannah's husband, David. You're the social worker, *jah*?"

Raven looked up and smiled. "Yes, I'm Raven Meadows. Nice to meet you, David."

She went through the necessary questions and their answers were sufficient. They wanted to be foster homes because Susanna told them there was a shortage of them. That was true. Many foster children now lived in group homes. They had the resources and their children all looked happy and healthy. Everything was fine, except Hannah now acted distant. Her husband asked his wife if something was wrong, but she dodged the question with a huff. How could a woman who appeared to be warm suddenly turn so cold?

Raven wrapped up the interview and said good-bye to all the smiling children. The young ones only spoke German. She'd had German in college and tried to converse, and they laughed. She laughed, too. "I have a bad accent, huh?" she asked, turning to David.

"*Jah*, you do," he said with a twinkle in his eyes.

.

Chapter 5

 oshua bit into an oatmeal whoopie pie. Since his mom started dialysis he was home alone more, and had time to think…of Raven. He felt so drawn to her, but it was an impossible situation. Maybe he had been too hard on Lottie. Women needed to feel loved, just like a plant needed water. He thought back to the last church service. After the meal, she'd made it clear from her body language and encouraging tone she wanted to court again. But she lacked the depth Raven had. Raven had a hard life, yet doted on the boys, when deep down, she was hurting. No one was doting on Raven. He was more than willing to, but it was like taking the forbidden fruit.

He thought of Lawrence Turner. A bachelor who needed a wife. Raven said she was going to his church with the boys. When he drove past the Ellington Town Square during the Fall Festival, he saw them together, eating cotton candy and laughing. Joshua sighed. He was jealous. Lawrence had come over to visit Eb yesterday when Raven was over to gather more papers. He saw them meet in the yard to talk and could see Lawrence was attracted to her. How could he not be? She was beautiful not only to look at, but her heart and spirit touched him.

He shook his head. What was he thinking? Maybe if he courted Lottie again he'd see what he first saw in her. Maybe he was drawn toward Raven because of loneliness. Joshua bowed his head and said a silent prayer.

~*~

Raven tried to be nice to Lottie, but the girl was annoying, being too soft spoken and prissy. If a stray hair fell out from under her prayer *kapp*, she'd quickly conceal it again, gently tucking it in. She was petite and looked too fragile to do farm chores. Most likely, she spent her days quilting or knitting, never bothering to visit the sick woman who lived down the road, not helping Joshua with the messy things that came with caring for his mom.

Lottie put a piece of apple pie in front of her "I just warmed it up for you. I hope you enjoy it."

What could she say? She jogged to stay fit. With the threat of snow a foot deep on Halloween, as the boys claimed, she knew her jogging days were limited. "Thank you," she found herself saying against her will, and took a bite. Too sweet, just like the maker.

Soon Lottie's parents came into the kitchen. The father was a husky, macho-type Amish man and the mother too meek. Raven greeted Eli and Mary and got through the questions as quickly as she could. She had to admit the more they talked, Mary and Eli were wonderful couple.

But jealousy gripped her when she was around Lottie. She felt like she was in junior high. Why? Raven said her good-byes to the three younger Miller boys and was enchanted. They wore the same style clothing as the adults, and they looked like little men.

She got into her car and headed back to Appleton. Raven looked at the gray blanket of clouds that reached across the sky. Blackbirds by the hundreds lined telephone poles, getting ready to make their flight south. She thought of Florida, and for the first time, Brandon. He was so shallow and she was glad she broke it off. She'd tried for a year to have a heart to heart talk, but to no avail. Blamed herself for the walls she put up, but since she met Joshua, she knew it wasn't her. Brandon could have listened when she mentioned anything about her past, but didn't. Joshua did the way he pulled the words out of her by simply caring.

Raven looked at the clock. The boys wouldn't be home for an hour. She pulled into a driveway, turned her car around and headed back to Cherry Creek. She wanted to see how Susanna was feeling, and drop off the knitting needles she'd gotten at the craft store in town ....and see Joshua.

~*~

Joshua saw Raven's car pull and park behind his Aunt's Hannah's buggy. Her sharp words were fresh on his ears. Beware of Outsiders. He grinned when he saw that Raven rapped on the side door and not the front. She was learning the Amish ways. When she entered, he could see she was freezing. Her cheeks were read as cherries. He put on the tea kettle as he looked over at his aunt, who stared at Raven with obvious suspicion.

"Hello Joshua, Hannah," she said. "Have I come at a bad time?"

"*Ach*, no, you're always welcome," Joshua said, not being able to wipe the smile from his face.

"Can I see your mom? I got her some knitting needles."

"She's sleeping," Hannah said. "Had dialysis this morning and will be sleeping most of the day."

Joshua pulled out the chair at the head of the table. "Sit down and have some hot chocolate. We finally found one we mix with hot water that's *goot*."

Raven sat down and looked up at him. "Is there anything that needs done? Any farm chores?"

"Are you serious?" he asked.

"I'll send Lester and Joe over if you need help in the barn," Hannah said. "You should have let us know."

He didn't need help in the barn. With his *mamm* away three times a week for dialysis, he had plenty of time on his hands. He wanted to talk to Raven and turned to her. "We could use a driver. If you'd like to help. *Mamm* goes to the dialysis clinic in Randolph. Do you know where that is?"

Raven nodded. "I can find it. I'll give her a knitting lesson to help pass the time."

"Joshua, we have enough drivers already," Hannah said, glaring. "Bruce volunteered."

"*Mamm* would feel more comfortable with Raven." Joshua could see she wanted Raven to leave. He turned to get a mug out of the cabinet and spied Eb at the birdhouse. He hoped his aunt wouldn't notice, but she did.

"What is Eb up to now? He's in your yard," Hannah said.

"Eb's outside?" Raven blurted. "Oh, I want to see him. Thank him for all he did for me and see how much he charges for a big oak table like yours. Appleton needs a bigger one."

Joshua wanted to plead with her not to go. "Aren't you staying for hot chocolate? We have left over oatmeal whoopie pies."

She smiled at him. "I'm sorry, Joshua, I have no appetite. I'll see you later?" she asked.

He looked deep into her green eyes. Was this some hidden message she wanted to go on a buggy ride?

~*~

When Raven shut the door, anger arose within her. Why was Hannah so protective of Joshua? He wasn't a child. Relieved to hear Eb was outside, she had a reason to leave gracefully and thank him for all he'd done for her. It'd been over a week and she never had time to stop by. She ran to her car and grabbed the brown scarf.

"Hello, Eb, how are you?" she asked. Shock registered on his face. "I'm not Amish, so I can talk to you," she reassured him.

"I wanted to thank you for helping me when I milked the cow. And I made you this." She put the scarf around Eb's neck.

"Aw, my dear girl. *Danki*. Will come in handy soon." He probed her eyes. "I've been thinking of you. Why were you crying so hard when milking the cow?"

She searched his expression. He was actually concerned? He called her "dear girl," not upset he was disturbed in the middle of the night. "Milking a cow brought back some bad memories."

"Of what, honey?"

Raven felt moisture in her eyes. "My childhood. We had a cow I used to milk and, well, it made me think of a hard time in my life."

"It's good to cry. I go to the bottle; I'm sure you know. Joshua yelled at me for scaring you when you first came here. Said I was drunk. Don't remember and I'm sorry."

"Oh, don't worry about it," she said. "You know there's help to get off alcohol. Lots of programs. I can get you literature."

"*Ach*, I've been getting help. Pastor Lawrence and I are studying the Bible. Do you read the Bible?"

Heat rose into her cheeks. "I started a few weeks ago, and I have to admit, I like it."

"Well, I pick it up and read it when I feel the urge to reach for the bottle. It's been working, but Lawrence insists I go to a program at a church in Jamestown. Offered to take me and all, so I started last week. It's twelve weeks, or steps, or something like that."

"Oh, the Twelve Steps Program. It's excellent."

"So you've been to one?" he asked.

"I helped lead one in college. It's something I studied and have training in." She looked at this sweet man and the thought of him being shunned bothered her. It sounded so severe and would set back anyone going through Twelve Steps. He needed friends and family. She'd been tossed aside and Joshua was right; she wanted to make sure no one felt discarded.

"Eb, would you like to come to Appleton sometime for dinner? When you see the size of our table, maybe you can give us a quote on a large oak table, like the one you made for Hannah and Susanna."

"I'd be happy to," he said, eyes glistening.

~*~

The boys gathered in the living room as ordered. Raven had noticed over the past month that Cliffy hid in Chuckey's shadow too much. When a foster home became available at Susanna's, she was sure Joshua could help him overcome his fears. Maybe Timmy, too. Same problem, but he was a loner. Joshua did say they wanted a few boys. Starting with two would be wiser than taking three.

She looked at the others; Ethan, Chuckey, Bud, and Toby. They all seemed fine and didn't need extra care. If Lottie's home became available, maybe she deserved Bud and Chuckey. She held back a grin. They'd turn her quiet, simple Amish life into fireworks. Maybe Toby and Ethan would fit in with Hannah? She nervously twisted her pen around a long piece of black hair that ran over her shoulders. Wish they could all live here together...with me...

"Where's Mr. Rowe?" Bud asked, putting his feet up on the wooden coffee table.

"Feet down, Bud," Raven said. "He's driving for the Amish this morning."

"Is he taking Mrs. Yoder to diagnostics?" Ethan asked, looking pleased with his new vocabulary word.

"It's called dialysis, Ethan. Yes, Mr. Rowe drives her once a week and I will too."

"We pray for her at Bible Club," Chuckey piped in. "We're too young to get tested to be a match."

"Tested? For what?" Raven asked.

"To give her one of our kidneys," Chuckey said.

Raven sat down in one of the overstuffed chairs and put her binder on her lap. "You boys were all willing to give a kidney?"

"*Ya,*" Bud said. "We're too young and Mr. and Mrs. Rowe are too old," he chuckled.

"You know boys, I find this all very extraordinary. You'd all actually go through surgery to help Mrs. Yoder? You must really like her."

Toby raised his hand. "We hardly know her." He cleared his throat. "Pastor Lawrence got tested but he's not a match, and he said it was the least he could do, since Jesus gave his life for us. So, we all, well, just agree with him."

Raven put one hand over her heart. "I'm glad I came here to Appleton to meet such fine young men." She willed back tears. "Our little meeting today is about Halloween. Mr. Rowe said you'll be handing out apples."

The boys all groaned in unison.

"You know how Mr. Rowe feels about apples. He bought a bushel off the Amish and wants them all washed and polished. And wants me to remind you he did this for a living when he was your age."

"Sorry, Miss Meadows, but it's embarrassing," Chuckey said. "Kids don't want apples."

"It means so much to Mr. Rowe. You'll do it for him with smiles, right?"

Bud stuck out his lower lip and blew out air, making his fine brown bangs fly. "Mr. Rowe's hard to say no to. I've lost ten pounds since we went on a diet. Has me eating carrot sticks of all things." He broke into a smile and got up to high five Chuckey.

"We'll make Mr. Rowe proud we live here, right guys?"

They all got up and fist bumped each other. Timmy came over to fist bump her. She made a fist and knocked his. Great, Timmy's coming out of his shell!

"Thank you for your cooperation boys. Now, I have a surprise. I have an Amish friend who wants to give you boys a hayride. What do you say?" They were all quiet and gawked at her.

"Too childish for you or something?"

Ethan raised his hands. "We really don't know many Amish people. Are they nice? I mean, do they want to be friends with us?"

Raven hadn't realized the boys had such little contact with the Amish community. How short-sighted! If they were going to be in Amish foster homes, she needed to plan other activities as well.

~*~

Susanna sat in her rocking chair, knitting. The wide circular needles Raven bought were easy on the eyes. She feared needles would be too cumbersome. Dialysis was making her feel stronger and she was thankful she had something new to do to pass the long hours at the clinic. The nurse even told her how knitting was good for her health, to her surprise. She looked out the window at the large snowflakes falling almost horizontal, the wind being so strong. From the circle letters she received from friends in Pennsylvania, it was like they lived in Alaska compared to them. They'd never heard of a foot of snow on the last day of October, but here it was, without fail.

She thought of Rueben. At the first singing he had the courage to ask to drive her home. It was the last day of October, and he got the buggy stuck in the snow. He admitted later he planned it that way. They'd cuddled under the warm buggy robe and had their first kiss, his lips so warm against the harsh wind. He was like that today, too. Rueben warmed her heart every night when they held hands and kissed good-night.

Susanna sighed. Joshua needed the comfort a good spouse could bring. She thought of Hannah's accusation that he was falling for an Outsider … Raven. Now Hannah was encouraging Joshua to pay attention to Lottie. She didn't know which one scared her more because Lottie didn't fit Joshua like a glove, how her Rueben fit her. Lottie was too passive, too feminine, that it seemed unnatural. She didn't want to think badly of Lottie, but breaking her courtship with Joshua showed poor character. If she couldn't stand by him in hard times while courting, how could she during marriage? Susanna put her knitting into a basket and clasped her hands.

Dear Lord,

> *You see my faithful loving son, Joshua, day in and day out serving his family. I know you honor those who honor you. I pray for his future wife, Lord. Reveal your loving kindness to her. I pray she know you not in lip service, but in her heart. And I pray*

she love my son, and the love would grow into a beautiful family, like you have blessed me with. I pray this more fervently than for a kidney, Lord. My son's happiness means more to me than my life. I know you're a big God and can answer both prayers, but you know my heart, and how it aches for my son.

In Jesus name,

Amen

Chapter 6

$\mathcal{J}$oshua knew the boys would have fun skiing Amish style, so he hooked up the sleigh and waited for Raven to pull in. Over the past two weeks they'd tried to have a hayride, the snow kept ruining their plans. Maybe the boys would like this better.

The thought of seeing Raven again was troubling. As much as he gave it over to God, he still preferred her to Lottie. There was depth in Raven he admired. She'd had more struggles than most people, but she was still reaching out to others. On her visits to their place to finalize papers for foster parenting, she'd told him her concern for Eb. He needed healthier foods, so she collected leftovers from Appleton. And Eb lacked work, so Raven hired him to build a table and china cabinet. She even put up ads all around Jamestown and on the internet, and more orders were coming in. Shame filled him. Raven had a way of seeing needs…How stingy he was in giving Eb only twenty dollars.

Joshua soon saw the Appleton van come down the road, and his mouth grew dry. He had to guard his heart against these feelings for Raven. She wasn't Amish. He saw her get out of the van, and she wore a black coat with gray fur. When she looked at him, the blue hat made her green eyes look turquoise. Their eyes locked and he found himself drawn in and he didn't look away for a few seconds, then he turned to the boys. They seemed apprehensive being on an Amish farm, just as Raven had warned him. He greeted them all with a handshake and told them to call him Joshua.

"But you're an adult. We should call you Mr...?" Bud asked.

"My last name is Yoder, but we Amish aren't formal, calling people Mr. and Mrs. Just call me Joshua, okay?"

The boys nodded in unison. "How's your mom?" Chuckey asked. "Did you find a kidney yet?"

He was surprised the boys knew about his *mamm*. "No kidney yet."

"Well, we pray for her every day and especially on Bible Club night. The whole church is praying," Ethan said.

"Well, isn't that something," Joshua said. "*Danki*. We can use all the prayers we can get." Pastor Lawrence's whole church was praying for his *mamm*? Lord forgive him for being jealous of the good man of God. He was English and had a chance with Raven.

"Boys, do you remember how disappointed you were about the hayride?" Raven asked.

The boys groaned and nodded.

"Well, Joshua was looking for a clear day, but this snow is unbelievable. So he thought of something else you'd like to do. Ski."

"We're going to Cockaigne?" Toby gawked.

"*Nee*, you're going to ski here," Joshua said, grinning.

"How?" Bud asked. "There's no hills!"

"Are you going to teach us how to cross country ski?" Chuckey asked. "It's lots of work. I don't like it."

Joshua knew the boys would never guess. "I've asked one of my cousins to come over to help show you Amish style skiing." He turned toward the barn and yelled for Lester. He soon saw his cousin appear and smile at the boys in a knowing way.

Lester got into the sleigh and rode it to the back of the house. Joshua put on his skis and hung onto the noose he made in rope that was attached to the sleigh. He signaled for Lester to go and soon the sleigh was moving, pulling him along.

"It's like water skiing," squealed Cliffy. "I can't believe it."

Joshua yelled for Lester to speed up and soon he was racing across the field, skiing on the fields used for grazing. He continued to ski in a large circle a few times until it was slick. He let go of the rope with one hand and waved to the boys. He saw them all clap their hands, and Joshua shouted for Lester to pull him in. He soon glided to a stop in front of his audience. "Who's first?" he asked. He saw all the hands go up except Raven's. "Aren't women supposed to go before men?"

Raven's eyes grew round. "Not me. I was never good at skiing."

Soon the boys were chanting, *Miss Meadows, Miss Meadows, Miss Meadows.*

She threw her arms up in the air. "Okay, I surrender. I'll try it, but I'll fall." She went to Joshua and took the wooden skis. Joshua got down and put the leather latches around her boots, making sure they were tight. He handed her the rope, and whispered, "You don't have to do this."

She whispered back, "Oh, yes I do. I teach the boys to be brave, and they learn by example." She looked toward Lester. "Can you start slow?"

He nodded and soon they were off. Joshua watched as Raven held rigidly to the rope. "You need to loosen up in case you fall," he yelled. He saw her flex her knees a little. "That's better." They all watched her in admiration as she made her first circle.

"She's doing great!" Chuckey yelled, clapping his hands.

"Go Miss Meadows!" Cliffy screamed.

Joshua looked at Cliffy, the one Raven was worried about. She was teaching him a valuable lesson, even if she was scared stiff, literally. "Loosen up, Raven," he yelled. He saw her flex a little but then stiffen again, and watched as she struggled to turn the skis, and then crash to the ground. He led the way as they all ran to help her up, but she was face down in the snow, not moving.

"Oh my gosh! She's dead!" Bud yelled.

Joshua bent down, turned her over, and laid her in his arms. He looked down and saw one eye open and wink, and then she shut it again.

"We killed her!" Chuckey said. "We shouldn't have made her do it."

"We need to pray, right now!" Ethan said, trying to be calm. "God could raise her from the dead." He got on his knees and prayed. The other boys joined him. Raven still lay motionless.

Joshua looked somberly at the boys. "Look at it this way. An Amish funeral is cheap. Only costs twenty-five dollars for a pine casket."

He felt Raven wiggle in his arms then bursting with laughter. She slapped his arm. "Oh, so you don't care like my boys do." She stood up and looked at the kneeling boys. "I was only kidding. I'm fine."

All the boys got up and charged her, trying to give her a hug. She fell over in the snow, but only laughed. She made a snowball and threw it at Cliffy and then got up to run. Cliffy made a snowball and hit her back. Soon, there was a full-fledged snowball war going on. Joshua watched Raven play with the boys. She'd make a *wunderbar mamm*.

~*~

That night, Joshua closed the door to the barn and looked over at the snow drifts piled up against its walls. He leaned against the wind, covered his mouth with his scarf, and trudged to the house. He noticed his *daed* had brought in ample firewood for the night, and nodded at him, sitting in the rocker by the woodstove, reading the *Die Botschaft*. Joshua stomped the snow off his boots, took them off and put them by the fire, and sat at the table. "*Daed*, don't' you think we should check on Eb? It's mighty cold out there."

Rueben put the paper down, and leaned his head against the back of his rocker. "He's shunned."

"I know, but it just doesn't seem Christian-like to not check."

Rueben's eyebrows shot up and he leaned forward. "Son, we can't feather his nest outside the flock. We've talked about this before. He needs to miss the community, repent and be restored."

"Why can't we help him be restored, though? Raven is..."

Joshua saw his *daed's* eyes darken. "Because it's our way. This is Eb's second winter on his own, and maybe he'll miss the People more and return."

"Makes me feel bad."

"Son, look at Job. Are we not told in the Bible to consider his sufferings?" He shifted in his chair. "He never cursed God like Eb, and Job suffered more."

"Well, I'm glad Raven's helping him. She saves food from Appleton and brings it to him. Pastor Lawrence's trying to help, too."

Rueben hissed. "He'll never change. He made a mess of his *rumspringa* and tried to drag down other men with him. He could do it to you."

Joshua saw a fire in his *daed's* eyes he'd never seen before. What was he talking about? Did Eb try to drag his *daed* down when they were young? The deep red of his daed's face started to bother him and he got up and fetched him some water. "*Daed*, what is it? Calm down."

Rueben took the water and leaned his head back again. "Son, you don't know the real Eb. He got baptized, taking the Amish vow, but he never lived out our ways. Sometimes I think that fire was the judgment of God."

Joshua felt his own anger rising now. "God wouldn't let a man's wife and daughter die because of his sin. And he helped me stay out of sin during my *rumspringa*."

His *daed's* eyes slowly softened. "What are you talking about?"

"I was getting a little wild when I was seventeen. I was sneaking out with some English to go to Jamestown, and Eb knocked some sense into me. He even helped me stop lying when I was a kid, so we go a ways back."

Rueben folded his hands and sighed. "I didn't know that…"

~*~

Raven cherished the times she could snuggle up and read, and this blistering cold night made her feel all the warmer in her bed. She looked at the title of the book Lawrence gave her. *More Than a Carpenter.* He said her doubts about Jesus being God would slip away once she read it. She had to admit she liked Jesus, from what she read in the Book of John, and hoped he was right.

She also thought of Lawrence's question. Would you like to go out sometime for dinner and a movie? Yes, he was handsome and kind, but why did she compare him to Joshua and not Brandon? She didn't even think of her former boyfriend in Florida, unless he emailed her. She thought of Joshua more than she wanted to, and caught herself replaying over in her mind how it felt to be in his arms when she fell in the snow. He just seemed to fit her. She'd never talked about her past to anyone but she felt so safe with him.

Raven thought of him skiing Amish-style and had to stifle a giggle. The Amish had more ways of having fun than she ever imagined. Amish kids were always outside playing in the snow, sledding or making snowmen. Most

American children were inside, hooked up to electronics. She was prejudiced against the Amish when she first came to Appleton. Her only impression of them came from her childhood; that they were wimpy men who wouldn't fight back. How her views were changing.

She picked up the book and thought of Lawrence again, and how he looked at her. If it wasn't for Joshua, she'd say yes in a heartbeat to a date, but she needed to get Joshua out of her mind before she did. She could just say yes to coffee or something very casual, and that she'd just gotten out of a bad relationship…with Brandon…

~*~

Joshua chopped wood and looked over at Eb's. The house looked sad. Pealed paint and even a broken window replaced with a board. He'd helped rebuild after the fire, several years ago. Couldn't Eb see the goodness of God through the People? He thought of the days and weeks of tearing down the rubble, and replacing it with a new home where he would maybe raise a family again. Why'd he have to go and turn to the bottle, and in his rage, turn against God and the People?

A car pulled into his driveway and Raven got out with a large box. Joshua noticed Eb hadn't shoveled the walkway leading to the house. Sticking the ax in a piece of wood, he got the metal snow shovel and made his way over. "Raven, how are you?"

"I'm doing fine. How about you?"

"Well, concerned about Eb and I'm sure glad at least *you're* checking on him. I'm going to shovel the driveway and stairs so you don't hurt yourself when you come over."

"That's thoughtful of you, but Eb's shunned. You don't want to get in trouble. How about I ask Lawrence to do it?"

He tried to read her when she said his name. Did she feel something for the pastor? "I'll do it. Should have been done last week."

"How's your mom?"

"Getting used to dialysis. She's knitting everyone scarves. Says it helps pass the time." He looked at the concern in her eyes. He'd never seen it in Lottie's. He drew near to her and took the box, his hands overlapping hers, and turned when he heard the clopping of horse's hoofs. It was Lottie and her mother, Mary. Lottie gawked at him then snapped her head, looking straight ahead.

Joshua jiggled the doorknob and opened the door. "Eb," he yelled.

He heard a shuffling sound and soon Eb emerged. He was in his pajamas and robe with a brown scarf around his neck. "Stay right there, Son, I have some kind of flu."

"I can take you to the doctor," Raven offered. "Where's your thermometer? We need to take your temperature."

Eb walked over to an overstuffed chair and collapsed. "I'm sorry, dear one, I don't have a thermometer."

She went over to feel his forehead and quickly turned to Joshua. "He's burning up. Can you make me a snowball?"

He ran outside and took some snow from the front porch rail and pressed it together. "Here, this should bring it down."

Raven took the snow and put it on Eb's forehead. She broke off a piece and wiped it on both cheeks. Eb closed his eyes and moaned. "What hurts, Eb?" Raven asked.

"Everything. Mostly my head and joints."

She kept the ice on him for two minutes then felt his forehead again. "He's burning up. We need to get him to the ER."

~*~

Susanna sat up in bed, admiring her new quilt. It was warm and made with love. By the glow of the oil lamp, she saw each square had a flower embroidered on it and the name of its maker in small letters on the bottom. She was thankful Mary and Lottie had stopped in to visit and deliver the gift. Maybe she was wrong about Lottie and overly sensitive about her son's feelings.

She knew these quilts were usually made for those who were terminally ill. That she was, no denying it. All the people tested had not produced one donor match. She'd thought of putting an ad in *Die Botschaft* but it was illegal to solicit for a kidney, but knew many other people would get tested if they knew of the need.

She laid her head on the pillow and thought of the shouting she'd heard the other night. Rueben was getting nervous, she could tell, but there was something in his voice as he shouted about Eb's *rumspringa* days. It was guilt. But why? What was it about Eb that made him so cautious, always wanting him to keep his distance from Joshua? Was there something Rueben knew about Eb that she didn't know? None of it made sense. She soon saw Rueben come in and slip in beside her, concern on his face. "Joshua still isn't home? No trace of where he went?"

"None," Rueben mumbled. "It's not like him to up and go without saying a word."

Susanna took her husband's hand. "You carry a lot on those shoulders of yours. I'm still here to help."

He squeezed her hand. "You're sick and need rest."

She leaned toward him. "What happened during your *rumspringa*, Rueben? I've asked before and you make light of it, but I can tell it haunts you."

Susanna felt his hand stiffen and pull away. The silence in the room mocked the whistling wind that beat on the windows. Nothing made her husband turn cold as ice, unless she brought up the wild oats she guessed he'd sown in his youth. Rueben and some other fellows got a car and drove it to Jamestown and Salamanca. Everyone looked the other way, since they were allowed to explore the outside world to make sure they wanted to make a permanent commitment to the Amish faith.

Susanna could only think of one thing that could linger so long in his memory. Unrepentant sin…the sin of sexual immorality. "Rueben, I may not be here for you to ask me to forgive you, so I want to say right now, that I do."

She looked over at him and saw a tear glide down his cheek and felt him take her hand. "Eb was the ring leader and I can't forgive him. He kept taking us to a bar and I had too much to drink." He turned to her. "It was only once, as God is my witness. She meant nothing to me."

Susanna felt a stabbing pain in her chest, and swallowed hard. "Only once, you say?"

"*Jah*, one big mistake. I told Eb I'd never go down with him again, and I didn't."

Susanna prayed immediately for grace. Her instincts were right. He'd been with another woman before they were married and he blamed Eb for his sin. She didn't think such a confession would hurt so much, but it did; she closed her eyes and prayed for strength. "I forgive, Rueben, and I'm not vain, but was she pretty?"

"She was an Indian. From what I recall, yes, she was pretty, but I barely remember her. It meant nothing to me. We were all young and foolish."

She heard the sound of a car pulling in the driveway. Rueben got up and looked outside. "It's Raven's car and Joshua's getting out."

Chapter 7

$\mathcal{J}$oshua sipped his morning coffee and thought of Raven. How tenderly she cared for Eb while they waited for hours in the emergency room. She wanted to take care of him, too, insisting he stay at Appleton in a spare room. Jim and Marilyn were wise to protest, since the boys could all get sick.

So, she was at Eb's right now, sleeping on his couch. She'd go to work and check on him throughout the day. Raven even gave him her old cell phone and charged it in her car every time she visited. From what she'd said, she knew what it was like to be left alone and afraid when a little girl. Her aunt never kept the promise her dying mother asked her to keep. To care for Raven.

He'd promised his *mamm* many things, if she should go on to eternity, and couldn't imagine breaking his promises.

Raven's heart was pure gold, but who loved her like a woman needed to be loved? She'd mentioned she had no feelings for her old boyfriend in Florida. It felt too natural for him to want to take her in his arms and he barely knew her. He'd known Lottie since they were *kinner* but he still felt like there was a barrier between them.

Joshua heard a buggy pull in. It was Bishop Byler. Such a nice man to always be checking on his *mamm*. He greeted him at the door, and soon knew this was a serious matter.

"Joshua, I need to have words with you, in private."

"*Daed's* in the barn and *mamm's* asleep. Sit down." He grabbed the blue speckled coffee pot and filled a cup, placing it in front of the bishop, and then sat across from him. "What's the matter?"

Bishop Byler cleared his throat loudly. "You know Eb's a shunned man, yet you're seen over at his house. Why?"

Joshua grimaced. Lottie and her *mamm* saw him over at Eb's yesterday. It was clear they reported it. "*Jah*, I know he's shunned. He was sick. We took him to the hospital."

"Oh," the bishop stroked his long salt and pepper beard. "Well, you had that right. We don't withhold the hand of fellowship to anyone in true need." He took a swig of coffee. "So you only go over to Eb's for emergencies then?"

"Well, I shovel his sidewalk sometimes."

"Eb's not too elderly to do that. He's only in his fifties. Why would you do that?"

Joshua didn't have a good reason to help Eb. He had to admit what was inside. "I miss him."

"We all miss him and pray he returns. I pray this with all my might. Until then, no contact unless an emergency. He needs to feel the sting of being away from the flock."

Joshua shifted on the oak bench.

~*~

Light jolted Raven as she tried to open her eyes. She climbed out of bed, and with eyes shut, she made her way over to the window blind and pulled it down. *One down, two more to go*, she thought as she stumbled around the room. Her feet felt like lead and her head throbbed. When she got all three blinds down she slowly opened her eyes. The pain was still there but not as sharp. Exhausted, she fell back into bed and thought of Eb. She must have caught what he had. Maybe Joshua did, too.

Raven reached for her cell phone and called the house phone and soon heard Marilyn's voice. "I'm sick. Joshua was exposed. Can you make sure he knows? A flu could kill Susanna." Marilyn said she'd take care of everything.

She laid her head on her pillow, thinking of Eb. Who would check on him now? She reached for her phone again.

"Lawrence, Eb's sick and now I am. Can you take the box of food to him and see how he is?" He kindly offered to do anything to help and Raven told him she was grateful and hung up.

The pain in her head wasn't going away and she covered her eyes with a spare pillow. Soon a knock was heard at her door. "Miss Meadows, are you okay?"

It was Cliffy, and her heart melted. Not only was he overcoming his shyness, like she had, but he was learning to care for others. "I'm fine Cliffy. Just have the flu."

Soon Timmy's voice was heard. "Miss Meadows, Mrs. Rowe wants to know if you want to see a doctor. She said she can take you. I think you need to go."

This was her first job as a social worker for children and she had nothing else to compare it to, but was getting very attached to these boys. "Timmy, I'm contagious and don't want anyone around me. I'll drive myself."

Another knock. It was Chuckey. "Not a good idea. We can get Doc Mast to come here." He sighed loudly. "Thanksgiving's next week. We need you better."

Her head was throbbing, and she couldn't take this noise much longer. "If you think so, get the doctor."

She heard a stampede descend down the staircase and held her heart. This warm sensation she felt toward the boys must be love. But they'd have to leave when she found homes. Nausea swept over her so she closed her eyes and tried to not think about the future. The Bible said to not fret or worry about tomorrow. He took care of birds and He'd take care of her.

Raven thought of Joshua. He seemed nervous helping a shunned man, but did it anyway. Maybe he wasn't committed to the Amish and maybe he'd leave. She noticed how he looked at her. His eyes glowed with kindness and they pulled her in. She'd never been able to tell anyone so much about her past, and the more she opened up to him, and he accepted her, she felt deep feelings of fear and guilt being pulled out. The shame of not being wanted all seemed to be fading the more they talked. She'd heard Lawrence teach the boys that there was no fear in love. Was she falling in love with Joshua?

~*~

Joshua heard a car pull in the driveway. He gave his *mamm* her pills and went to the front door, hoping it was Raven. It was Pastor Lawrence.

"Raven caught the flu. She wanted someone to come by and tell you. She's concerned you caught it and might pass it on to your mother."

82

"*Danki*, I do feel strange. Weak."

"You look pale. Maybe you should get someone to help your mother until you're better. I'd stay away from her."

He was touched at the concern the pastor showed for his *mamm*. "If you could get word to my aunt, I'd appreciate it. She can send help. Do you know Hannah and David Byler?"

"No, but can you draw me a map?"

"It's easy. Just go straight down this road a mile. You'll see ski lifts on the left and Byler on the mailbox on the right."

Lawrence nodded. "Great view of Cockaigne from their place. I ski there all the time." He took Joshua's hand, and shook it. "Our whole church is praying for your mother."

"*Danki*," Joshua said.

~*~

Lottie was glad Joshua was sick and Hannah had asked her to help the family. Now here she was, cooling Joshua down with a cold towel. She'd opened his shirt and placed her cold hand on his chest, and he took it in his, but said the unthinkable. He called her Raven. How could he? She shook him until he was awake. "It's me Lottie."

He opened his eyes. "Raven, I knew you cared…"

Lottie's temples started to throb. How could this be happening? Joshua was hers. When his *mamm* died or got better, they would pick up where they'd left. She hadn't really called the courtship off, only took a break. It was morbid being in this house, helping him care for his dying *mamm*. She gently slapped his face. "Joshua, it's me Lottie. You're delirious. You don't know what you're saying."

Joshua looked at her fondly. He reached for her and she put her head on his chest. She took her fingers and ran them over the blonde hair on his chest. She knew Joshua still considered them to be a couple. He reached for her bonnet with one hand and pulled it back. Her hair was exposed and she was glad. He'd be her husband someday anyhow.

Lottie helped him pull the hair from the bun she had at the nape of her neck. He kissed it. She looked at him and could stand it no longer, and kissed his mouth. She hadn't had a kiss from him in well over a year. She kissed his cheeks and then his mouth again. He grabbed her and kissed her passionately and then held her tight, like he would lose her, and then kissed her again.

~*~

Raven heard the knock on her door. She fluffed her pillow and sat up. "Come in."

"Happy Turkey Day," they all yelled.

Raven saw the boys pour into the room. Toby and Ethan carried silver trays. "We made you breakfast," Toby said.

Ethan placed a tray on her lap. "Now you can watch the Macy's Day Parade."

She tried to hold back her emotions, but it was useless. No one had ever made her breakfast in bed before. She dabbed at the tears that were forming. "Thank you so much. I'll enjoy this and then come downstairs. We can watch the parade together."

"Doc said bed rest," Bud said. "Tomorrow you're allowed to get up."

Bud was being bossy, but it was so cute. "Can't I watch the parade on the big screen TV?"

Bud looked at her somberly, and then grinned. "You're asking me?"

"Yes, I've been sleeping around the clock all week. How do I know what the doctor said?"

"I talked to the doc, too," Chuckey said. "I'm sure you can come downstairs."

Bud took his chubby hand and felt her forehead. "No more fever. Okay, you can come downstairs, but we're still doing all the chores on your list until tomorrow."

Pride swelled in her chest. "You boys followed the chore chart?"

"Mr. and Mrs. Rowe had to remind us when we forgot, but all the chores are done," Cliffy said, smiling broadly.

Raven felt like giving Cliffy a big hug. He was overcoming his shyness for sure. She felt a wave of fatigue and put her head back on the pillow. "Thanks for the breakfast boys. Now go get yours."

They smiled and said their good-byes. She looked at the tray Toby put on the side of her bed. It had mail on it, so she leafed through it and found a card...*from Brandon?* She opened it with shaking hands, still feeling tired. It was a card that read, Thinking of You.... She opened it and read the card's poem. It was romantic. He wrote something on the bottom:

Raven, I never should have let you go. I'm coming up during Christmas break. I love you.
Brandon

Her mouth grew dry. He didn't ask if she wanted to see him. What nerve. He let her go! He didn't own her. Coming up for Christmas meant a long stay, since he was a teacher and had Christmas to New Year's Day off. She felt more fatigued than before. Raven put the breakfast tray on her nightstand and let the mail fall on floor, and then buried her head in her pillow.

~*~

Joshua woke up, surprised to see Lottie in his room. She smiled and pulled her *kapp* off. "Lottie, why are you here? Where'd Raven go? And put your *kapp* on."

"Joshua, don't you remember?"

"Remember what?"

She sat next to him on the bed. "You know. Our times together." She leaned over to kiss him.

He pushed her back. "Put your *kapp* on. Your hair is for your husband to see."

"You will be my husband, silly." She started to unpin her bun.

"Lottie, I don't know what's going on, but stop. Put your hair in your *kapp*. You're breaking the *Ordnung*."

"*Ordnung* kind of rhymes with boredom, wouldn't you say?" She leaned toward him again. "We're home alone. Your *mamm's* in the hospital and your *daed's* with her."

Joshua felt like he was in a bad dream. "Why's my *mamm* in the hospital?"

"She got the flu, like you did."

"Is she okay?"

"Your Aunt Hannah stopped by with food. Said to pray for her."

Joshua pulled back the covers and saw he was in his long john underwear, and quickly covered himself again. "Lottie, please leave. I need to get dressed to go to the hospital."

She put her hand on his shoulders and pushed him back in bed. "I've already seen plenty."

Joshua blushed. He must have been awfully sick, because he didn't remember anything. What did she mean? "Why didn't my *daed* take care of me, or another man?"

"Your *daed* was sick. I took care of him, too." Her eyes brimmed with tears. "I've worked so hard, only to have you be short with me."

He took a deep breath. "We appreciate it, but there's nothing between us anymore. Why are you acting so strange?"

"I still love you, Joshua. I know now you feel the same…"

~*~

Susanna adjusted the oxygen tubes that went up her nostrils. She looked at Rueben sitting in the recliner next to her bed, and her heart went out to him. He'd been sick, too, but came to her as soon as he could. She loved this man of hers and was glad the air was finally clear between them concerning his past. She blushed to think she cared if the woman was pretty. How vain…

The sunbeams poured through the vertical blinds on the window. Susanna was thankful for sunny days, even though the nurse had told her it was frigid outside. Her heart was like that at times. Susanna thought of her fear of dialysis. It tried to get its icy grip on her and paralyze her, then she'd read her Bible and the light of God's Word told her to fear not. Then fear held her back again. No amount of coaxing from Rueben or Joshua could make her move forward. She'd refused dialysis until death was knocking at her door. She was glad Rueben told them to start the whole process. It wasn't as bad as she'd feared.

Susanna thought of the good news, too. Her cousin, Sarah, was a match. She would be donating a kidney as soon as all the paperwork went through. They'd go to Pittsburgh for the transplant right after Christmas. She closed her eyes and thanked God. Such good news to get on Thanksgiving Day.

Soon a knock at the door was heard and she saw Joshua and Jim Rowe enter. Her son looked at her as if in shock. Did she look that bad?

"*Mamm*, I heard the good news. You're getting a kidney for Christmas, *jah*?"

She reached her arms out to the son she loved so much. The son who put his life on hold to care for her. Now he could move on...

~*~

Raven felt the wind whip at her cheeks as she got out of the car. She was so glad to be back to work and visiting the Yoders. It had been two weeks since she saw them.

She noticed a buggy; probably someone bringing a meal, and ran to the side door and knocked. Joshua opened the door and a look of dread spread across his whole face. Was something wrong with Susanna? Raven stepped inside and he took her white coat and blue hat and scarf.

"Joshua, I'm so glad you're better. We all caught that flu from Eb."

"*Jah*, and it was a bad one at that." He shifted his weight.

"Thank you for coming over to help take care of me. I was too forward. I'm sorry."

"Joshua, what do you mean?"

"I kissed you. Don't you remember? And you were here, I saw you as plain as day."

She wished he'd take her in his arms and kiss her for real, but had no idea what he was talking about. Out of the corner of her eye she saw red hair and a dainty figure. It was Lottie. She swayed over and put her arm through Joshua's. "I've tried to tell him he was delirious. I nursed my man back to health. He just got us confused."

My man? Was he courting Lottie again? With Susanna getting a transplant, she could be the center of attention again. How typical of such a selfish girl.

"Can I talk to you privately?" Joshua asked, his eyes were pleading. "In the living room?"

She saw Lottie pull her arm out of his and march out of the room, and then she heard feet bang up the stairs. Joshua put his arm around her and led her to the living room. They sat beside each other on one of the benches. "She's not my girl. Please tell me it was you who came here and helped me. I did kiss you and need to apologize."

"It wasn't me, Joshua. Do you think it was Lottie you kissed? She was taking care of you, right?"

"Well, she was taking care of me when I woke up. But you helped, too. And I kissed you."

"I became delirious too and thought the boys where aliens when they cared for me. I was afraid and yelled for help. They still think it's funny. Your mind plays tricks on you. You thought Lottie was me. You kissed her, not me." Her heart skipped a beat. His natural reaction was to kiss her. She fidgeted with her hands and the ticking of the pendulum clock made the silence awkward. Out of the corner of her eye, Raven noticed Joshua's face was turning red, so she took his hand. "Don't be embarrassed."

To her surprise he cupped her hand and stroked it. He looked up and she saw longing in his blue eyes. Joshua put his hand on her back to pull her closer. Time stood still, until she heard Lottie gasp as she entered the room.

Joshua pulled away from Raven, and seeing how awkward he felt, she bent down and opened up her brief case. "Here are the papers stating you're approved to be foster parents. How will this work, though, with Susanna leaving for her transplant?"

"I'll be here. My *daed* will be with her the whole time. It'll be two months before they're home…"

"Who will take the place of your *daed* on the farm?"

"My cousin, Lester."

"I'll need to run a background check on him, but it can be expedited. Cliffy is peeking out of his shell, but needs to come out the whole way. I was thinking of placing him here. You'd be good for him. Also, I think Timmy still feels invisible. He needs more attention and I know you can deliver on that, too."

"*Jah*, I can. I feel invisible sometimes, too. We can be *goot* company for each other."

For the past three years Joshua had been isolated, spending his time caring for his mom. Raven took his hand. "Joshua, you'll be free after the transplant. Your life will go back to normal, right? And I'll come over to visit."

He squeezed her hand. Lottie made her presence known by coughing loudly. She walked arrogantly over, and putting her hands on Joshua's back, said, "I'll be here to keep Joshua company." She massaged his shoulders.

Raven knew leaving was her best option, wanting to tell the silly girl exactly what she thought. "I need to go. Can I see Susanna before I leave? I bought her more yarn."

"She's sleeping. Don't disturb her," Lottie said, eyes narrow.

Joshua took Raven by the hand and led her toward the stairs. "My *mamm* will wake up for you to say hello. And she'll want you to see the shawl she finally finished." He turned and glared at Lottie before following Raven up the stairs.

Chapter 8

$\mathcal{J}$oshua watched as Raven took his *mamm's* hand and stroked it. He hadn't seen Lottie show affection like that toward her. He pulled up a chair for Raven to sit in and sat in the other one in the corner of the room. He noticed Raven's response to his *mamm*; she looked like a flower opening up in the spring.

If he married, it needed to be a girl who really loved his *mamm*. Yes, she'd have a new kidney, but she'd still need lots of care. Doctor appointments, blood tests, medicine adjustments, and that's if they were blessed. No, Joshua would be nearby to care for her until her dying day. If only Raven were Amish, he'd have no hesitation to make his feelings known.

How could anyone get to really know Lottie? She was always fickle, but over the past year, something changed her. How she tried to seduce him needed to be told to the bishop, but she'd only say he kissed her first. Didn't she understand he wasn't in his right mind? She also mocked the Amish ways, saying *Ordnung* rhymed with boredom. No baptized girl would talk like that. The *Ordnung* was agreed upon by all in the community and if she had some complaint, it could be brought up for discussion. How many times had natural gas stoves been talked about and it was a decided no in the end? Did Lottie want something changed that was forbidden? Was she flirting with worldly ways? Was she straying from the flock? Was he the only one who knew and did he need to help her?

~*~

Raven plopped on one of the overstuffed chairs in the living room. She had three homes for the boys and Appleton could now accept more clients. It would be an hour before the boys came home from school and she soaked in the peace and quiet. She thought of Susanna and what she said about God. Raven would read the book of Matthew the Amish held in such high esteem. She'd pay attention to some story on the mountain. If she had questions, Susanna nudged her to ask Lawrence Turner and spoke highly of him. She had read all the books he'd given her, but still had so many questions. Lawrence suggested going out to eat to talk about it more.

Her cell phone rang and she saw it was Brandon. Fear swooped over her. Raven froze not knowing what to do, so let it ring and didn't pick up. Why was she so afraid of him? Saying he wanted to come up to visit her for Christmas made her sick. When would she be able to talk to someone like she did Joshua and Susanna? She felt transparent for the first time. Maybe she needed more practice. Her phone rang again; it was Brandon. She answered the phone.

"Hello?"

"Raven, I've missed you so much. How are you?"

"I'm fine. Really love it up here in NY again."

"You said you hated that state. Don't you miss Florida at all? Or me?"

She didn't want to be rude, but she needed to be honest. "Brandon, I've moved on."

"I know my temper scared you, but I've changed. Couldn't we just forget my stupidity and pick up where we left off?"

"I don't know, Brandon."

"You met someone else? Please, don't drop that bomb on me."

"No, I've changed. I'm getting, well, I'm getting religious. Reading the Bible and liking it."

She heard him fumble for words. "I'm not a believer in anything, but if it means a lot to you, it doesn't matter to me…"

It hit her like ice water being thrown in her face. There was something about God or her spirituality, or whatever you called it, and it did matter a great deal to her. She and Brandon hadn't seen eye to eye on this and it was part of the wedge that formed between them. How could someone go through life without wondering how they got there? Maybe it's why she respected the Amish and Lawrence so much. They seemed to know God was real. "I need time to think, Brandon. You really caught me off guard."

"I'm impulsive; I admit it. It's why I didn't call you: to give you space. You run like a scared deer when someone gets too close."

His words sent a sharp pain to her chest. He was right about her running away but he said it in a way that shamed her. She'd told Joshua she had a hard time opening up, and yet he accepted that and wanted to know how to help.

"I'll call you when I'm ready to talk, Brandon." She hung up the phone and threw it in her purse. She may not be able to be with Joshua, but something about the Christian men she'd met seemed so much better than Brandon. He lacked depth. Maybe she should pay more attention to what Lawrence was trying to teach her, and him too.

Raven heard a knock at the door and tried to regain composure. She opened it, surprised to see Lawrence and Eb. "Come in. It's freezing out."

They stepped inside and she saw Eb look at her with tenderness. He reached out to her and embraced her. "You saved my life. *Danki.*"

For some reason she didn't pull away, saying it was nothing. "You're welcome, Eb."

He took her by the shoulders and she saw tears were in his eyes. "You okay, dear one?"

"Oh, fine. I've been over the flu for a week. Didn't you see me pull in to the Yoder's? I meant to stop but had lots to catch up on." Raven looked up at Lawrence and noticed the genuineness of his smile. Brandon was so shallow in contrast. "Would you two like some hot chocolate? I was going to get some ready for the boys. They'll be stampeding through here in no time."

"We can't stay," Lawrence said. "Eb's here for a reason. Go ahead, Eb."

She saw him take off his black wool hat and fiddle with it. "Joshua told me I was drunk and made a pass at you. I have no recollection of it, but know Joshua doesn't make up stories. I'm so sorry."

The shame in his eyes moved her and she reached out and hugged him. "Eb, you don't need to apologize. You already did."

She felt him hug her tight. His body started to shake and tears fell on her shoulder. He pulled her back and looked intently at her. "No matter my loss, I have no excuse to turn my back on God and turn to liquor." He looked up at Lawrence for reassurance.

Lawrence put his large hand on Eb's shoulder. "Well said." He looked down at Raven. "Eb and I are doing a program similar to Alcoholics Anonymous. He's been sober for a month now and is going back and making amends to people he cares about. People he feels he may have offended. He made a list and we're almost done."

People he cares about? She was someone on that list? Raven took Eb's hand. "I am so honored I'm even on your list." She hesitated, not sure whether to ask what was on her mind. "Have you made amends then with the Amish? "

"God's working on my heart concerning that. Some things take more time."

She knew from Susanna that Eb felt abandoned by God since his wife and child were taken, but here he was talking about God. She looked up at Lawrence. He must be a good Bible teacher to get through to Eb, and didn't look away when his chocolate brown eyes held hers. The next time he asked her to go out to dinner to discuss the Bible, she'd say yes.

~*~

Joshua looked at his Aunt Hannah in disbelief. "You want Lester and Lottie to stay with me during the transplant? Lester, yes. Lottie, no."

Shock registered on his aunt's face. "I thought you two would be announcing your wedding in the spring."

"Who told you that?"

"Well, no one, I just assumed. You two courted before and I know you took a break with your *mamm* being so sick, but isn't it natural to pick up where you left off?"

"She broke our courtship because she felt neglected. She's not the one for me."

"Joshua, she needs you," his aunt blurted out, eyes round. "She's been hurting, too. She's twenty-one and wants a family. Was just waiting for things to calm down. She hasn't courted anyone in a year."

He hadn't looked at it that way. Maybe Lottie was straying from the Amish ways because she needed him to keep her on the straight and narrow. She hadn't courted anyone in a year, which did show dedication. But he felt nothing for her; someone else was crowding his heart. But Raven wasn't Amish. He looked at the concern etched on his aunt's face. "I'll think about what you said, but I don't think it's wise she stay here while my parents are gone. I can manage."

"I think it would be nice to have this place done over before your *mamm* gets back, and a woman's touch is needed. If not Lottie, who else will do it?"

He had over thirty female cousins who could come over and stay. One of them would have willingly stayed with them over the past two years. They were only really needed during March and April, when the sap was running and making maple syrup consumed their time. "How about Lottie come over in March, when she's really needed?"

"Joshua, I'm trying not to be rude, but this place looks shabby. We couldn't paint and varnish with my sister being sick, but she'll be gone. Lottie will have this place spick and span. You need new curtains, too." She put both hands on her hips and held her ground.

"Let me talk to Lottie before I say yes…"

~*~

Joshua was glad it was a full moon. Traveling at night was much easier. He looked up at the clear sky and was amazed at the star-studded blackness. The heavens declare the glory of God, Joshua thought. He heard an owl hoot, but all was silent.

He hadn't been out at night for a buggy ride since he courted Lottie. She'd snuggle up against him and they'd talk of their dreams for the future. When he asked her to marry him last year and move in with his family, helping to care for his mamm, she recoiled. She wanted her new house with a large living room so she could have her friends over to quilt. She reminded him of his promise to build a new house. How they argued. He accused her of being selfish, and she said he was insensitive and demanding. Was he? Why was she willing to help now? He'd soon find out.

As Joshua approached the house, he saw a car parked down the road from it, near the cornfield. He pulled in the driveway, hopped out of the buggy, and made his way to the side door. Mary answered.

"Come in and have something hot to drink."

"How are you Mary? I hear you've been approved to be foster parents."

"*Jah*, Raven stopped by to tell us. She seemed sad, though. I think she's more attached to those boys than she'll admit."

"She has a big heart," Joshua said. "We'll have to make sure the boys visit her."

"Poor girl doesn't have folks, can you imagine? Being alone in the world like that?"

"It makes her all the more special; she gives out of her lack, like the woman in the Bible who gave the two coins, all she had."

He saw Mary look at him, eyes wide. "You speak so fondly of her."

"I do? Well, she's a trusted English friend, like the Rowes'." He wiped some snow off the bottom of his trousers to escape her penetrating gaze. Was it so obvious he cared for Raven? "I came to visit Lottie."

Mary smiled broadly. "Well, she went to Wal-Mart, but I'm sure she'll be home soon. She's been gone a few hours."

"I'll come back another time. Beautiful night for a drive." He nodded to Mary and walked out onto the porch. He saw the same car he'd seen on the road pull in the drive way and Lottie sprung out.

"Joshua, how *goot* to see you."

A male driver, his age, opened his door and didn't look at him. He opened the trunk and started carrying in grocery bags. He brushed past Joshua as he entered the house. When he came back out he looked at Lottie sternly, and then grinned. "Call me when you need a ride."

He saw Lottie turn red and put her head down. When the car pulled out of the driveway and down the road, she looked up at Joshua. "He's a new driver."

"I saw you parked down the road. What's going on?"

She looked down again, fumbling for words. "He, ah, said his car didn't sound right and stopped to check on something."

"Why not check it in the driveway, in clear view of the family?"

Anger shot out of her eyes. "Because his car made a bad noise down the road. You don't drive a car and he does. I think he knows best."

Joshua couldn't argue with that. He didn't know a thing about cars. "Why a male driver? Women take women on long drives."

"His *mamm* was supposed to take me but she's sick. He did a good deed and took me instead." He saw her draw close to him and her face soften. "Are you jealous?"

By the moonlight, he saw her brown eyes had yellow flecks. She looked beautiful. He cleared his throat. "Lottie, can we talk?"

She put her arms on his shoulders. "I think I know what this is about."

"You do?"

"*Jah*, Joshua. The way you acted toward Bruce told me everything. You were jealous, because you love me and want to court again." She pulled his neck down to kiss him. "Let's take a buggy ride, like we used to."

He didn't know what to say. Maybe he was jealous, but it didn't mean he loved her. "Okay, for a short ride. We need to talk."

~*~

The boys sipped hot chocolate and sat around the kitchen table stringing popcorn. Marilyn kept popping more corn on the stove and replenishing the large stainless steel bowl that sat in the middle of the table. Jim sang along to a Bing Crosby White Christmas LP.

Raven thought of her grandmother. They'd strung cranberries for the birds to eat this time of year. Christmas was celebrated but not really a religious holiday. It was a time to think about the animals that needed food to make it through the winter. Respecting nature was a Native American custom she relished. Her grandfather planted pine trees on their land, just so the birds could nestle behind the needles. He also grew his own bird food. She never tired of taking the huge sunflowers that dried in the attic and pull out all the seeds in the center. She helped him cut the millet plants and hang them to dry, then collect the seeds and mix them with the sunflowers. How proudly her grandfather went out to the tin trays scattered throughout the reservation, making sure he kept up with the birds' needs...and he always took her along.

But her Aunt Brook made fun of her parents and their love for the birds. She didn't care who was hungry...even her niece who spent many hungry hours in the attic. Raven was reading the book of Matthew like Susanna told her to. She was learning how God cares about one little sparrow in need. He did see her all alone in that attic and her case worker took her out and put her in a place she was cared for.

Wonderful memories of her first foster home came back, when Granny Nora taught her how to knit. Her wrinkled hand had cradled hers as she taught her how to hold the yarn and needles. Learning how to cast on was easy, Granny praised her for a week for being so talented. Learning the difference between a knit and purl took time, but she was soon following patterns. Her first project was a scarf, and then more complicated things, all outfits for her doll. Yes, good things came out of foster care. God had his eye on the sparrow, and he was looking over her, just like they sang in church.

She heard the doorbell ring and looked up at the clock. It must be Lawrence to pick her up for their date. Jim got the door and soon Lawrence appeared in the kitchen. "Looks like we're having fun here. Want to string some up for the tree at the church?"

Bud looked up. "I will. I'll string as much popcorn as you've got."

Jim chuckled. "You eat more than you string." He patted his stomach. "Remember?"

Bud threw a piece of popcorn at Jim. "I know. Some of us are on diets." He grinned as he continued to work on his string.

Raven got up and went to stand by Lawrence. "You boys have your homework done?"

They nodded in unison.

"Cliffy and Ethan, did you get all the multiplication problems done?"

They nodded, and then they all stared at her. Soon they all burst out laughing. "What's so funny?"

"Nothing," Chuckey said.

"No, tell me."

She turned to see Lawrence had her white coat in his hands. He'd gotten it off the hook in the entryway. "Can I help you on with your coat?"

The boys roared. Bud yelled, "*Ew*, Pastor got a date."

Raven could feel heat rise in her face as she let Lawrence help her with her coat. Bud was a little funny bone and she'd get him back. "Actually, you see the color of my coat, right Bud?"

He nodded.

"Well, it's white for a reason. You can get married in a white coat in the winter, on the Indian Reservation. It's a custom." She looked at Lawrence and batted her eyelashes. "We're getting married tonight, aren't we darling?"

To her surprise, Lawrence took her and dipped her, his face close to hers. "I've dreamt of this moment since the day we met." He stood up and scooped her in his arms. He turned to Bud. "You want to come to the wedding? Be the ring bearer?"

Bud was a statue with a wide open mouth. Raven looked around the room. Everyone was, even Marilyn and Jim. "Boy, I'll have no problem fooling you on April Fool's Day. You're all so gullible."

"No, we're not," Jim said. "Maybe what you said is believable. You two look really great together."

Chapter 9

Joshua asked the waitress to bring more hot chocolate. He looked over at Lottie, and she looked as nervous as he was. Not many Amish came to the Grainery, but he felt he needed to get her out of his buggy. The way she was cuddling beside him didn't warm his heart like it used to.

"Are you warmed up enough to go home now?"

She glared at him. "I was warm in the buggy. We've gone riding after a singing in much colder weather."

"Lottie, we're not courting anymore. You're not the same girl and I'm not the same man."

"What could have possibly changed, Joshua? The Amish life is slow. Not much change to really affect anyone."

Joshua stiffened. Was she really that shallow? "My *mamm's* been facing death, and I see in her that she has no regrets, at least concerning who she married. My *daed* cares for her sacrificially, and always has. I want a marriage like theirs."

She reached over the small table and took Joshua's hand. "I love you. I'd do the same for you."

Her words were hollow. "Your actions don't match your words. You didn't show much love by ending our courtship when my *mamm's* diagnosis turned terminal.

Other women came and sat with her, bringing presents…loving her. You did nothing."

"It's too morbid for me, Joshua. Watching someone die scares me."

"It scares everyone," Joshua said.

The waitress put two full mugs of hot chocolate with whip cream on their table.

"*Danki*," Joshua said. He looked over at Lottie who again had tears spilling down her cheeks. Was he too hard on her? Maybe he was so used to being around someone who was sick. But he thought of Raven, who knew of his *mamm's* condition. She stopped by whenever she could. They'd formed a bond in three months that he'd never had with Lottie. "Please don't cry."

"Joshua, I'm more emotional than usual, I know. But maybe it's because I care so much about you. Won't you let me make it up to you somehow? Let me show you I am that caring woman you once loved?"

Joshua looked at her and sighed. Out of the corner of his eye he saw a girl with long black hair in a white coat. He turned to see it was Raven with Lawrence Turner. He felt his heart jump up in his throat and jealousy stirred within him. He watched as Lawrence pulled out the chair and took Raven's coat. Joshua wished he could change tables and be with her. She not only looked gorgeous tonight, but her countenance had changed. She looked more at peace. He couldn't pinpoint why, but he wanted to be her hero, her rescuer. Was it love? Was it pride? Shouldn't he be happy she was discovering God loved her? Others too?

"Joshua, I see your English friend, Raven, has a boyfriend. Why don't we go over and say hello."

Before he could stop Lottie she'd gotten up and headed toward their table. He followed and when his eyes met Raven's, she gave him a look that confused him. Was she jealous he was with Lottie? Lottie chattered on about how they were out on a buggy ride and had to stop in to warm up or freeze to death. Raven's face turned red and she looked at him as if in search of an answer.

"I had important things to discuss with Lottie. We need a female helper when my *mamm* goes to Pittsburgh for her transplant. Lottie offered to help."

He saw the tension in Raven's face ease. "Joshua, you can count on me to help, too. You're mom has helped me in many ways and I'd be happy to come over and repay her kindness."

Without hesitation, Lottie blurted out, "What has Susanna done for you? She's too ill to do anything. Did you ask her to teach you to quilt, like so many *Englishers* do?"

He saw Raven bite her lower lip and look down. She slowly looked up with misty eyes. "Susanna's shown me the love of God. She made Him real to me." Raven looked over at Joshua. "Now, Lawrence is teaching me the Bible."

Joshua's eyes locked with Raven's. "I'll tell my *mamm* what you said. She'll be mighty encouraged. She can't do much but pray and love…"

Lawrence looked at him in admiration. "Those are the two most important things to do." He reached out to shake Joshua's hand. "Tell her we have our church and half the town praying for her."

Joshua smiled and shook his hand firmly. "*Danki.*"

~*~

Joshua was relieved to get home. Lottie unnerved him to his core. She was so emotional and lacked purity. Amish girls didn't throw themselves at their boyfriends. By yanking on his neck and trying to kiss him, when they were no longer courting, was not attractive. In the buggy she'd made the most preposterous suggestion. They get married as soon as possible? It was like being in a bad nightmare.

Seeing Raven was like seeing the first spring rain: totally refreshing. So his *mamm's* love was affecting her, helping her receive God's love. He thought of the hard look she gave him when they first met. Miracles still happened because Raven was a different person. Her inner beauty now matched her outer. He remembered what his *daed* said about his *mamm*. It was her loving spirit that made him pursue her. How could he, though? Should he just tell her how he feels and ask her to be Amish? She seemed too attached to her electronics and modern ways.

He was shaken from his thoughts when he heard a car pull in the driveway and honk a horn. Joshua ran down the stairs and saw it was Lawrence and Raven. He ran to the car, barefoot, and saw terror in Raven's eyes and ran to her side. She opened the door and stepped out. "Appleton's on fire. We just got a call. Can you come with us and help?"

Eb ran over from the house. "What's the matter, dear one?" When Eb reached her she fell into his arms and clung to Eb.

~*~

Raven gasped when they pulled into the driveway, and the tears ran freely down her cheeks. All the boys were outside, and she ran and embraced them. They were all staring motionless, in shock.

"Where are Marilyn and Jim?" Lawrence asked.

"In the hospital," Bud said, in a monotone voice. "Marilyn left the pan on the stove and it caught on fire. They tried to put it out. "

"They told us to run outside," Toby said, teeth chattering. "I stayed back and kept telling them to leave. Mr. Rowe said he had to get the box."

Raven got down on her knees. Mr. Rowe could have been seriously injured, but he was thinking of the boys. What love and dedication. The box held all the boys' paperwork. Without it, they'd be put into emergency foster homes. All the documents she needed to get the boys in good homes was in what Jim called the "Important Box".

She felt someone get down in the snow beside her. It was Eb. She embraced him and sobbed. "Did you lose a lot of your stuff, Raven?"

She hadn't even thought of her things. Then Raven remembered her doll, and all the clothes she'd knit for it over the years. Horror-stricken, she screamed, "My doll!" Her side of the house wasn't on fire, and she charged toward it. A firefighter tried to stop her, but she got around him and ran into the building, and charged up the stairs. She felt the heat pour into her lungs and she gasped for air, and then two arms pulled her from behind.

~*~

She woke up and saw Joshua holding her hand. A paramedic was taking her pulse. "Where am I?" She looked at Joshua, wondering why she was inside an ambulance. He grabbed her in his arms and held her tight. Eb asked questions about her rag doll. Then Raven remembered what she did. How foolish. "Joshua, I'm so sorry."

He laid her down again and she looked at him. He had black soot on his face, streaked with tears. He took her hand and kissed it.

"I'm so sorry I put you in danger. I don't know what came over me."

A steadier stream of tears flowed down his cheeks and he couldn't talk. She heard the paramedic ask him if he needed something for shock. Joshua shook his head no, just clung tighter to her hand. What was he trying to say to her he couldn't get out? He seemed as bottled up as she used to be. Or did he get bad news about Marilyn and Jim? She turned to the stocky paramedic. "Where are the Rowes?"

"They were taken to the hospital, but they'll be fine. You'll be fine too; it's your friend here I'm keeping an eye on."

She looked at Joshua. "Joshua, everyone is fine." Raven turned again to the paramedic. "Can we talk in private?"

He nodded and walked away.

"Joshua, look at me. You're shaking and need to take something for shock."

He squeezed her hand. "I realize something…"

She put her hand on his cheek. "What?"

"I love you…"

Was this some kind of dream? "What?"

Eb climbed up in the ambulance. "You're staying at my house, Raven. You and all the kids. Lord knows I have spare rooms."

Reality set in. "I need to place the boys in foster homes."

Joshua stroked her hand. "They can stay with Eb until tomorrow. We can sort it out in the morning."

"Joshua, I need to follow rules. He's not a licensed foster home."

"Well, I am. They can all stay at my house."

Raven got up to hug him. She whispered in his ear. "Thank you, my knight in shining armor."

"Is that a *goot* thing?" she heard him ask.

~*~

Raven opened her eyes and was jolted to see a room with all white walls, dark blue curtains pulled to one side, and wooden floors. She was not at Appleton, but in Eb's house; most likely all her worldly possessions taken in the fire. Pans clanked downstairs and the smell of bacon wafted into the room. Eb's care warmed her heart and she quickly wrapped a small quilt around her shoulders.

She'd fallen asleep in her clothes and longed for her cozy pajamas.

Descending the plain oak staircase, she remembered her first day at Appleton, when Marilyn yelled that breakfast was ready. It was odd how she felt more at home in a simple Amish home, not a grand Victorian. Eb was standing by the black woodstove cracking eggs into a cast iron skillet. "Morning, dear one. How do you like your coffee? Black or with milk?"

Raven didn't know if it was the trauma of the night before, or the kind man's way of looking at her, but she soon found her chin quivering. She let the tears fall down her cheeks, unashamed, and let Eb engulf her in a hug. "You've been through a lot. But you need to keep up your strength. I made you an Amish breakfast."

She let Eb guide her to the oak table. "Thank you, Eb. I'll take my coffee black."

Eb sat a plate before her and then a mug of coffee. Raven gawked at the massive amount of food. "Is this Amish style? I'd weigh a ton if I ate like this every day."

"If you were Amish, you'd work it off. No sitting around looking at those boxes."

"Boxes?"

Eb snickered. "I call a TV a box. Don't' know why people watch other people live. Why not just live yourself? Makes no sense to me."

Raven looked at Eb, now sitting across the table. He was being serious and it made her wonder why she did watch other peoples' lives so much. To escape her own? She jumped when someone pounded on the front door;

her nerves were so unraveled. It was a woman's voice asking to speak with her and she got up and went into the living room. A short, stout police officer stood firmly at the front door. Her stern black eyes, the same color as her skin, made Raven know she meant business.

"You must be Raven. I'm Officer Carter and I need to speak with you about the boys. They'll need to be placed today into foster homes. I understand they're all living next door, with Mr. Yoder?"

Raven felt like her knees would give out and asked the officer to come sit at the table. Eb asked her if she wanted breakfast and coffee, but she declined. He also asked if this talk could wait until they were done eating, but she said she was on a busy schedule.

"Can the boys stay together today, even though they'll have a foster home by tomorrow? They're pretty traumatized by the fire and need each other."

The officer sighed. "I sure do wish I wrote these rules. No, they'll need to be placed today."

"But I don't have any clothes. I need to contact the insurance agent and make arrangements."

The officer hit her forehead. "I'm sorry. Almost forgot. I have some of your clothes in my car. Your room was spared from a lot of damage. It was the other side of the house above the kitchen that got completely ruined. I'll get the box."

Eb quickly got up and asked if he could get it for her, but the officer looked at him like he was daft. "I can lift a box. Don't trouble yourself."

Raven grabbed at her black hair, fury rising in her. Why couldn't this wait? She couldn't absorb all that was happening and wanted to visit Marilyn and Jim in the hospital, not work at getting the boys acclimated into new foster homes. Soon the officer came back and plopped a box on the table. Raven stood up, peaked inside, and saw her rag doll lying on the top. She gasped and took the doll in her arms. "Thank God. She's all I have…"

"No she's not," the officer said, curtly. "You have all these clothes and –"

"All I have left from my grandmother," Raven snapped. She put her head down and sobbed as she clung to the rag doll. Raven trembled as she sat down, memories of her grandmother flooding her. How she wished she was here now to just hold her, but Raven soon felt Eb's hands on her shoulders and heard him ask the officer to leave.

~*~

Joshua was glad the boys stayed over; they sure did lighten up the house. They had managed to use the outhouse, only when it was absolutely necessary, running out at the last minute. When they got back they complained of the cold…and the smell. He'd never seen boys act like girls.

They dug into the stacks of pancakes he put on the table and was impressed that they all asked who was saying grace. Bud offered, and thanked God that Mr. and Mrs. Rowe were okay and to bless them, and then the food.

Bud looked up at Joshua. "Can we see Mr. and Mrs. Rowe today? Make sure they know we miss them?"

Joshua spied Raven walking across the yard. "Miss Meadows is coming over. I'm sure she has something planned." He watched as Raven got closer, and thought of the confession he'd made last night. That he loved her. How foolish, acting on sheer emotion. He'd have to talk with her and tell her that he was sorry for speaking so carelessly.

But when she entered the room, all he wanted to do was hold her. She looked so lost and it was apparent by her red eyes, she'd been crying.

"Hi everyone," she said looking around the kitchen. "Where's Susanna?"

"She's upstairs in bed. Can't be in crowds."

"Even this little a group?"

"*Jah*, and she's tired, too. Will most likely be in bed until the transplant."

"I'll visit her as much as I can, being next door. It must get lonely." She turned to look at all the boys seated at the table. "Boys, I'm so sorry, but I got orders that you need to be placed in foster homes today."

The boys all moaned. Bud raised his hand. "I want to see Mr. & Mrs. Rowe."

"We can stay here with Joshua," Chuckey belted. "We know where the outhouse is and everything."

Raven put her hand up. "It has to be done today. Timmy and Cliffy, how would you like to stay here with the Yoder's?"

Timmy raised a timid hand. "And where's everybody else going?"

"You boys will all be living close to each other. Pastor Lawrence will be coming to help take everyone to their new homes. He really cares about you boys."

Joshua didn't know he could be so selfish, and shame filled him. Here was Raven trying to help the boys along with Pastor Lawrence and he was jealous and sulky. He took a deep breath and tried to focus on what Raven was saying.

"Bud and Chuckey, you're going to live with the Millers. Remember Eli and Mary Miller? They have a daughter, Lottie, and three younger children. You could be like big brothers to the little ones."

Joshua grinned. She'd chosen both outspoken boys to be in Lottie's house. He could see Lottie's face, huffing over this decision. Bud and Chuckey would certainly put her in her place.

"But we want to stay together," Bud insisted.

Cliffy stood up, panic stricken. "I want to be where Chuckey is. He's my best friend." A sob escaped. "Why are you doing this to me, Miss Meadows?"

Joshua saw Raven tremble as she pleaded with him to understand. Bud got up and told everyone to listen to Miss Meadows, and then embraced Raven. She thanked him.

"That leaves Toby and Paul. You'll be with Hannah and David Byler. They make good ice cream all year long and…you'll live right across the street from the ski resort."

"Can we go skiing?" Toby asked. "Maybe take lessons?"

Raven forced a smile. "I'm sure it can be arranged." She turned to Joshua. "Maybe Mr. Yoder can take you Amish skiing."

"How about we put something on the calendar so you all have something to look forward to?" Joshua asked. "Maybe we can ski in a day or two."

Raven looked at him through blurry eyes. "Thank you, Joshua. The boys need clothes and placed in their homes today, but I think in two days we can plan to ski, Amish style." She cocked her head to one side. "Can I talk to you privately?"

"*Ewwww,*" echoed around the kitchen, but Chuckey got up. "She's marrying Pastor Lawrence, remember guys."

Joshua grimaced. Marry Pastor Lawrence? Of course. He proposed to her at the Grainery over dinner.

Raven clapped her hands to make the boys stop talking. "It was a joke, remember. I'm not marrying the pastor."

"She has a boyfriend coming up from Florida," Bud belted out. "Don't you guys hear anything when she talks on the phone?"

Raven gasped. "Bud, you are out of line. What do you do? Listen through my bedroom door?"

Bud put his head down. "It gets boring at the house. Your life's like watching a movie. Sorry…"

Raven asked Joshua to speak with her in the living room. He didn't know why, but he felt furious. She still talked to her boyfriend? The one she said she didn't care for anymore? Why? But he was talking to Lottie, too. Raven sat next to him on the bench, and he wanted to dart up and go to the barn to cool off.

"Joshua, I picked Timmy and Cliffy for you since they're both shy and I think you'd be good medicine for them."

He bit his lower lip. "Ok. That's fine."

Raven took his hand. "Are you alright? You seem like you're in a bad mood. Were the boys too much to handle?"

Joshua wanted to say life was too much to handle. His *mamm* might be dying and the girl he loved wasn't Amish. "The boys were *goot*. No problems at all."

She squeezed his hand. "Joshua, Brandon isn't coming up here. I told him no and that I cared for someone else."

"Lawrence?"

Raven put her head on his shoulder. "Don't you remember last night? You said you loved me...and I love you."

Relief swelled his heart and he couldn't help but put his arms around her.

nsert chapter nine text here. Insert chapter nine text here.

Chapter 10

Raven looked through the boxes of clothes and sighed. She'd just packed to come up to Ellington a few months ago, and was unpacking again, in another strange place. She looked over at her rag doll sitting on her bed; did she need to knit her another sweater for a new home? Would she ever stop moving? Staying with Eb was offered, so she took it, not thinking about the fact that is was totally off the grid. How would she charge her cell phone? She depended on that Smart Phone to keep her life straight. She'd just have to keep it charged in her car.

Raven thought back to all Lawrence had explained to her about a loving advocate...an advocate for her. She'd seen God loving her through Susanna, that was for sure. The woman's eyes were pure sunlight that calmed her. She thought of Susanna's upcoming surgery and all her pettiness seemed to ease, except for the gnawing feeling of being alone...abandoned....again.

Eb knocked on her bedroom door. "Need any help?"

"If you don't mind, I'd like to be alone..."

Eb came closer and put his hand on her head. "You're most likely exhausted. It's not right having the government boss you around so, but you English have to comply."

"What do you mean?" Raven asked.

"Well, if this happened in the Amish community, someone would just take the family in. No government involved."

"But how do you know the homes are safe?"

"We know each other. Well, they used to know me...but...I turned from them and God."

"Because of your wife and daughter that got killed?"

"*Jah*, I felt like it was my fault. A judgment from God. Not real Amish thinking, I know for sure. When they argued that it was God's will and His sovereignty...well, I know better...it was my fault."

"Eb, what could you possibly have done? I'm learning that God really loves us and –"

"You don't understand. I sinned years ago, and I know it. That has to be the reason it happened, because if a loving God would allow it, I don't want anything to do with Him."

Raven tilted her head. "You don't really believe yourself. You turned to the bottle because when you drink, it's easier to agree with those words of guilt."

"Guilt?"

"What else would you call it? And guilt is one of the deadliest emotions. So painful, it drives people crazy." She crossed her arms. "You think about it Eb. When you're tempted to go to the bottle, how are you feeling? Guilty for your wife and daughter's death? How can that be healthy or right?"

Eb lowered his head. "How'd you get so smart about all these things?"

"I studied addictions in college. We all have some addiction…sometimes to something that we can't name. A feeling of emptiness sometimes is safer than reaching out and accepting love."

Eb's eyebrow shot up. "Are you talking about love of a family or a fellow…that lives next door?"

Raven grinned. "Is it that obvious?"

"*Jah*, but Raven, you're not Amish. Will you convert for Joshua?"

She sat back down on the oak floor and continued sorting through clothes. "We've only known each other for three months. I can't make a lifelong decision like that. I don't even know what's involved."

"I do," Eb said with a wink. "I have books that explain it all."

"And you're willing to go through them with me?"

"*Jah*, I am."

Raven knew how much Eb coming back to the Amish meant to Joshua. Maybe if Eb went through the books again, he'd return to his faith. Maybe that's why all this happened.

.

~*~

Raven lay in bed, knitting a sweater for her doll, exhausted over the day's events. Placing the boys in homes so soon after the fire was traumatic. Even though Joshua had promised to take them skiing in a few days, they wanted to visit Marilyn and Jim in the hospital instead. Lawrence was nice enough to drive them, even giving them winter projects to learn to take their minds off the fire. Chuckey and Bud asked if Lottie could teach them to bake pies, both having a craving for sugar, and she couldn't help but chuckle. Lottie would soon learn who was bossier. Paul and Toby would learn basket making from Hannah and David, and Timmy and Cliffy would learn how to whittle all kinds of animals from Joshua. Of course, all the boys would learn how to milk a cow, gather eggs…live without electricity.

Tomorrow afternoon she and Lawrence would drive the boys to Jamestown and she was sure to find out their real feelings as they spilled them out so freely to the Rowes'. She bowed her head and said a prayer for her boys

She'd study all the books Eb gave her about the Amish faith tonight by the glow of the oil lamp. But there was a haunting feeling in the light. She stared at the flame and saw something she hadn't thought of in years. The candles that lit the attic at night. Raven could see the light from the bedrooms below through the cracks in the floor boards. The house being ancient and in ill repair, was drafty and cold, and sometimes she had to warm her hands on the candle flame.

A feeling of emptiness overwhelmed her, of being abandoned. The only thing that took that feeling away was reading the book of John, the first passage she'd learned from Lawrence, about God wanting to be our advocate and wanting to adopt us, not leaving us orphans. She grabbed her Bible and skimmed through until she found the passage. No, I will not abandon you as orphans—I will come to you. Raven hugged the Bible and rocked back and forth. She wasn't alone; she was adopted by God Himself, and He wouldn't leave her.

Raven had told Lawrence about her past, about the abuse. Being a minister she felt he knew what she was supposed to do. Forgive. Did that mean she'd have to go find her Aunt Brook and Uncle Ram and talk to them, something she vowed never to do? Couldn't she just forgive and let it be between her and God? She put down her knitting and picked up the book Rules of a Godly Life, and flipped through the pages. Many of the rules dealt with simple things, like minding your own business and not being nosey, but when she came to the one on forgiveness, she read it slowly.

Permit not envy or hatred in your heart, nor carry a grudge against anyone. God loved us when we were His enemies and therefore He expects us to love our enemies for His sake. It is but a small thing for us to forgive our enemies, in comparison to what God has forgiven us. Even though you may think your enemy unworthy of your forgiveness it is well worth doing it for Christ sake.

Oddly, the words didn't sting. Somehow she trusted this Jesus she was coming to know. If forgiveness was something the Bible commanded, then she'd do it. Raven picked up the sweater she was knitting. She'd seen prayer shawl books in the craft store. Jesus had said to love your enemies and do good to them. But surely He wouldn't want her to make a shawl for her Aunt Brook, and she pushed the notion out of her mind.

Raven walked over to a window, seeing a full moon. Such a clear night revealed a star-studded sky. A feeling of peace enveloped her. She strangely felt at home in Eb's house. Raven looked over at the Yoder farm and saw through the kitchen window Timmy and Cliffy doing something at the table. Why were they up so late? Her throat tightened when she saw a girl walk past the window. She couldn't help but stare. Was it Lottie? What was she doing over there? She saw an oil lamp brighten the front of the house and soon saw Joshua walking into the living room, the woman behind him. By Joshua's body language, it didn't appear he was very happy. It was Lottie! When she made advances toward Joshua, he backed away. Anger grew within her. Why was Lottie so forward toward Joshua? So clingy?

She continued to watch, the small windows blocking most of her view. What was she missing? After a few minutes, Lottie came out on the side porch, slamming the door as she left the house. What on earth? She saw Joshua come out after her, but Lottie quickly got into her buggy and pulled the horse forward to the back of the driveway, turning the buggy around, and then snapped the reins to make the horse trot. Joshua tried to stop the horse, grabbing onto its bridle, but to no avail. Lottie urged the horse forward and was soon onto the road, leaving Joshua behind in the driveway, snow from the buggy wheels spitting up in his face. But why did he fall to his knees? Was he upset she left? Did something happen to Susanna?

Even though in her pajamas, she needed to go and see what was wrong. To be there for Joshua if Susanna was taken. Dear Lord, no! Raven put on her boots and winter coat and ran down the hallway. She heard Eb snoring, so wasn't concerned noise would wake him up. She made her way outside, the cold slapping her in the face. How brutal the winters were in Upstate New York.

Raven trudged through the snow, seeming to not make much progress, it being a foot high. Although the farm wasn't far away, it seemed like an eternity to reach it. When she did, she banged on the door and Timmy answered it. Not wanting to startle the boys, she tried to appear calm. "Timmy, why are you and Cliffy still up? It's ten o'clock."

Timmy yawned. "Well, we were supposed to go to bed at nine, but Lottie came over, now Joshua's real upset. We're worried about him."

"You two go up to bed, now. I've come to talk to Joshua."

The boys gladly agreed and headed up the back steps off the kitchen to their loft bedroom. She went into the living room, and saw Joshua, on the bench, his head in his hands. "Joshua, is your mom alright?"

Joshua turned to her, as if in shock. She'd never seen his face so contorted. "My *mamm's* fine," he said and raked his fingers through his hair.

Raven sat next to him. "I was ready for bed, but was watching the full moon. I saw Lottie leave here. What's going on?"

Sweat beads were on his forehead and he clenched his hands together, shaking his head.

"Joshua, can I do anything to help you?"

He reached for her and drew her close. She felt him trembling and rubbed his back. "You need to tell me so I can help."

"You'll find out soon enough," he said, gasping for air. Joshua pulled away from her and got up, pacing the room. "Too much is happening. My *mamm's* so sick, the Rowe's are in the hospital, and now Lottie's having a problem."

Raven stiffened. "You must care about Lottie to be so upset, or is it that serious?"

"I can't talk about it…"

"Are you sure everything is over between you two?"

"What do you mean?"

"Well, if you didn't care so much for her, her problems wouldn't affect you so much. You must still feel for her…"

Joshua put his hand up. "I can't talk about it."

~*~

Lawrence was like an anchor to her over the next few days, going with her to visit all the boys and now Marilyn and Jim again in the hospital. She bought Marilyn some yarn, circular needles, and a pattern book to make dishcloths. Most likely Marilyn had forgotten the patterns she knew as a child. And knitting would calm her and occupy her time.

When they got to Jim's room, she watched as Bud and Chuckey tried to gently hug Jim. His right arm was bandaged but he hugged them back with his left.

"Are you two eating too many Amish pastries? I thought we were on diets?" Jim winked.

Bud let out a laugh. "Well, Mary, I mean Mrs. Miller, she makes pies every Saturday, enough for a whole week. We have pie for breakfast a lot and dessert after every meal."

"And they make candy in the snow," added Chuckey.

"You mean pour syrup in the snow until it hardens?"

Chuckey cocked an eyebrow. "How'd you know? Did the Amish teach you to do that?"

"No, I did it as a kid and my kids did it, too," Jim said.

"Have Gary and Larry been here to visit you a lot?" Lawrence asked.

Jim couldn't hide his smile. "I've seen them more over the past week than usual."

"Well, that's good," Lawrence said.

Raven looked closely at Jim's face. He looked younger. Were the boys aging him, or was it that he was seeing his sons more? He turned to her. "Raven, how are all the boys doing living off the grid?"

"Fine, I think." She turned to all six boys. "Do you like living Amish style?"

Timmy and Cliffy shook their heads yes. Toby and Ethan shrugged their shoulders, and Bud and Chuckey rolled their eyes. Bud sighed audibly. "We've been stuck with Lottie."

"What's wrong with her?" Lawrence asked.

"She's like living with a time bomb. Gets so upset and cries over everything. I mean, she yelled at me for putting too much salt on my meat. She's a little nuts."

Concern etched Jim's face. "How about living without electricity?"

Chuckey moaned. "I don't like it, but like Bud said, it's trying to live with Lottie that's the hard part."

Raven clenched her jaw. She'd have to sit down and talk with Lottie over her behavior. Whatever her problem was, she needed to show some self-control. Lottie was upsetting too many people.

"When are you getting out of here?" Bud asked Jim.

"Well, in a few days. Mrs. Rowe will, too. We'll stay with Larry until Appleton is remodeled."

Chuckey jumped up and down. "I knew it! Appleton could be fixed!" He gave the boys a round of fist bumps. "Then we can all go back."

"I like it with Joshua," Timmy said. "Not that I don't miss Appleton, Mr. Rowe. But I like the farm animals."

"Me too," Cliffy said. "And with Susanna being sick, we're helping Joshua a lot. I love milking the cow best."

Jim beamed. "I knew it. Good hard work on a farm is what every boy needs. I milked a cow when I was a boy," he said. "When I wasn't selling apples."

Chuckey laughed. "We know. You sold a ton of apples when you were a kid."

"Yes, I did." He turned to Toby and Ethan. "And how are you boys doing, living Amish-like?"

Ethan pursed his lips. "Not sure yet. It's only been a week."

Toby looked up. "Well, I like it better than I thought, but don't want to hurt your feelings, Mr. Rowe."

"Aw, I want you happy. Can't live at Appleton forever."

"Why not?" Chuckey and Bud blurted out in unison.

Jim cocked his head back. "I thought you wanted to be adopted."

They both shook their head, and Bud spoke up. "We miss Appleton. It's home for us."

Raven knew she had to speak with Lottie as soon as possible, and it made her stomach do a flip. Something about that girl was so irritating, and she didn't think it was jealousy over how much Joshua cared. Something made the boys not want to be in the same home as her.

Her mind turned to Joshua. She cared so much for him, but he'd seemed so fickle over the past few days. He said he'd take the boys Amish skiing but changed his mind, saying he had an important meeting. When she pressed him further, to see if it was about Susanna's health, he seemed irritated with her and flippantly said it was personal. Even though they lived next to each other, the distance between them had grown. He must regret saying he loved her, since she wasn't Amish. But he didn't know she was reading all she could about the Amish faith, and agreed with most everything. She only really struggled with minor issues like being a pacifist, having been in the military, but she had only enlisted to get an education and have an income. Raven knew she needed to talk to Joshua, too, but maybe wait until after Christmas.

Chapter 11

Susanna turned to look at all the snow beating up against the window. The Amish were encouraged to live in pace with nature, but sometimes nature moved too fast. She tried not to think of her upcoming transplant, and savor her time at home for Christmas. Although weak, she had her rubber stamp collection out and Timmy and Cliffy helped her make cards, something she looked forward to every year. She felt such love for these two boys and knew the Lord had placed them in her life to love, and to her surprise, they were a comfort to her.

She looked over at the boys sitting at the oak table, intently making cards. They didn't have enough ink on the stamps at first and Joshua taught them to press the stamp down hard against the ink pad. The boys were afraid ink would spill out and stain her table. Such thoughtfulness. They were also so eager to bring up her meal tray on days she just couldn't get out of bed. Although talking wore her out, she could always listen. The boys chattered non-stop one on one, but appeared shy when together with the whole family. When visitors came, the boys tried to blend into the woodwork.

Especially when folks came over with meals, which were getting more regular. Susanna couldn't help but notice Lottie was over more than usual, following Joshua around like a baby duck. Why did she like Raven, who wasn't Amish, better than Lottie? Susanna put down the card and pen and pulled her prayer shawl tight around her. She didn't want to meet her Maker without a clear conscience, and if the surgery didn't go well, it would be soon.

She bowed her head and confessed to God her dislike for Lottie. She had a *mamm's* heart, wanting her son to marry a girl that would build him up, not tear him down. Lottie was too emotional lately, and it never did settle right that she'd broken off with her son because of her illness. It wasn't the Amish way to not live for others...to be so selfish. She felt her prayers were going nowhere. The more she prayed for Lottie, the more fear rose in her heart concerning her son. He wasn't his usual self either. She'd asked repeatedly what was wrong, but he only forced a smile, saying everything was fine and to enjoy the Christmas season. She knew exactly what he meant. Rueben said the same thing...enjoy the Christmas season. It might be her last.

~*~

Raven put another log in the woodstove and snuggled under the warm afghan Susanna made years ago. She used to have a little store selling all kinds of things she made, when she was healthy. She opened another book Eb gave her but was soon interrupted by a car that pulled into the driveway. She could see through the window it wasn't Lawrence. Maybe an Amish driver Eb hired? Raven watched as a tall man wrapped from head to toe in winter garments walked to the house. When he knocked, she slipped on her moccasins and ran to the door. When he pulled the scarf off his face, she stepped back.

"Brandon, I told you not to come. And how did you know I was here?"

Brandon stepped inside and took her by the shoulders. "We need to talk, face to face."

"But it's over. Can't you understand?"

Brandon stomped the snow off his boots. "Where can I put these?" he asked, pointing to his feet.

"On the black mat," she said, but wanted to yell Nowhere. Leave!

He took off his parka and gave it to her and then unlaced his boots. "Are we alone?"

"Eb's upstairs…"

"Who's Eb?" Brandon asked in a demanding tone. "Your Amish boyfriend?"

Raven shook her head. Brandon was so immature. "No, he's a friend who's housing me since Appleton burnt down."

"I heard about that in town. The locals told me you were living among the Amish and gave directions. Had to go from farm to farm, asking where you were. The people next door told me you were here."

Raven cringed. Most likely Joshua had spoken to him.

"*Ya*, real nice folks, next door. Asked me in for hot chocolate. The man with the long beard looks like Rip Van Winkle."

"So you met Rueben?" she asked.

"Met the son too, but he was kind of edgy. When I said I was your boyfriend, he blushed like a girl. Kind of funny. Think he has the hots for you."

As he moved closer to her, putting both hands on her face, she pushed him away. "I'm not your girlfriend."

He grabbed her around the waist and roughly pulled her to him. "I've missed your feistiness, too."

He put his hand on the back of her neck and forced a kiss on her. She slapped his face. "Stop it." She tried to break free, but he had her around the waist. "Brandon, you're hurting my back. Let go!"

He released her. "You looked like you were starving for a kiss. Don't you miss me at all?"

"If I missed you I would have told you to come and visit, but I've changed. A lot. I see our relationship was based on physical attraction alone. It's not enough. We couldn't talk."

Brandon pulled at his knuckles, cracking each one. He sat on one of the benches. "How about we backtrack then? Start over as friends."

Raven looked at him evenly. "You live in Florida, and I'm staying here. Long distance wouldn't work."

"We could try, couldn't we?"

Raven forgot the darker shade of blue Brandon's eyes became when he was upset. How could she tell him she loved an Amish man, when Joshua was giving her such mixed signals? Seeing Lottie over at the house so much made her feel more hopeless. Her mind turned to Lawrence. He would never act so rude, grabbing her and forcing a kiss. No, he was her friend. If anything ever developed she had that as a foundation, and was so fond of him.

Brandon got up and went near her again, putting his hands on her shoulders. "What do you say? We could start over." He pulled her to himself, cradling her head against his chest. "I love you, Raven."

Surprised she felt nothing at all toward him, only distrust, she pushed him away again. "Brandon, it's over. I'm sorry."

"Who is it?" he yelled. "I can tell there's someone else."

She couldn't look into his eyes. "You need to leave. There are hotels at good prices in Jamestown."

He threw his hand in the air. "I just got here. My flight back home isn't for a week. I took off a whole week to spend with you –"

"And I told you not to come. I meant it. This relationship is over."

"You're turning Amish or something? Being brainwashed? Maybe this will bring you back to reality." He grabbed her head and forced a kiss so hard it hurt. He pulled her up against him and pulled down her turtleneck sweater and roughly kissed her neck.

She slapped him and yelled for him to stop. She saw Eb, standing at the foot of the stairs, mouth gaping. "Eb, help me!"

Brandon didn't appear to hear, only continuing to act like an animal. Eb yelled for him to let her go. Brandon turned to him and scoffed. "Go away, old man."

To Raven's horror, Eb walked back into his room. The Amish were pacifist. Fear and anger gripped her. She felt so violated, but then Brandon had done this while they were dating. Why didn't she see the lust before? As he continued to devour her, she remembered her self-defense class, but not one move came to her mind, which was racing now. Her back ached and his rough goatee was bruising her neck. The only thing she could think to do was knee him where it would hurt. But what if he only got angrier? How could she have dated him? She felt she deserved to be abused, just like when she was a child. No more! Raven mustered up all her strength and kneed him. He groped in pain, but grabbed her wrist so tight she yelped. She saw the rod iron poker near the woodstove, and tried to reach for it.

He started to pull her toward the steps. "Let's go up to your room," he snarled, "You've always resisted me."

Her mind whirled, not knowing what to do, but saw a car pull into the driveway. It was Lawrence.

Eb walked down the steps, angrily holding a cell phone up. "The police will be here soon. Let her go."

Brandon looked over at Eb, a smirk on his face. "I'm not stupid. Amish don't have phones."

"I'm not Amish!" Eb shouted. "Now let her go."

She felt Brandon release her and she ran to Eb. Soon Lawrence was in the house talking to Brandon, and then a police car pulled up. Raven buried her head against Eb's chest, feeling ashamed. How could she face Lawrence; who knew she'd dated such an animal?

When the police got there, she saw Officer Carter again, this time directing her attitude toward Brandon. Her male partner took Brandon by the arm. "You want me to throw him in the slammer for attempted rape?"

Raven looked at Brandon sheepishly. "No, just get him out of here."

"Are you sure? I mean —"

"We were just making out," Brandon snarled.

Officer Carter charged over to Brandon and got up on her toes, and grabbed his collar. "From what I hear, a woman was telling a man to stop. When a woman says no, she means it, Buster. Understand? No, means, no!" She looked over at her partner and then spun around to face Raven. "Are you sure he's safe to be in society?"

"Yes. He's an ex-boyfriend. Upset that I broke things off."

Officer Carter turned to Brandon. "Where do you live?"

"Florida."

"Then get your tail-end out of this state in twenty-four hours or else."

Brandon turned to look at her, as if to apologize, and then headed out to his car. She was shocked to see Officer Carter wink at her. "Giving people twenty-four hours isn't even a law. Need anything else, just call 911."

Raven let Eb guide her to the kitchen table and put on water for tea. Lawrence sat beside her. "I'm so embarrassed."

Lawrence gently took her hand. "Raven, it wasn't your fault."

"No, I'm embarrassed that I dated someone like that. Such an animal."

"You're changing. From all our talks, you realize that you have a God who loves you with a pure love…"

She couldn't deny that she'd never noticed how impure Brandon was, until she knew what pure love felt like.

~*~

Joshua saw the police car over at Eb's. Now he could go over to the shunned man's house, because there was some kind of emergency. What could have happened that Pastor Lawrence was there too?

He trudged through the snow toward Eb's. He saw deer munching at frozen stumps of cornstalk in the field across the street. One looked at him as if he could read his thoughts. He was going batty. Too much stress. Too many problems.

When he got to the house, he didn't bother to knock but just walked in. He took off his boots and Eb soon appeared from the kitchen. "Come on in, Joshua. Making tea. Join us."

After putting his boots on the black rubber mat, he walked into the kitchen, but stepped back when he saw Lawrence and Raven holding hands. He knew it. All along she'd been dating him. The boys had said she was going to marry him in her white coat, out in the snow. Even though it didn't make sense, since the Amish didn't have the same customs. Raven turned to look up at him, her eyes seeming to search his. For what?

Eb broke the silence. "Raven's old boyfriend was up. He wasn't too nice. I called the cops."

"But you don't have a phone…"

Eb pulled a cell phone from his pocket. "Yes I do. Lawrence got it for me. If I have the urge to drink, I call him, and he comes over. Been mighty helpful."

Jealousy over Lawrence again consumed Joshua. Jealousy was a sin, and one he'd been committing ever since he met Raven Meadows. God didn't lead us into temptation, so was it clear he needed to stay away from Raven?

Raven followed Eb's orders and snuggled up in bed. What she'd experienced with Brandon was exhausting, but emotions were surfacing that fatigued her more. How could Joshua act so coldly, and not even ask if she was alright? And why did Lawrence tell her the church doors were always open if she needed time to sort things through: the house fire, living with Eb off the grid, and Brandon's abusive behavior. Lawrence had called it abusive. Didn't all men have needs, like she was told?

Raven reached for her new knitting supplies that she bought at the craft store. Everything she had from this comforting craft was destroyed in the fire, even the needles that Granny Nora had gotten her. All the yarn she'd collected, some expensive alpaca. And the sweaters she knit for her doll were gone, too.

She took her doll and touched the faded pink and blue paisley print of the doll's dress. Her bonnet that matched was faded as well. Raven took off the hat, seeing the tiny holes on the dolls head. Her attempt to give her doll yarn hair had failed. Why no one put hair on the doll was a mystery. And why black boots instead of nice shoes? Her grandmother had given her the doll on her fifth birthday, and oddly, it was an anchor in her life; a constant along with knitting, until now. She had God. A God who said He would never leave her alone, like an orphan. She could face whatever lay ahead because He was with her.

Raven thought of the church program all the boys were involved in. It was called "Emmanuel, God with us." Yes, she could sense He was with her, and she actually felt sad for Aunt Brook and Uncle Ram, the more she prayed for them. Maybe someday she'd have the courage to go to Salamanca and find them. They could have peace with God, too.

Fatigue washed with peace soon overtook her and she grabbed her rag doll and surrendered to sleep.

~*~

Susanna couldn't sleep again. One side effect of all her medicines was insomnia. Loud voices from downstairs continued. Joshua and Rueben were talking about a baby? When their voices got loud enough to really hear, Rueben hushed Joshua.

She was not only cut off from the people physically, but in many ways emotionally. Rueben shielding her from stress was thoughtful, but awkward feelings enveloped her when friends visited, always feeling like they couldn't share their hearts because she might get upset. Yes, she had enough trouble of her own, being on the transplant list for three years, but it was a joy to share other people's burdens. It was partly why she needed foster *kinner*, someone to love and help.

Susanna heard Joshua pound his feet as he ascended the stairs. Soon Rueben came up and laid on the bed next to her, worry etched on his face.

"What's wrong, Rueben?"

"Nothing. Not really."

"So something's wrong?"

She felt Rueben gently put his arm around her middle and she patted his hand. "Don't shut me out. I'm not as fragile as one of my teacups."

Rueben moaned. "*Jah*, you are, until you get your transplant." He arched himself up on one elbow. "Looking forward to going to Pittsburgh and getting your transplant over with? When you're feeling better, we'll have a new life."

Susanna knew something was wrong and Rueben needed to talk. "Love, can you talk to the elders about what's ailing you?"

Rueben moaned. "Nee."

"Why not? They're always filled with wise counsel. God chose them to help us."

"Some shouldn't have been picked at all."

"But they drew the lot. I may be too ill to help you, but you are Amish and know we believe in order and church authority. Go to them. Listen to what they say."

Rueben touched her long grayish-blond hair. "You rest now. Don't fret yourself. I'll listen real hard to what the bishop and elders say."

Susanna hadn't heard such concern in her husband's tone in a long while. She closed her eyes and asked God to help Rueben, the man she loved with all her being. Then she prayed for Joshua. His behavior was so baffling. She put him in God's capable hands.

Chapter 12

$\mathscr{R}$aven had watched Little House on the Prairie over and over in foster homes. They were the family she found to be a constant. How silly, she mused. But as she looked around the church with all the live greenery put up in the windows and the tree decorated with green and red paper chains, for a moment, she was Ma Ingalls waiting for her kids to perform in the Christmas program. But for the first time she longed to have her own children. Always content to have a cat, she now desired to have children? Maybe she missed having a pet.

Lawrence stepped up to the podium to welcome everyone to the Christmas Eve service, all put on by the children in the church. He said how many hours they'd practiced and his chest seemed to puff out, so proud of the children. Lawrence was ready to turn thirty; she wondered if these children filled a void in his life, not having a family of his own. He faithfully checked on each boy from Appleton, asking them questions like a social worker would. He was making her life easier.

She looked at the bulletin. It had a single candle on the front, with "Emmanuel, God With Us" across the top. The children all came from their seats and lined up behind Lawrence. He took a guitar and started to strum. In harmony they all sang:

Emmanuel, Emmanuel.

Wonderful, Counselor!

Lord of life, Lord of all;

He's the Prince of Peace, Mighty God, Holy One!

Emmanuel, Emmanuel.

The children repeated the lyrics several times and then just sang Emmanuel over and over again. Raven thought she'd heard this song before. She opened the bulletin and saw the song lyrics. At the bottom it said, Words and Music by Amy Grant. Her mind wandered back to middle school; someone had given her an Amy Grant CD in foster care, and the songs helped her during those rough years. But it was Christian music, and it didn't bother her back then.

What had hardened her to Christianity as she got older? Before she came to Appleton? Was it the media, portraying them as a hate group? People who were narrow-minded and had no tolerance for people who didn't fit into their agenda? Maybe it was them saying there's only one way to God.

How her opinion changed when she came back to New York and it all started with the love of Susanna Yoder; her embrace just made her know God was love. But the boys seemed to carry the most weight with her, as she watched them sing. These children in Dickens' time would be called orphans, all had so much hope and resilience. She never had that growing up, and some foster parents were as wonderful as Marilyn and Jim.

Raven looked over at the Rowes seated across the church. Jim had his arm in a sling and Marilyn had a bandage on her cheek, but here they were, watching their boys. Chuckey and Bud weren't adjusting well to living with the Millers, always asking to go live back at Appleton. Something was wrong and she had such limited access to them. Should she get them a cell phone? The Amish prohibited them and she wanted to respect their culture. She'd have to see if there was something battery operated so they could communicate with her. Raven closed her eyes and prayed for Bud and Chuckey.

~*~

Joshua sat in-between Cliffy and Timmy. How attached he was becoming to these boys. They'd shared what they knew about their parents and he found it hard to believe anyone could be so cruel to a child. He thought of Raven, so many hours spent sitting in an attic. The times he chanced talking to Eb, he'd told him that Raven was working on forgiving her aunt and uncle, even planning on visiting them, even bought yarn to make her aunt a shawl. What courage. What a heart.

He found his mind wandered too often to Raven. But everything had changed now. He had to listen to the elders and bishop. Joshua looked over at Lottie and their eyes met. His *mamm* always told him that the eyes told so much. Her eyes seemed to say, "I got you," or worse, "I tricked you."

He looked at the candles and greenery the *kinner* had placed in the schoolhouse windows. He stared at a single flickering candle. Light my path, Lord. I need to see clearly.

~*~

After the church program, Lawrence announced there was a bag of candy for all the children lined up at the back of the church. Raven looked up at Bud and tried not to laugh. He was staring at Jim, rubbing his belly. When she came to Appleton she was sure the church had been bribing the kids to come with loads of candy. These boys were the bridge to her newfound faith and she was so thankful.

Lawrence greeted everyone as they left the church, but the usual crowd stayed longer to talk. He came up to her with a present. The boys howled in unison, "*EEEWWWWW.*" She laughed and said, "Not getting married yet." Lawrence chuckled and handed her the gift. She looked up into his mellow brown eyes and thanked him, and then ripped the paper to see a CD called *Peace on Earth.*

"This music's so peaceful. I know you need some...peace..." Lawrence said.

"Thank you. I'll listen to it...in my car. With no electricity, no CD player." She noticed Lawrence seemed a little nervous. Maybe she was projecting her own anxiety. "I really appreciate you helping me get through the whole ordeal with Brandon. You helped me see it wasn't my fault, but I'm so afraid of him coming back."

"Well, Officer Carter is, too, or she wouldn't have given you her personal cell phone number. I wish you'd press charges."

Raven stared at the CD cover. "No, let's just leave it alone. Living with Eb is just what I need, so peaceful. I just wish I could talk to the boys. Actually, I'm worried about Bud and Chuckey. I thought of getting them walkie-talkies, but they need to be charged."

"No, they're battery powered. I have one in case of an emergency." He looked down at his feet and then smiled at her. "Actually, I've had one since I was a kid. I've always thought they were fun. Want me to pick one up for Bud and Chuckey?"

Raven laughed. "You men aren't going to have all the fun. How about I get a couple and give them to the boys. One for me, too. We can all talk."

"Sounds good." Lawrence looked past her, over at the boys. "Looks like we have an audience. We should give them something to talk about."

Raven nodded in agreement. Lawrence put his arm around her and they headed out of the church. They walked down the sidewalk. Raven put her arm around Lawrence, and turned to see all six boys gawking at them.

Lawrence got down on one knee, and the boys started to cheer.

He took her hand and whispered. "Raven, will you go on a date with me?"

She bent down. "Are you kidding?"

"No, I'm serious."

Raven looked at the boys, frozen little snowmen, and she nodded her head yes. The boys jumped up and down in excitement. Raven looked down at Lawrence and winked.

~*~

Cliffy and Timmy talked with the other Amish boys their age. Cliffy tried on an Amish black wool hat. Joshua walked over to the boys. "You don't look Amish with that red hair."

"Lottie has red hair."

"Well, you can hardly see it under her *kapp*." Joshua saw Lottie walking toward him.

"I heard that. *Jah*, I have red hair." She pulled Joshua down to her and whispered, "And soon you'll get to see it without the *kapp*, like when you were sick."

Joshua squirmed. "We'll see about that."

Lottie stomped her foot. "*Jah*, we will."

Joshua looked over at the group of boys, all their eyes as round as the full moon.

"What's wrong with her?" Timmy asked.

"*Ya*, she's nice one minute and mean the next." Cliffy said. "She's like a yoyo."

Joshua told the boys they needed to go. He wanted to have a peaceful night with his *mamm* and daed. Maybe the last Christmas Eve they'd share together. As they were leaving he had to walk past Lottie.

She stepped in front of him. "Joshua, I'm sorry I'm so emotional. But you understand why, *jah*?"

"*Jah*."

"Are you going to ask me over to your place? It is family time."

Joshua shook his head. "My *mamm* said she wants to spend time with Cliffy and Timmy. Put a puzzle together."

"Why does she care so much about those boys?" Lottie blurted.

"As Christians we're to care for orphans and widows, *jah*?"

A forced smile spread across Lottie's face. "Okay, Joshua. But will I see you tomorrow?"

Joshua couldn't believe how self-absorbed Lottie was. She knew his *mamm* and *daed* were leaving for Pittsburgh the day after Christmas. So much needed to be discussed and many people offered to help, but not Lottie. He thought of what the elders told him, and nausea washed over him. "I need to go. Not feeling too *goot*."

Raven woke up and quickly got on her robe and slippers. She was going to cook a Christmas breakfast for Eb as a surprise. She tip-toed down the steps and smelled coffee. When she went into the kitchen, Eb had pancakes stacked high on a plate in the middle of the table. He was making scrambled eggs and turned to look at her. "Merry Christmas, dear one."

Was this really happening? She'd never had anyone make her a Christmas breakfast, and this was a feast. "Oh, Eb. Thank you." She went over to embrace him. "I wanted to surprise you."

"You English get up so late."

"Eb, remember, you're not Amish anymore."

"Well, I'm used to getting up with the roosters. Anyhow, this isn't all for you. I'm making breakfast for the Yoder's next door."

"But you're shunned…"

"It's Christmas, shunned or not. And Susanna leaves tomorrow and I want to see her."

"Well, let me help then. I'm going over too. I want to say good-bye. She'll be missed."

"You stir these eggs while I cut up this here fruit."

Raven knew Susanna was on such a limited diet, not allowed most of the food Eb was preparing, but didn't feel right saying anything. The whole family was going through a lot and surely with four men over there they'd gobble it all down in no time. Cliffy and Timmy seemed to be turning into men…maybe a little too fast. But the Amish kids all seemed like little adults. As long as they were happy, she supposed it was alright.

"Raven, what's your favorite Christmas memory?" Eb asked.

"Well, it wasn't celebrated too much when I was a kid, being raised on the Indian Reservation. My grandparents exchanged presents, though."

Eb slowly turned to look at her. "You're Indian?"

"Yes, I was raised in Salamanca. I'm half Seneca."

"And half what else?"

Raven didn't know why but she felt close enough to Eb to tell him she was an illegitimate child. "It was a teenage pregnancy. I never knew my mom or dad. My grandparents raised me and they're gone."

Eb held on to the side of the counter and didn't say anything. Raven knew the prejudice some people had against Native Americans, but thought Eb knew. She also spilled the beans about being illegitimate. Would Eb change his opinion of her? Withhold the love he'd always shown? "Eb, what's wrong?"

"I, ah, I'm not feeling too *goot*. Tired all of a sudden. You go ahead and take this here breakfast over to the Yoder's."

Raven put her head down. "I understand."

~*~

Filled with confusion and feelings of rejection, Raven packed up the breakfast in a basket, covered it with a tea towel, and headed over to the Yoder's. How could such a nice man like Eb be prejudiced against Native Americans or illegitimate children? Well, her grandparents warned her that this could happen so she always told people she was French, but for some reason she let it slip to several people, feeling that Christians were supposed to love everybody. She had a lot to learn, obviously.

Would Eb want her living at his place? Her mind raced as she ascended the steps leading to the side door. When she saw Joshua the emotions she was carrying were too much. She wanted to just sit down and have a good cry, but knew how to hide her emotions well. Anyhow, she needed to be professional since Timmy and Cliffy might overhear.

"Merry Christmas, Joshua. Eb made this breakfast for you all."

Joshua gave her a concerned look. *"Danki.* Are you alright?"

"Fine. I'm just fine. Would like to see Susanna before she leaves, just a short visit?"

Joshua stepped back to let her in. Timmy and Cliffy sat at the table. "Merry Christmas, boys."

"Merry Christmas, Miss Meadows," they said at the same time, mouths full of food.

Raven would normally give them a mini lesson on manners, but today was Christmas. Joshua took the basket and Raven tried her best to get the snow off her boots before taking them off. She felt Joshua's eyes on her, as if he could see through her, like he had in the past. The blue eyes she once found peace in she would not surrender to, or reveal any hurts. He seemed to have cut her off, most likely since she wasn't Amish, even though she considered converting. Obviously by Lottie's many visits, the church controlled most everything in Joshua's life.

"Can I see Susanna now?"

"Follow me…"

She walked behind him up the stairs and into Susanna's room. Raven needed one of Susanna's hugs; a hug that made her feel loved. But she was here to see Susanna, to lend strength, not take it. She bent over and kissed her on the cheek. "Merry Christmas. And just think, in the new year, you'll have a new kidney, and a new life."

Susanna was sitting up in bed as usual, unable to lay flat. So much water retention could fill up her lungs and she wouldn't be able to breathe. She was as white as the snow, but reached for Raven's hand. "*Danki*, dear one."

Dear one. That's what Eb called her…used to call her. She willed back tears.

"Raven, you seem upset. What's wrong?"

"Nothing. I'll miss our talks…"

"You have a phone, *jah*?"

"Of course. I'll write down the number and you call me when you're up to it."

"Well, may not hear from me for a while." She looked over at Joshua. "Did you tell her any details?"

"*Nee,* slipped my mind."

"Well, I'm awful weak and talking tires me. Can you explain?"

"*Jah, Mamm.* Raven, she needs to sleep. Want to go downstairs?"

Susanna squeezed Raven's hand. "I'll call you. *Danki* for everything."

"Everything?"

"Bringing the boys to me. I love them so."

Raven kissed her cheek again, and said good-bye. When she got out into the hallway, the realization that she may never talk to Susanna again overwhelmed her. The woman who talked to her for hours about her faith, the woman who didn't fear death, the woman that took in foster children just to love them….what if…what if…

"I know," Joshua said. "We're all asking the same thing."

"Asking what? You can't read my mind…can you?"

"Well, you're thinking it's the last time you might see *Mamm*. She'll be gone for two months. She'd appreciate it if you called. She's really fond of you…"

"I'll call her. For sure."

"We put her in the arms of Jesus and leave her there. It's all we can do."

Raven nodded. "I need to get back."

"Let's talk in the living room."

Numbly, Raven followed him downstairs and took a seat in one of the Amish rockers, not wanting to sit on the bench with Joshua.

"Raven, what's wrong? You don't look *goot*."

She looked over at the clock on the wall. Back and forth her emotions went, just like the pendulum. She took a deep breath, hoping to clear her mind. "I'm fine. What do you want to talk about?"

"You. You're pale and seem so unhappy. Want to talk?"

She knew it was Christmas and Susanna was so ill, but she lost composure. "I'm not a doll to take down and put back up on a shelf when you feel like it."

Joshua cocked his head back. "I don't play with dolls."

"But you do understand my meaning, though, don't you?"

"Not really."

Men! "Let me explain then. I can't be in your life one minute and out the next."

"Raven, you're not out of my life, unless what the boys tell me is true."

"What?"

"That you're engaged to Lawrence."

Raven put up both arms in a huff. "It was a joke. The boys are always teasing."

"Those boys are smart. Maybe they see something between you two."

"Joshua, I don't mean to be rude, but I don't see that any of this is your business."

He bent over and put his head in his hands. "I wish it could be…"

"Then why did you shut me out of your life?" she said, louder than she intended and lowered her voice. "Three weeks ago when Appleton burnt down you said you loved me, and then did a one-eighty, even though I said I would turn Amish for you." She stared at the floor. "You acted like you didn't care at all when the police came."

"You were holding Lawrence's hand."

"He was there for me because he cares. Joshua, you don't; it's obvious by your reaction."

"*Jah*, well, I meant what I said before…I do love you, but a big stone got stuck in the hay rake."

Raven wasn't sure what he meant, but obviously something was holding him back from seeing her…someone…"If you really loved me, nothing would hold you back. I see Lottie over here a lot."

"Can we talk after *Mamm* and *Daed* leave? I've been mum about a lot of things because I don't want to upset her. Only *Daed* knows…"

"Knows what? Is your *mamm* worse off than you're letting on?"

Joshua looked at her, eyes tender. "Your love for my *mamm* is what I've always wished for in a wife…but…"

"Joshua, you didn't answer my question. Is Susanna not going to make it?"

"Can you come over tonight, around nine, after the boys are in bed?"

"Sure."

Chapter 13

ℛaven walked into Eb's house, confused. She saw Eb was eating but he avoided eye contact with her and she took it that he didn't want her around. "I'm going to go to the church; Lawrence told me I could always go there and I…I want to just sit and read my Bible today."

"Okay."

He didn't ask her to spend Christmas with him. He obviously was a deeply prejudiced man. She went upstairs to get her Bible and the CD Lawrence gave her. She looked over at her rag doll, and wanted to take it. Every time she'd run away in the past, she took it. But she was twenty-four, and in a few weeks twenty-five. You are not a child anymore, Raven Meadows!

Raven left the doll on her bed and grabbed her Bible and CD and darted down the steps, not even saying good-bye to Eb.

~*~

The empty church mirrored her heart, alone on Christmas Day. She looked down and saw a bulletin of the Christmas Eve service on the end of the pew. Lawrence was pastor and janitor and was most likely too tired to clean up the mess from Christmas Eve service. She looked behind her and saw more bulletins and round paper candle holders. After the candlelight service, church members were encouraged to take their candles home as a reminder that Christ was the light of the world.

Well, she'd clean the church for Lawrence as a surprise; cleaning always made her feel in control. Feeling too emotional to read her Bible, she got up and started the task. She saw a wastepaper basket in the back of the church and then went searching row by row, picking up anything left behind. Candy wrappers abounded since Lawrence had made little bags of candy as gifts. What a kind man.

As she went through the church, Raven thought of the people who sat in their usual places, as if they were permanently marked. The Sarver family had her over for dinner after only two visits to church. Then the Ott family. What a jokester Carl was and his patient wife, Debbie, who sat each Sunday in the back pew, waiting for her man who was usually the last to leave, talking up a storm. The Rachuna, Wendle, and Taylor families all felt like family…but they weren't.

Raven put the overflowing basket back in the corner, and sat down in the front pew. *Lord, I don't have a family. A real one.* She remembered her first impression of the town: something out of a Thomas Kinkade picture. How she had loathed the perfectness, and now she knew why. Each house seemed to smile, since it had love inside. A family. Something she didn't have.

The back door opened and she jumped, afraid it was Brandon. But it was Lawrence.

"So, Miss Meadows. Why are you in church today?"

Raven saw the concern in his eyes, trying to hide it by being light-hearted. She was tired of being strong, always putting up a front. "I had nowhere else to go…"

Lawrence looked around the tidy church. "You didn't have to, Raven, but thank you. I was going to clean today."

"On Christmas?"

"Have nowhere to go either…was hoping to fly home to Colorado but couldn't afford it, being as poor as a church mouse."

"Maybe you need a raise?"

"It was a joke. A poor one, I guess," he smirked. "No, I just decided this year to put the money into an African village. The cost of a plane ticket started a piggery."

"A what?"

"A pig farm. So, here I am alone on Christmas, too. Want to go get something to eat?"

Raven had taken for granted Lawrence's kind and gentle ways. She expected it from a pastor, but was now seeing him differently. She remembered having to go to church in foster homes, and some pastors weren't very nice, some very arrogant. She smiled at Lawrence. "I'd love to, if any are open."

Lawrence hit his forehead with his hand. "You're right. Most places are closed for Christmas." He jutted out his chin and scratched it. "You could come to my place. I can cook."

~*~

Lawrence walked her to the car. "I had a great Christmas with you, Raven." He bent down and kissed her cheek. "And I'll talk to Eb. I don't think he's a prejudiced man at all. Like I said, Christmas brings back memories, and you never really get over losing a wife and daughter."

Raven couldn't believe what a nice day she'd had with Lawrence. She looked up sheepishly into his soft brown eyes. "I hope you're right. I can't live with a man who looks down on my heritage."

He put his hand on her shoulder. "Why not ask Eb what's bothering him? He may open up."

"Okay," Raven said, feeling so much better. She hugged Lawrence. "You're such a good friend."

He held her close to him. "I'd like to be more…" She didn't pull away. "When are we going on a real date?"

"Soon…very soon," she said, feeling the warmth of his arms wrapped around her.

~*~

Raven pulled into Eb's place just long enough to tell him she'd be next door. She was late, promising Joshua she'd be over at nine. Susanna and Rueben would be leaving early in the morning. She'd just go over and tell Joshua it was better to talk tomorrow.

She pulled into the Yoder driveway and carefully walked to the side door. Buggy wheels made icy tracks in the snow and she was sure to step over them. Raven knocked softly, and saw Joshua come to the door. He put his index finger to his lips, and whispered that he didn't want to wake anyone. It was ten o'clock, after all, he said.

"I'm sorry. Just stopped over to say we can talk tomorrow."

Joshua staggered over to the kitchen table. "I was worried. Where have you been?"

Raven looked at Joshua's eyes, which were rapidly aging. "I spent Christmas with Lawrence. Lost track of time."

He stared at her for a while, as if struck dumb. He clenched his fists and put them on the table, twiddling his thumbs rapidly. "So, he's your boyfriend now?"

Joshua looked ill, so she didn't answer his question. Only sat across the table from him and grabbed his hands to stop his fidgeting. "What is it? Something's wrong?"

Joshua looked up at her, eyes hollow. "Are you up for a talk?"

"Of course. We English stay up later than you Amish. We don't have cows to milk at four a.m." She saw Joshua's head go down again. Trying to lighten up this conversation was impossible.

He tightened his grip on her hands. "Raven, I love you."

A chill blew through her. "And the Amish have a problem with that..."

He looked up but avoided eye contact. "Nee, because you said you'd convert. It's...Lottie."

"You love her, too?"

"Nee, I don't. But I have to marry her."

Raven bolted up. "What?"

"She's pregnant."

Raven felt pressure on her face and wanted to shout at Joshua, but only turned to leave. Joshua ran after her and held her from the back. "Let me explain."

"Joshua, I know all about the birds and the bees."

He turned her around and took her by the chin. "I do, too, and I don't think I'm the *daed*."

"Think? How can you not know?" She turned her head, having a hard time looking at the first man she really trusted, who deceived her.

"She said it happened when I was sick. I was delirious and don't remember anything."

Raven almost laughed at the absurdity of it all. It was worse than a soap opera. "Let me get this straight. Lottie's pregnant, and says it happened when you were sick, but you don't remember anything?"

"You had the same flu and were delirious, too."

Raven's mind flashed back to when Joshua apologized for kissing her when he was sick. It was Lottie he kissed. "Joshua, let me try to understand. She got pregnant but..." She needed to sit down, and headed toward Susanna's rocker. Joshua didn't take his hands off her. When she sat down, he knelt in front of her, taking one hand.

"Lottie says I'm the *daed*. Told her parents who told the bishop and elders. They're telling me to do the right thing and marry her. My name will be tarnished forever if I don't."

Raven leaned forward. "Maybe Lottie's lying."

"That's what I said. But the elders, bishop, and my *daed* believe her."

"And your mom? Does she believe Lottie?"

"*Mamm* doesn't know. Too much stress."

Raven moaned. Susanna could see through things clearly. "Did you tell them your side?"

"*Jah*, I did. But they said delirious or not, they'd seen us court over the years, and they believe her. They want to have a wedding real quick before she shows." He gripped her hands tighter. "My *mamm* doesn't know. When she comes home, we'll have the wedding then. Real small one."

Why wasn't he putting up a fight? He must still love Lottie. She turned her head. "Joshua, you say you love me, but you don't, or you wouldn't marry Lottie. We've only known each other for three months; you two courted for years. Your loyalty is with her…"

"I've never felt love toward Lottie like I feel for you."

"Then why are you going to marry her?"

"Because if it is my baby, I want to be the *daed*. Be responsible."

"Why not wait until after the baby's born and have a blood test taken?"

"It would make Lottie look mighty immoral. What I'd be saying is I'm not the *daed*, but someone else is. So it would look like she's been with more than one man."

"And why do you care so much, Joshua? Because you still love her."

"No I don't…."

~*~

Eb passed the sausage to Raven. "I need to apologize about my behavior yesterday. I wasn't myself."

Raven nodded. "When you heard I was half Native American, you changed."

Eb's head shot up. "What are you saying?"

"You don't like Native Americans."

Eb swung at the air. "That has nothing to do with anything. There's not a prejudiced bone in my body."

"It's alright, Eb. I've seen prejudice before. I recognize it."

Eb's eyes grew round. "Now look here. I don't lie. Ask Joshua Yoder. I had to pound in that boy that being truthful is one of the most important things in the world. I'm not prejudice. My past just came up and hit me in the face yesterday, that's all."

"Your wife and daughter?"

"Christmas has a way of bringing lots of emotions out. So, you just forget about any notions of me being prejudiced."

Raven still felt tired from her talk with Joshua last night, and wanted to change the subject. "Susanna leaves today…"

"I know. Maybe I'll see Joshua more when they're gone."

"Eb, don't go getting him in trouble. He already has enough…"

"What's wrong? Something gone wrong with Susanna?"

"No, I think she's doing pretty well. He has a lot on his mind, though."

Eb scratched his beard. "He's like a son to me, Joshua is. It's been hard not being able to talk. Maybe if you invite him over, and you two talk then –"

"I won't be talking to Joshua much."

"Why not? I thought you two were friends."

"Well, we are. But I'm busy with all the paperwork from the fire, and checking in on the boys. Appleton can be saved and now I have to help Jim and Marilyn. Actually, the boys, Lawrence and I were all planning on doing some repairs to help save money."

Eb snapped his finger and pointed at her. "You smiled when you said Lawrence. I knew it. So, he doesn't want you seeing Joshua because he's jealous."

"The imagination you have. My goodness, how you run with things."

"You're not only smiling, you're blushing. You like the pastor a lot."

"Eb, I'm not five. I do go out on dates. And yes, I think a lot of Lawrence."

~*~

Over the next few weeks, Raven was surprised by all the help they got to fix up Appleton, but never expected the Amish to show up in droves. Even though temperatures dipped below zero, Amish crews came and Jim played contractor. The insurance money came in, and Jim kept telling his depression era stories about saving money and doing things on his own. He wasn't going to hire a contractor, feeling the Amish and English could work together and save money.

It was interesting to see people from her church working right alongside the Amish, chatting and laughing. Some days the Amish broke out in song, singing in German and in harmony. With the boys back in school, and Marilyn still recovering from the fire, she was the only female in the house, steaming off all the wallpaper.

When she first came to Ellington, Raven thought the wallpaper too extravagant. How silly. The boys had a home they could be proud of. She steamed a part of a wall, and then went up on the ladder to reach the top of the ten foot ceiling. Someone was coming down the hall singing slowly, as if in mourning and she turned to see Joshua, hunched over as if sick.

"Joshua. Are you alright? You look sick."

"I'm not sick," he said as he passed by.

"Joshua, wait." She scurried down the ladder. "Any word about your mom?"

"She's doing *goot*, but in lots of pain. Allergic to most pain medicines, but they're doing their best."

"You must miss her. Ever think of taking the bus to Pittsburgh?"

"It costs money, and we're all saving for her new medicines when she comes home."

"'We're all'. Who's that?"

"The Amish. Our *Gmay*, or church as you call it."

"The Amish will pay for her medicine? Why?"

"I don't know. We've always done things that way. We're all paying for the transplant."

Raven gasped. "But that could be a million dollars."

"I know. Our settlement can't pay all that, so others are giving money. Someone put an ad in *Die Botschaft* and lots of funds are pouring in across the country."

She read this Amish newspaper since Eb subscribed to it. This was the good side of the Amish she liked, unbelievable generosity. But why they were treating Joshua so severely she couldn't overlook. Everyone could see he looked horrible. "Joshua, how are you really doing?"

Joshua's once twinkling blue eyes now looked gray and he wouldn't talk. "You're so unhappy. You can't go through with this wedding."

"I have no choice. I'll be a *daed* and it's time to be responsible."

Raven stomped her foot. "Joshua, you are too responsible. Who took care of your mother for three years? The problem is, you're too responsible...."

"Why should you care? I see you with Lawrence all the time."

Pain and anger shot from his eyes and Raven had an overwhelming urge to hold him; to see the once happy Joshua she knew; the man who had such peace and strength. She'd told him about her abusive past, and it was one of her first steps toward healing. She took his hand. "Joshua. I miss you. Our talks. You helped me once; let me help you."

He put his other hand on top of hers. "I've missed you, too. But how can you help me? I'm like an animal in one of my traps." His chin quivered and he blinked uncontrollably.

"Joshua, you need to see a doctor for your nerves. You've been under too much stress."

His eyes seemed to slowly focus on her. "You really care, don't you? Even though I'm going to marry Lottie, you still care."

"Yes, I care a lot."

"Then I'll go to the doctors. Can you drive?"

"I'll call and make the appointment," she said.

Chapter 14

*R*aven went home, too tired to walk. As usual, Eb had dinner ready with hot coffee to warm her up. "Thank you, Eb," she said as she collapsed in an Amish rocker in the living room. "I'm too tired to eat."

"Then you're too tired. You're not going tomorrow to that house. I am."

Raven looked at Eb in disbelief. "You're shunned."

"Not by Jim Rowe," he said with a twinkle in his eyes. "Anyhow, there's lots of English there. I'll stick around that boyfriend of yours."

"Eb, Lawrence isn't my boyfriend. We're just casually dating and seeing where it leads."

"Sounds like dating to me." Eb walked over with a tray of food. "Now eat."

"Yes, Papa," Raven said.

Eb sat in the rocker next to her. "I wish I were your *daed*."

"I never knew him. Like I said, I was an illegitimate child. My mom had a teen pregnancy."

Eb leaned closer to her. "Did you know your *mamm* at all?"

"I never knew her either. She left right after I was born. My grandparents raised me."

Eb's brows furrowed. "Where's your *mamm* now?"

"My grandma said she ran away and never saw her again. She was heckled by people for getting pregnant, and couldn't take it anymore, I suppose."

"What was her name? Do you know?"

"Flower. Of all things. Flower Meadows. Native Americans name people after things in nature. My hair was black when I was born, so they named me Raven."

"Well, it fits you real nice, though." Eb got up and went into the kitchen. Raven found Eb so refreshing. He accepted her just as she was. How many times had children been so cruel, saying neither parent wanted her? She saw Eb come in with two mugs of coffee.

"How old are you, Raven?"

She didn't know why all the questions, but January was a long month and cabin fever set in, making people climb the walls. "I'll be twenty-five on February 9th."

Eb started to choke on his coffee, gasping for breath. He took a deep breath and grabbed her mug. "This is too hot."

"Eb, are you alright?"

Eb ignored her and took the mugs in the kitchen. "Do you mind if I go out with your boyfriend? These four walls are falling in on me."

She knew it. Eb needed to get out more, which explained his mood swings and non-stop questions. She'd just read tonight and take Eb's advice, and not go to Appleton tomorrow. Maybe take Joshua to the Express-Med in Jamestown for a check-up.

~*~

"Today? But I'm working on the house," Joshua said, as Raven entered the kitchen.

Cliffy and Timmy were at the table, eating breakfast. "How are you two today?"

"Okay. How about you, Miss Meadows?" Timmy asked.

"You look tired," Cliffy said.

"She needs to see a doctor, too, *jah*?" Joshua said, eying Raven.

"Then we'll both see the doctor this morning." She smirked at Joshua. She heard a buggy pull up the driveway and cringed. Not Lottie!

Cliffy ran to the window. "Looks like your girlfriend's here."

Raven sighed loudly, not even trying to hide her disdain for this girl who was ruining Joshua's life. But she had to remind herself that Joshua had chosen her. He loved her.

Lottie acted as cold as the wind that accompanied her into the room. "Why are you here?"

"I'm taking Joshua to the doctors. He's sick."

"I'll take him."

Raven rolled her eyes. "To Jamestown in your buggy?"

"No, we have a doctor here in Cherry Creek."

"Lottie, I can take myself to the doc here. I'm going with Raven to Jamestown today," Joshua said, evenly.

Suddenly, Lottie's shoulders shook and tears sprung from her eyes. "You're trying to take him." She charged at Raven. "You know my condition. He's mine and you can't have him. You're trying to take my husband."

Raven looked at Timmy and Cliffy. This was not appropriate behavior for children to see. So much lack of self-control in an adult was scary. "Cliffy, Timmy, come with me."

Joshua raised his hand. "Wait! What's going on?"

"We like it here," Cliffy protested.

"Can I have a word with you, Joshua Yoder, in private?" Raven asked.

He motioned for her to go into the living room. When Lottie followed, he told her to stay in the kitchen.

Raven crossed her arms and looked at Joshua severely. "I will not have my boys be subjected to a woman who lacks such self-control."

"She just started crying. My *mamm* cries at times."

"Let me tell you something, Joshua Yoder. If you plan to adopt those two boys like you say you want to, I won't consent to Lottie being their mom. She's unstable."

"She's pregnant and all emotional."

"I'm a woman. I see things men don't. My boys deserve a mother who is…normal."

Joshua put his head down. "Then I won't be able to adopt them."

Raven felt the strength go out of her. He was willing to lose the boys for Lottie. "I want to talk to Cliffy and Timmy."

~*~

"Boys, no one can hear you up here, so don't be afraid of saying anything. Okay?"

Both boys nodded from their twin beds.

"You most likely know Joshua and Lottie are getting married. Can you see her as a mother?" Cliffy raised his hand as if in school. "Yes, Cliffy."

"Why would Joshua marry her? All they do is fight."

"Really? Timmy, is that how you see it? They fight all the time?"

"*Ya.* Don't know why he's marrying her. She's weird."

Raven rubbed her temples, trying to prevent a headache. "Are you afraid when they fight?"

"Freaked out," Timmy said. "I mean, she's always screaming over something little. Mrs. Rowe never did that." He shifted his feet. "I miss her."

"Me too," Cliffy said. "She'd never throw things across the room."

Raven grabbed at her hair. "She throws things? Like what?"

"Well, the other night Joshua made a really good stew and she thought it needed more salt. Joshua said something about watching how much salt she ate; she got out of her chair and got the salt shaker, and then threw it hard at Joshua. Hit him in the head good." Cliffy put his hand on his head. "Joshua said it really hurt."

"She doesn't act like an adult," Raven said through clenched teeth. "What did Joshua do when this happened?"

"Yelled real loud and told her to leave," Timmy said.

Raven cleared her throat. "And did she leave?"

"*Ya*, in a huff," Cliffy said.

"Joshua will be marrying Lottie, in March, when Susanna gets back. How do you feel about that?"

"I feel sorry for him," Cliffy blurted out. "She's nuts."

"Timmy, how do you feel about him marrying her?"

"Just like Cliffy. I mean, Miss Meadows. Joshua is the nicest man I know, next to Mr. Rowe and Pastor Lawrence. Why wouldn't he want to marry someone nice, like you? You'd make a great mom."

A lump formed in her throat; she realized for the first time she wished she could be their mom. She looked at each boy fondly. "Do you feel safe with Lottie here? Please tell me."

"We can handle her," Cliffy said. "And if we have a problem, we have our walkie-talkies."

Raven grinned. "It is fun talking to you on them. Do you talk to the other boys?"

"*Ya*, and we spy. Feels like we're in a movie."

Raven could see the boys were happy and couldn't help but open her arms and ask for a group hug. She prayed these precious boys would find the parents that deserved them.

~*~

The whole way to Jamestown, Joshua wished he could take Raven in his arms. Would this love for her go away once he married Lottie? How he needed his *mamm's* advice, since she had a discerning heart and could see through things. Such wisdom he missed. His *daed* not defending him still hurt. Saying he'd seen him court Lottie for years, and how he even had a crush on her in school, in eighth grade. How ridiculous. But it hurt more that his *daed* thought him capable of being immoral. He always heard if you point a finger in judgment, you have four pointing back at you. Was his *daed* ever in an immoral relationship before he got married? Joshua shook his head, trying to figure it all out.

The roads were icy and Raven clung to the steering wheel. "Joshua, we'll be late and may miss our appointment. Maybe have to take a later one. But you need to be seen today. I've seen nervous breakdowns before."

"I appreciate you doing all this, but I'm not too bad off."

"You may not see it, but you've developed a nervous twitch on your right eye and you stutter at times."

"I know. This whole thing with Lottie couldn't have come at a worse time. Got a letter from my *daed*, and he said *mamm's* having some problems. Blood work shows her new kidney's working, but not as good as they'd hoped."

Raven turned to him quickly and then eyed the road. "Will she make it?"

"They're confident she will, but this recovery is harder than anyone thought."

"Would she like a visit? Seeing you would cheer her up."

Raven was in such sharp contrast to Lottie; it stunned him at times, not knowing what to say. If he did go to Pittsburgh, his *mamm* would see right through him, and she'd force him to tell her. Him planning to marry Lottie could kill her. But he needed advice…

"Joshua, what do you say? Want to go to Pittsburgh? It's only a four hour drive. No need to reimburse for gas."

Looking out at the ice pelting the car, Raven was as good as a hot fire on a cold night. She had such warmth....he put his hand on her shoulder. "I can't, but *danki* just the same."

"Why can't you go? Need permission from the bishop to leave the cloister?" Raven groaned. "I'm sorry. I didn't mean to say that."

"*Jah*, you did. You think the bishop controls my life."

"He does. Look at what's happening to you. You're being pressured to marry someone...it's wrecking your health."

"They only want what's best. Told me they knew of a case where a man got drunk and got a woman pregnant years ago. He said he didn't remember, but ended up being the *daed*. They look at me being delirious, and think it's the same."

"Whatever..."

Joshua saw the frustration on Raven's face. She did care for him. "If I could get evidence, I'd be a free man...free to be with the woman I really love."

Raven slowed the car and pulled into a parking lot. "I can't drive in this storm and talk at the same time. These roads are bad."

Joshua took Raven's shaking hands in his. "Maybe you need to see a doctor for your nerves, too."

Her green eyes met his. "You may be right."

He put his hand on her cheek. "Do you know I pretend we're Timmy and Cliffy's parents? Cabin fever can make you do strange things, but when I think of being a *daed*, I think of those two boys....and you."

"Then why are you marrying Lottie?"

He released her and slouched in his seat. "I'm asking the same question."

~*~

Susanna looked at the IVs pumping pain medicine through her worn out body, and tried to be thankful, but felt panicky. Was it the medicine doing tricks with her mind, or was she supposed to be praying for someone? She prayed daily for her family, but today, something was urgent. Dear Lord, help whoever needs help.

She saw a group of Amish women in the hallway, but they wore other colors besides black and blue. Must be Mennonite, she thought. They came back down the hallway and into her room. An elderly lady with silver peeking out from her black bonnet smiled at her and hugged a present. "So you're Susanna Yoder."

"*Jah*, I am. Do I know you?"

She came over and sat next to her bed. "I'm Deborah Weaver, from Smicksburg. This here's my knitting circle I've told you about."

Tears sprang from Susanna's eyes. Tears of joy. She'd written circle letters to all these women, and on the day she felt the most despair, here they were in her room. She tried to sit up, but pain shot through her middle. But since the bed elevated her some, she could look at them all. "So *goot* to see you all."

Deborah got up and placed her hand on each girl's shoulder and said their name. "Maryann, Lizzie, Fannie, Ella, Ruth, Lottie, and Becca. We have old people like me, and young ones like Becca."

Susanna remembered how these women had solved so many problems together. For some reason she thought of Raven and her love for knitting. Maybe when she recovered, she and Raven could start a knitting circle, too.

"Granny, are you going to give her the present?" Becca asked.

Susanna didn't want to laugh, because it hurt, so she steadied herself. "Who's Granny? Deborah?"

"*Jah*, they all call me that. I love these girls like my own. Only had boys. How about you?"

"I have a son and daughter. Ann and Joshua. Ann lives in Ohio, but is here visiting me now. Went out to lunch with my husband."

"Well, it's nice she could be here." Deborah started to put the present on her, but Susanna pushed it back, "Please, don't. The pain…"

Deborah jumped back. "I'm so sorry. Do you want me to open the present up for you?"

"I'm sorry. The new kidney is put in the front, right here." She motioned to her left side. It's where the incision is. Awfully painful for a while."

Deborah opened the gift and Susanna clasped her hands and bit on her knuckles, trying not to cry. "It's so beautiful."

"This here blanket was knit with love. We passed it around, just like a circle letter, so everyone here helped make it."

Deborah moved closer and Susanna felt the soft yarn. "Did you spin this wool?"

"*Jah*, I did. Was going to dye it, but felt it looked nice in nature's colors. Notice the black mixed in with all the creams and whites. I had a black sheep, and there's his wool."

Susanna reached for the blanket and rubbed it against her face. "It's so soft."

"If I put it on you, will it hurt?"

"Nee, it'll keep me warm."

The women took the edges of the large blanket and together placed it on her. Love seemed to pour from the blanket, making such a difference to her aching body. She'd have to knit for people who were ill; it really was something.

"We'd like to pray for you. We call some of our prayers casting off prayers. We cast all our cares on God, because He cares for us. Is there anyone you need to cast on God?"

Susanna took inventory of all the people in her settlement who needed prayer. Too many to count. But someone she needed to cast on God. Lottie. She had such bad feelings for this girl that it haunted her in dreams. "Lottie. Her name is Lottie, and I want us to pray for her."

~*~

Joshua nodded at the doctor and thanked him for his advice, and shook his hand before leaving the room. He went into the large waiting room. The Express-Med was part of the hospital's ER and packed. Many looked too ill to be sitting up. He scanned the room again, and in the corner saw Raven with Lawrence. Jealousy again overcame him. A sin he kept committing. He slowly walked over and nodded at Lawrence, but couldn't make eye contact. This was the man trying to steal Raven's heart. Ashamed at such childish thoughts, he sat down in a chair across from them.

"What did the doctor say?"

"Just too much stress all at once, with my *mamm* and taking in the boys."

"Did you tell him everything?"

What was she thinking? Lawrence didn't know about Lottie. He stared at her coolly. "*Jah*, everything."

Lawrence hit his knee with his hand. "I need to make my rounds. So many down with the flu. Raven, I can follow you back home if you want to stick around Jamestown. The roads are bad."

Didn't Lawrence realize he was a man, capable of keeping Raven safe? No, he didn't know how to drive a car, but could help just the same. Why did some people treat the Amish as if they were stupid? How many flat tires had he changed for the English?

"We'll be fine. I've driven in worse weather."

Lawrence put his arm around Raven. "Are you sure?"

"I'm sure," she said, smiling warmly.

"Well, call me if you need anything." He turned to Joshua. "Any news about your mom?"

"She's in a lot of pain."

"Well, if she needs anything, or if you do, just…use one of the kids' walkie-talkies," he said with a grin.

Raven embraced Lawrence before they parted. "Better head home."

They walked out into the parking lot and sleet pelted them. "I hope this isn't freezing rain." Raven stared at the parking lot. "Ice is forming. I need to listen to the radio."

She got into the car and was preoccupied with flipping through stations, trying to get weather updates. It was times like this Joshua was glad to be Amish. The English fought nature while the Amish moved with it. If it was raining down ice, stay home. He tried to tell Raven this morning it looked like snow clouds were coming in mighty fast, but she ignored him.

When he got in the car, he heard a weather warning, but it wouldn't be in effect for another hour.

"We'll be home before this big storm hits."

"But the wind off Lake Erie could make it come much sooner."

"The weatherman has radar. They know what they're doing." She pulled on to the main road, and clung to the wheel, biting her lower lip. She pressed on the brake and got traction. "No ice yet. Good."

As they made their way out of Jamestown and up Route 62, the snow and ice blew horizontal. Raven made the windshield wipers move wildly. "Need to get on my snowshoes."

"Do you have a pair?"

"It's just an expression. Means I need to get used to all the snow. Not be afraid to drive in it."

Joshua didn't talk, since she was concentrating so much on the roads. But why could she listen to the radio? He thought of Lawrence, and started to put one and one together. They were dating and she was ignoring him. He sighed loudly.

"What's wrong?" Raven glance at him.

"Nothing. Keep your eyes on the roads."

"I am."

The more he heard the radio, the more rejected he felt. Is this how Raven felt when she saw him and Lottie together? If so, it was a horrible feeling, yet she still made an effort to be his friend, caring about his *mamm*, taking him to the doctors. Such a selfless person...

He saw a truck headed their way and it was swirling. "Dear Lord," Raven yelled. "Stay on your side!"

The truck seemed to only disobey, sliding further into their lane. "I need to do something!" Raven screamed, and then jerked the car off the road and they bounced violently through a corn field, until the car finally stopped.

Raven stared ahead, shaking all over. She looked so afraid, Joshua couldn't help it. He reached for her and took her in his arms. "We're alright. You did a *goot* job."

She looked straight ahead, and then buried her head in his chest and cried. He stroked her hair, trying to calm her down. He rocked her back and forth until her stiff body relaxed. She looked up at him, eyes still bewildered. "Can you hold me a little longer?"

"*Jah*, would be happy to…"

With Raven in his arms, dread over marrying Lottie overwhelmed him. How could he go through with it? Dear Lord, help me see clearly. He felt the warmth of Raven against him and his heart started to race. The desire to kiss her made it only beat harder…

Raven pulled away from him. "You're a nervous wreck, too. Your heart is thumping so fast."

Joshua turned to look out the window, feeling heat on his face, knowing he was blushing. Then he thought of Lawrence, and how hard it would be if Raven married him. He felt her hand on his shoulder and took it. "My nerves are wrecked over many things."

"Well, the car is fine, let's see if I can pull out of this field." She put the car in reverse and the tires just spun. Then she put the car into drive and moved a bit further. "We're stuck. I'm calling Lawrence."

"Wait, I can push."

"We'll need a chain. Someone needs to pull us out of here."

Joshua got out of the car and went to the front. He motioned for her to back up. When she did he pushed with all his might. Anger over everything in his life rose from within him and fueled his strength. The car moved backwards and he kept pushing. Even though they still had a ways to the road, he knew he could get Raven to a spot where there was no ice to get traction, and she wouldn't be calling Lawrence for help. And for that, he was glad. But this whole day gave him a lot to ponder. If he married Lottie, he'd lose the boys. Joshua looked at Raven through the windshield. And he'd lose her, the girl he loved…

Chapter 15

Raven and Eb got out another two-thousand piece puzzle. "How'd you get so *goot* at puzzles?" Eb asked. "Didn't know the English did them as much as the Amish."

"It's having good visual spatial relations. It's supposed to be hereditary." She thought of all the puzzles she put together at a young age. "My grandpa was faster than me. Must get it from him."

Raven got up to grab her ringing cell phone. The number wasn't familiar. Fearing it was Brandon, she answered anyway.

"Raven? This is Susanna Yoder."

Raven put her hand to her cheek. Susanna's voice was so weak; she sounded like she was over a hundred years old. "Susanna, how are you doing?"

"I'm alive so I won't complain. I've been thinking of you a lot…"

Raven heard strained breathing and a long pause. "I think of you all the time. The church is praying for you."

"*Danki*, I'm grateful….I got visitors today, and have an idea. Want to start a knitting circle?"

"I'd love that."

"We could meet at my place…"

Raven didn't know what to say. Susanna didn't know that Joshua would be marrying Lottie when she got home. Would Lottie be living at her house? If so, she wouldn't be going.

"Raven, what's wrong?"

"Nothing...."

"Is everything alright at my house?"

"Oh yes, nothing's wrong at the house."

A low sigh came through the phone. "I'm sorry. This medicine makes it hard to think. Seemed like something was wrong......How is Joshua?"

"Fine. He's just doing great," Raven said, a little too chipper.

Another long pause. "How are the boys? I miss Cliffy and Timmy."

"Oh, they love being in an Amish house. They like living without electricity. Said they feel like Daniel Boone."

"Who's that?"

"Oh, a man who lived without electricity, too, long ago."

The pause that followed was so long, Raven thought she lost the call. "Hello?"

"I'm here. Raven, what's wrong with Joshua?"

"Nothing. Nothing at all."

"You're not talking from your heart, I can tell. What's wrong?"

Raven pursed her lips. "He's a little worn out. Helping rebuild Appleton and raise two boys. I told him to slow down, and he's a man...not listening."

Raven was relieved to hear a chuckle on the other end.

"Hard to get men to slow down. I miss him. Is he going to visit?"

"Do you want him to?"

"Ach, Joshua's more than a son. Over these past years, he's become my constant friend."

Once again, Raven was overcome with emotion. She wanted to marry this son of hers. He was such a good man. But Lottie was ruining everything. "He's a good man for sure."

"And you care for him, but not Amish?"

She clenched her cell phone. Was it so obvious? Yes, it was true. She loved Joshua Yoder, but he was being controlled by an impossible group of men.

"People convert for love," Susanna continued.

Raven realized the pain medicines must be loosening Susanna's tongue to say things she would normally not. She was thinking out loud. "So, we're starting a knitting circle. What should we make?"

"Prayer shawls. For people on dialysis. Maybe for people you think of, too. My recovery will be almost six months and I'll have lots of time on my hands."

"Well, I'll look for yarn sales and stock up. When you get home, we can knit away."

"I'd like that. Ann may be coming up for a while. She's a knitter, too."

"Who's Ann?"

"My daughter from Ohio. She's here in the hospital with me. Sure wish Joshua would come…"

"I'll talk to him. Offer to drive. It's not that far."

"*Danki*, dear one."

~*~

Susanna hung up the phone. Something was really wrong with Joshua. She'd write him a letter, asking him to come. She could read his facial expressions and find out what was happening. Her mind turned again to Raven. Since she loved Rueben with her whole being, it was easier to spot a woman in love. Did Joshua know? Did he realize she could convert?

Susanna looked over at Rueben sitting in the recliner reading a book. "I think Joshua's coming to visit."

Rueben slowly put his book in his lap, and then pulled off his reading glasses. "Who said that?"

"Raven. She said she'd drive him. I'm writing to him tonight to encourage him to come."

"But you're ill."

Susanna sighed. "Rueben, you can't shield me from everything. Something's wrong and I need to see Joshua, face to face. Besides, I miss him."

"But Ann's here. Isn't she enough company? And the women from Smicksburg said they'd be back."

Susanna laid her head down. "I want to see my son."

~*~

Raven held on to the teacher's desk, gawking at Bud and Chuckey's teacher. "They told you that and not me?" She had to admit, she was hurt. She visited the boys regularly and they never said a word. Did they feel safer talking about Lottie out of the house, thinking Lottie could hear?

"Let me get this straight. The boys were in a car with an *Englisher* and Lottie, and they were afraid. The English man was speeding and Lottie was laughing in a way that scared them."

"That's what they said. This man went faster when the boys asked him to slow down. And the roads were icy. This happened last week."

Raven sat down at one of the student's desks. "Anything else I should know?"

"Well, I know young people who are in love kiss, but it seems like they were…passionate."

"Passionate?"

"Yes, Bud said Lottie was mad she had to take them along. So was the man. They asked them to stay outside and play for a while, but boys being boys, they saw things."

"Like?"

"Kissing. Nothing more. But Bud and Chuckey are awfully upset because they said she's engaged to someone else." She put her hand up. "That's all I have to say. Have another parent to see in a few minutes."

"Thank you, Mrs. Polk. There needs to be more teachers like you, who see their students are upset."

"They came to me. I can't prod. But thanks just the same," she said.

~*~

Raven knew this was going to be a long day. She needed to talk to the Miller family about this incident. Supper time was when all Amish were home, and she didn't care if she interrupted their meal. She marched up to the Millers and banged on the front door.

Soon Mary appeared. "Raven, you can use the side door. You're a friend."

"Mary, I need to talk to you and your husband, Lottie, Bud and Chuckey right now."

"But I have a roast on the table."

"This is an emergency."

Mary's eyes widened. "Step inside. We'll all meet you in the living room."

Raven collapsed on the Amish rocker, forgetting to take her boots off. Snow melted around her feet like a puddle. She pulled them off and when Mary came into the room, asked for a rag. Mary said not to bother, worry etched on her usually meek and mild face.

When everyone took their seats in the traditional circle of Amish rockers and benches, she looked over at Bud and then Chuckey. "I talked to Mrs. Polk today. She called a parent teacher conference. Now boys, just nod yes or no to what I'm about to ask you."

Both boys nodded vigorously.

"When you were in the car last week with Lottie and an English man, was he speeding?"

Both boys nodded yes.

Eli's head jolted to his daughter. "You out with Bruce again? We told you it was forbidden."

Lottie quickly got tears in her eyes. "*Daed*, we needed groceries and *mamm* told me to take the boys. How was I to know Bruce would speed?"

Eli turned to his wife. "Did you know she was out alone with Bruce?"

"Nee, I did not. I thought his *mamm* was taking them."
She narrowed her eyes. "Lottie, I told you to stay away
from Bruce."

Raven cleared her throat loudly. "Boys, was there a
smell of alcohol in the car?"

They both shook their heads no.

"Were you asked to stay outside the car so Lottie and
Bruce could have some privacy?"

Lottie stood up. "Everyone knows Bruce has lots of
problems and I only try to help him."

Raven kept her eyes on Bud and Chuckey. "Boys, how
long were you outside?"

"Seems like half an hour."

Lottie laughed. "You know how kids are. A minute
seems like an hour. It was only a few minutes."

"Boys, did you look into the car?"

They nodded.

"And what did you see?"

Bud looked sheepishly over at Lottie. "Kissing,"

Again, Lottie got up and laughed. "We were not. Bruce
just broke down about a family situation and I gave him a
hug. That's all."

"Boys?" Raven prodded.

Chuckey's face grew a deep shade of red. "Lottie, we
know you're supposed to marry Joshua. You talk about it
all the time, so why not be nice, instead of throwing
things at him?"

"I don't throw things at Joshua, unless we're playing a
game."

Bud shot up. "And you swear at him. Is that a game, too?"

Lottie put her hand on her heart, as if she was going to faint. "I would never...Bud. Joshua and I talk in German."

"Well, that's not how we hear it..."Chuckey said.

Raven asked to speak to only Bud and Chuckey. The family slowly filed out. They went up to the boys' bedroom. "What do you mean, she swears at him, and you hear? From Cliffy and Timmy?"

Bud grinned and pulled his walkie-talkie from under his pillow. "This has come in mighty handy. Timmy and Cliffy let us listen in on their arguments, Miss Meadows; it's like watching TV, only better because we know Lottie."

Raven couldn't help but grin.

"She's a good actress, honestly. She acts all sweet and perfect here when her parents are home, but with Joshua, she turns into Darth Vader." Bud made the deep breathing sound of the Star Wars character and went over to Chuckey. "Charles, I am your father."

Raven didn't know why she started laughing, since this was so serious. Most likely pent up nerves. "Boys, do you know when Bruce comes over here?"

"That's easy. All the time. Lottie thinks we don't know, but she meets him near the end of the farm. Being on the third floor, we can see everything for miles," Chuckey said. "She tells her parents she's going to check on some sick lady down the road, but she's playing a game. She gets in the car with Bruce."

Raven looked up, deep in thought. "I'll tell you what. When this happens, can you reach me by walkie-talkie?"

Bud jumped up. "Like being spies?"

"When you see Lottie walk down the road and you know Bruce is waiting, how about you tell me a code."

"Cool," Chuckey blurted. "How about S.O.S.? Mr. Rowe used that code in the war."

"Fine. Say S.O.S. That will be our secret code. Promise you'll do this?"

"Promise."

"Do not ever get in the car with Bruce again. Understand? I can't prove anything, but I'll get to the bottom of this."

~*~

On the short drive home, she thought of Joshua. Should she tell him about Bruce? Most likely Lottie would tell him the same story, and it didn't get him off the hook.

So many things she admired about the Amish, but they seemed stuck back in time. She'd watched old movies and seen shot gun weddings. That was what this was, only the Amish were pacifist.

When she passed Joshua's house, she decided to stop in for a few minutes. Raven made her way across the icy driveway, and knocked at the side door. She heard laughter inside and through the window saw Joshua and the boys were playing Dutch Blitz. Joshua came to the door and stepped back to let her in. She wanted to hug him, tell him he couldn't ruin his life by marrying such a girl.

Their eyes met and Joshua frowned. "Raven, what's wrong?"

"Just being neighborly."

"Want to play cards?"

"No, wanted to say hi to Cliffy and Timmy, too."

"Do you want some hot chocolate?"

Raven looked into Joshua's blue eyes. The eyes that pulled out the truth about her childhood. Now he was about to be trapped in an abusive marriage. Lottie would make him miserable. Tears filled her eyes and she wiped them, saying she had a cold. Joshua asked her to talk to him in the living room. He sat on the bench and patted the seat next to him. She sat down, and tried not to look at him.

"Joshua, don't marry Lottie. I can't prove anything now, but please, let's go down and talk to your *mamm*. She'd know what to do."

"Too much stress on her. Nee, I won't go down."

Raven took his hand and kissed it. "Joshua, you deserve better than Lottie."

She felt his arm go around her. "Raven, what's going on?"

She turned to him and looked into his eyes and then hugged him around the neck. "Don't marry her. I c-can't prove anything yet…"

"Prove that I'm not the *daed* of the *boppli*?"

She released him and looked at him evenly. "Joshua, please trust me on this. I'm going to clear your name."

He looked at her sheepishly. "You love me, don't you?"

She put her head down. "How could I not love you? No man I've ever met compares to you."

He smiled. "I thought you were going to marry Lawrence for sure."

"I realize now that I really do love only you."

Their lips slowly met and the most gentle, heartfelt kiss that was ever put on Raven's lips melted her heart. Joshua was so gentle, so unlike other men.

Joshua stroked her long black hair. "Last week, when you asked me to hold you, I did. Now I'm asking you to return the favor."

Raven wiped the tears that spilled on to her cheeks and wrapped her arms around Joshua, the sweetest man she'd ever know. Surely God would stick up for him and save him from an unhappy marriage.

Chapter 16

"*I* was ready to send a bloodhound out to find you! I was worried."

Raven staggered into the living room and plopped down on the couch. "Long, long day. Sorry, Eb."

"Well, maybe I worry too much. Feel like your *daed* or something."

Raven tilted her head and considered what Eb said. "I'd like that. Having you for a dad."

He grinned. "You would? Having an alcoholic for a *daed* wouldn't be a picnic."

"Recovered alcoholic, right? You've been sober how long?"

"Well. It's been Nov. 4th since I took a drink. So that makes it three months."

Raven pulled a boot off. "That's over ninety days. They say if you can do something for ninety days you've kicked a habit, although you'll always need to stay away from alcohol, you know that?"

"*Jah*, I do. But I don't need it anymore."

"So you don't feel guilty anymore about your family's death?"

Eb placed a tray full of food on her lap. "I'm thinking the bishop and elders were right all along. It wasn't my fault and there was no need to blame God."

Raven shrugged. "That bishop and those elders seem awful stern to me."

"Are they mean to you? But you're not Amish."

"No, but just observed something. Don't think it's fair."

Eb scratched his chin. "The bishop cried like a baby, pleading with me to not forsake God, and turn away from the bottle. I know if you talked to him, he'd listen."

"Really? I'm surprised. But I told an Amish person I wouldn't tell anyone about his secret."

"Well, then don't. But I'll be behind you in prayer, dear one."

Raven was glad to come home to Eb. He'd cared for her since the day he met her, and she was thankful he thought of her as a daughter. She needed family and hoped to find it eventually with Joshua. Susanna would be her mom…

"If your friend is innocent, the Lord will clear his name. Seen it too many times. The bishop and elders depend on it, too. They wait a while before passing a strict judgment, to see if the Lord shows up."

Raven wondered if the marriage being in March wasn't only for Susanna to be home, but for the truth to come out. She slowly turned to Eb. "Have the elders been talking to you lately? Have you had a change of heart toward the Amish?"

Eb's eyes glistened. "Let's just say I'm starting to see that God is good again."

"So you might be returning to the Amish? Sure would make Joshua happy if you did."

"And why is it so important to you that Joshua is happy?"

"He's a good man."

Eb wagged this finger at her. "Tell the truth."

"I am. The Yoder's are the nicest people and Joshua shouldn't be forced to –" Raven covered her mouth. "Oh, I can't say."

"Well, all I know is since I've seen how you hover over those boys, being their advocate, I'm seeing how much God is ours, like the Good Book says. And I'm seeing an amazing answer to prayer, but I can't say what it is now." He winked. "I realize God sees…and he redeems….he helps us like an advocate does."

Raven leaned forward. "Eb, are you alright? It seems like you're talking about yourself."

"I am, dear one. I am. God is a restorer for sure and for certain."

The way Eb looked at her, all sentimental, made her wonder if he just wanted to be alone and read his Bible at night, like he always did. "I'm going to turn in early. Long day and need to knit."

"What're you making?"

"A prayer shawl, for my Aunt Brook. When I knit I'll pray for her, and then I'll deliver it."

"So you found her?"

"No, but Lawrence has connections on the reservation and is looking into it." She walked over to Eb and kissed him on the cheek. "Good night."

"Good night, dear one….my girl. Oh, and remember, don't make plans on your birthday, at least in the afternoon. I have a surprise."

"I won't. Thank you."

~*~

Raven was running in the woods, not knowing which way to turn but followed the flickering light. She woke up to see a light flickering in her window. What on earth? She slipped on her moccasins and robe and went to the window. It was too dark to make out who it was. Brandon? It couldn't be. He'd left over a month ago. Maybe one of the boys was in trouble and needed her. She ran down the steps and looked out the bottom window. It was Joshua. Raven opened the side door to let him in. She braced herself, fearing bad news about Susanna.

But Joshua had hope in his eyes, and was as carefree as when she met him. He scooped her into his arms. "I'm free."

She shook her head in shock. "So the bishop found out about Bruce, and believes me?"

"I don't know what you're talking about." He swung her around. "And I don't even care. I talked to my *mamm* on the phone. She was so suspicious about me not going to visit, it was making her sicker. So, I told her about Lottie's accusation." Joshua took off his black wool hat. "*Mamm* said if I marry Lottie she'll shun me."

Raven grinned. "That's so funny...but what does all this mean?"

He took her hands. "Raven, I'd rather live as a man known for not being responsible and have you."

All the ridicule she'd endured, all the rejection and feeling of abandonment seemed to be peeling off, like old paint. She put her head on his chest. "I don't feel like I deserve you, or I would have fought harder."

"What do you mean?"

"I thought you'd naturally love Lottie. I didn't feel worthy of you…"

"Why? Why would anyone not love you?"

"I don't know….I lived a worldly life before I came here. Understand?"

Joshua tilted her head up and she looked into his unflinching blue eyes. "All have sinned, *jah*? And you asked for forgiveness?"

"Yes, many times."

"When someone sins in the Amish community, if they repent, all is forgiven and forgotten. We all know we're made from the dust, and are human. We make mistakes. It's the job of the community to restore." He shifted. "That's what they're trying to do with Lottie. Force a true confession. It's really for her own *goot*."

Raven couldn't take in all this goodness. Feelings of shame and unworthiness threatened to drown her. He took her and kissed her gently, but then with all his heart. "Raven Meadows, there is nothing that could make me change my mind about you, no matter how hard you push away. I want to marry you some day."

Raven gasped for air. "Oh, Joshua, I love you too, but so many obstacles… I'm not Amish."

"You said before you'd convert, *jah*?"

"Well, I was going to, but now I'm afraid. The leaders seem to have too much control."

"I'll be talking to the bishop tomorrow. He has a high opinion of my *mamm*, and what she says he'll take to heart. He's a *goot* man. I'm praying God will reveal the truth about this *boppli*, too."

"Well, let me tell you about this Bruce guy, and the boys' plan…"

~*~

Raven went back up to bed, floating on a cloud. Joshua would give up so much for her? She loved this man with all her being. So much, that it made to want to defend him more. Find out more about what was happening between Bruce and Lottie. She was certain he was the father, if she was even pregnant.

What a funny thought? If she was pregnant? She would be almost three months now, and still had a trim waist. But then again, she wore a lose apron. Raven laid down in bed, determined to not worry or let Lottie steal this magical moment. Joshua loved her unconditionally.

Being wide awake, she may as well make a few rows of her aunt's shawl. A prayer shawl meant praying for that person who you knit for. She thanked God for her Aunt Brook because… Raven couldn't think of anything to be thankful about. Then she remembered what Joshua said long ago. Raven had a hard life and tried to help other kids so they'd never go through what she did. If she had a pampered life, she may be blind to all the needs around her. She might not care about anyone but herself. She might be…Lottie. She did have a lot to thank Aunt Brook for…

~*~

Joshua heard a loud knock on his door the following afternoon. It was Lottie, and her *mamm* and *daed*. Eli took off his black hat and held it calmly in his hands. "Joshua, the bishop came by this morning and told us of your decision to not marry Lottie. Is this correct?"

"*Jah*, it is. I'm not the *daed*."

"Then you've fallen for the lies of Raven Meadows?" Mary asked. "About Lottie and Bruce being together, and that Bruce is the *daed*."

Joshua sat down. "*Jah*, I believe Raven and the boys. But I made my decision before anyone told me about Bruce."

Lottie stomped her foot like a child. "Raven and those boys cooked up this story to stop you from marrying me."

Joshua stood up. "Don't talk about Raven like that."

"Why?" Eli asked, visibly upset. "Are you attached to an Outsider?"

"Maybe I am."

Lottie ran toward Joshua and started to hit him in the face. Her *daed* pulled her back. "Lottie, you are Amish. We don't embrace violence." Eli led her to the door and told her to wait in the buggy, and then marched up to Joshua. "You've broken my daughter's heart. What happened to the Joshua Yoder who was upright and respectable?"

Joshua just hung his head and prayed that God would defend him. He'd done nothing wrong and hoped his innocence would be revealed.

~*~

Cliffy looked wide-eyed at Timmy. Sitting at the top of the steps they'd heard everything.

"It's *goot* that he dumped Lottie," Cliffy said.

"You said '*goot*'. You sound Amish," Timmy laughed. "I'm glad she's dumped, too. And I think Joshua wants to marry Miss Meadows. Think about it. If he does, she could be our *mamm*, I mean mom."

Cliffy elbowed Timmy. "*Jah*, I know. So we need to move fast. What if Joshua gets in trouble, like is shunned or something? Gets kicked out of the Amish? I want to be Amish, don't you?"

"I think so. I want Joshua as a *daed* for sure, even if he's young. Susanna and Rueben would be our parents, though, I think. Not sure what's going on."

"It doesn't matter. All the Amish act like they're one family. Look at all the cousins Joshua has."

"You know Toby and Ethan want to be Amish, say they like the big families, or just being in a family. But Bud and Chuckey don't like it. I'm afraid we'll all get separated."

Cliffy sighed. "When Appleton reopens in April, I want to stay here. Do you?"

"For sure." Timmy turned to Cliffy. "We'd be brothers, huh?"

The boys fist-bumped. Timmy ran to get his walkie-talkie. "Come on. I'm calling all the guys. We need to work on nailing this Bruce guy."

~*~

Over the next few days, Raven learned that her boys were working overtime trying to see if Bruce was with

Lottie, but to no avail. But Joshua was so confident he'd be cleared and he looked happy and healthy again, and in love with her. She'd have to trust that everything would work out.

Today was her birthday, and Eb had big surprise. But why was Lawrence going? She had to stop trying to figure everything out. She pulled a letter out of her jean pocket; a message Susanna set her, revealing her favorite Bible verses:

Lord, my heart is not haughty,
Nor my eyes lofty.
Neither do I concern myself with great matters,
Nor with things too profound for me.
Surely I have calmed and quieted my soul,
Like a weaned child with his mother;
Like a weaned child is my soul within me.
Psalm 131:1-2

Everything happening was too profound and great for her to grasp. She'd rest in the arms of Jesus, as the Amish often advised. God was in control, so she could quit white knuckling every situation in her life.

She saw Lawrence pull in from her bedroom window, and looked again in the mirror. She had on enough make-up, going with a more natural look. Raven grabbed her white coat and blue hat and went downstairs.

"Happy Birthday, Raven," Lawrence said. "Ready for your big surprise?"

"I don't know. You two are making me nervous. With this much fanfare, it must be something big."

She noticed Eb's eyes were misty. "What's wrong?"

"Nothing. Nothing at all. But you need to get your doll."

"My doll? Why?"

"It's part of the surprise," Lawrence said, his hand on Eb's shoulder.

Raven put her hands up in surrender. "Okay." Running up the steps she had a clue about what the surprise was. So many of her doll sweaters she'd knitted over the years were ruined in the fire. Eb must think she wanted doll clothes, but she wasn't that attached to her doll to go shopping for it. She'd act surprised no matter what he did for her, the dear man had been planning this for weeks.

Raven grabbed her doll and went downstairs. "We're ready to go."

Lawrence helped her across the driveway and into his car. Eb got in the back. She looked over at the Yoders, hoping Joshua didn't get the wrong idea about her and Lawrence. She'd see Joshua tonight and explain, not wanting to bring any more drama into his life.

Lawrence drove further into Amish country, and not toward Jamestown. "What's up here? Only farms…"

Eb patted her shoulder. "It's only a few minutes away." He told Lawrence which back roads to turn on to.

"I've never been down these roads. Are they even plowed?" Raven asked.

"I have a Jeep," Lawrence quipped. "I can get through anything."

Raven now knew why Lawrence was invited. They needed a four wheel drive. When Eb told Lawrence to pull into a little shop with a quilt sign on the front, she turned to him. "Eb, thank you! But Amish quilts are so expensive."

"A quilt isn't your present," Eb said in a shaky voice. "Grab your doll before we go in."

When they got out of the car and started towards the store, Raven saw that Eb was trembling. "Eb, are you cold?"

"Nee, I'm fine. Excited, is all."

When they entered the store, a middle-aged Amish woman met them. She seemed to know Lawrence and didn't shun Eb at all. Raven looked around to see every nook and cranny of the tiny store was filled with crocheted and woven rugs, baskets, table runners, homemade cards, wooden puzzles, lots of quilts hung up, and Amish dolls. She naturally went over to the dolls first. She picked one up and noticed it looked like her rag doll. It didn't have traditional Amish clothes but a pink and blue paisley dress with matching bonnet, just like hers.

Eb called her over. "Raven, this is Martha Mast. An old friend of mine."

"Nice to meet you, Martha." She held up the two dolls. "They look the same, only mine's faded. Got it from my grandmother years ago."

Martha took her doll and looked at it carefully. "Where does your grandmother live?"

"Well, she used to live in Salamanca."

"Ach, she could have bought it here."

"What a coincidence. Is there any way of knowing if you made it? Any special mark on the doll?"

Martha scrunched her lips. "Well, if I get a particular order, to make something special, I take orders, and before I put the black boot on, I write the person's name on the doll's foot."

Raven had to know if this was the woman who made the doll, the link to her grandmother. "The boots are sewn on. Is there any way of looking to see if her name is on the foot?"

"Easily. I have a stitch ripper handy at all times. Will only take a minute. Why not shop around while I take off the boots? I believe Eb wants you to pick something out, *jah*?"

"*Jah*, I do. But not a quilt." Tears filled Eb's eyes. "I'm sorry. I wish I could afford it."

Raven was puzzled over Eb's behavior. A cake with candles would have been fine. Why would she expect him to get her a quilt? Maybe he thought the English got really big presents. "Eb, I actually want another doll. I like the ones with the wine color dresses and black aprons."

"Well, go pick something out." He turned to go over and talk to Martha.

Raven tingled at the thought that her grandmother could have been in this very shop. That she picked the material for her doll and special ordered it would be such a treat. She had a hard time shopping as Martha took the boots off her doll, but looked around nonetheless. Raven noticed the even stitches on a crocheted rug. She'd heard the Amish made knitted rugs that were heavy duty. She'd love to see one and wondered if Martha made them. Maybe she could bring up a picture and show her.

She heard crying, and turned to see Eb embraced by Lawrence. "What's wrong?"

Lawrence motioned for her to come over, as he tried to calm Eb down. Martha told her to come back around her little counter. "I have something to show you."

Raven looked at Martha's face. She was smiling as if it was good news. But why was Eb crying? She made her way around the counter and Martha took her hand. "Raven, the person who ordered this doll for you wasn't your grandmother…but your *daed*." She held up the doll's foot for Raven to see EB written on the foot.

She blinked and looked again. "Whose initials are those?"

"They're not initials, but the name of your *daed*, understand?"

Raven leaned forward and held on to Martha. Lawrence came over and took her hand in one and Eb's in the other. "Raven, Eb's your father."

"What? How?" Raven felt too numb to talk.

"I came with Eb for moral support and to explain if his name was on the doll's foot and not Rueben's."

Martha got a chair and put it behind Raven, and she plopped into it.

"Raven," Lawrence continued. "Eb and Rueben Yoder had girlfriends during their *rumspringa*, or running around days. These girls lived in Salamanca and came here to have them pick out dolls. They both liked the same doll, so Martha said she'd make two dolls and they could pick them up. She marked the foot on one doll Eb and RY, on the other, for Rueben Yoder."

Raven put her head in her hands. "So you're saying my mother was in this shop?"

"Yes, and she picked out that doll. It was passed on to you by your grandmother. Something that was your mother's. Maybe you don't remember your grandmother telling you it was your mother's?"

Raven rocked back and forth. "I was five. I don't remember much. Just know my grandmother gave her to me." Her mother...her real mother... was in this store! She felt lightheaded and raked her fingers through her hair. And her real father was in this store...Eb!

She looked up at Eb, sobbing by her side, and she got up to embrace him. "I'm glad. I'm glad," is all she could get out.

She felt Eb cradle her head on his shoulder. "Me too...my dear one."

Lawrence put his arms around them both. "How about we go back to Eb's and he can tell you the story in detail."

Raven looked up to see other customers had entered the store.

"But Raven needs to pick out a birthday present," Eb managed to say.

She put her arm through his. "I already have my present."

Chapter 17

$\mathcal{J}$oshua asked the boys to clean the dishes so he could talk to Raven in the living room, and give her a birthday present. She'd been so emotional during dinner, and he knew she went somewhere with Lawrence, so was anxious to see where he stood.

He sat on the bench next to her and took her hand. "Raven, what's wrong?"

"Joshua, I just can't wait to tell you something. Eb is my *daed*."

"What?"

"I found out today at the doll shop in Leon. He bought my doll for my mom years ago when they were dating, during his *rumspringa*. His name was on her foot. Your dad and Eb had girlfriends in their teens and both girls wanted the same doll, so Martha Mast had to make two dolls and marked the doll's foot with the customer's name. "

Joshua looked out the window toward Eb's house. "So that's it. All these years my *daed* blamed Eb for leading him into a sinful *rumspringa*. He had an English girlfriend, too?"

Raven took his hand and grinned. "Joshua, I'm glad RY wasn't on the doll's foot, because I'd be your sister."

He saw the excitement in Raven's eyes, and didn't want to spoil the night, but he'd be having words with his *daed*. *Jah*, he was right. When you point the finger, you have four pointing back at yourself. When Lottie accused him of being the *daed* of her *boppli*, his *daed* believed her because it was something he would have done, or did when he was young.

He turned to Raven. "He always felt the house fire and losing his wife and girl was God's judgment for some past sin…"

"He told me all about that. Now he feels like it's such a miracle he found me, that God really loves him. He wanted to marry my mom. Remember when I first met Eb and he called me Beauty? He called my mom that."

"*Ach*, and he was drunk. You must look so much alike."

Raven lowered her head. "Being in that shop, knowing my real mom had been in there, made me happy and angry all at once. I wondered why she abandoned me, but Eb said they were going to meet and run off and get married but she needed more time to think. Never saw her again."

Joshua rubbed her back. "How about we celebrate you finding your *daed*?"

"Oh, I'm overcome with joy. Eb's like a dad already. It's awesome how God brought us together. I was drawn to him immediately, remember?"

He tilted her chin up and kissed her. "*Jah*, and do you realize you're half Amish?"

She chuckled. "I guess I will be, because Eb's going to repent and be reinstated in good standing."

"Ach, that's *goot* news…everyone will be relieved. We all love Eb."

"And since my father is Amish, I don't feel like I'd be denying my heritage by turning Amish too." She put one hand up. "Not saying I will, but am leaning towards it for two reasons."

"And what might they be?"

"The two men I love are Amish."

Joshua pulled her close. "I have a present for you." He pulled her up, leading her to a corner in the room. "It's under the quilt."

She looked at him and grinned. "*Danki.*" Then she pulled the quilt back to reveal a hope chest.

"Look inside."

She opened the mahogany top and squealed. "Such beautiful China." She picked up a cup. "So dainty."

Joshua took her hand. "I can't propose official like, since you're not Amish. But a hope chest is just that, *jah*? Something to give, hope of the future?"

"So we'd be unofficially engaged, is that what you're saying?"

"*Jah*, I want to marry you when God makes our path straight. I dream of you being Amish and my name being cleared. I think God put it in my heart, so I'm believing it will all happen."

"Oh, Joshua, I'd love to be your wife." She threw her arms around him and kissed Joshua until she was out of breath. "This is by far the best birthday I've ever had."

~*~

Susanna fidgeted with the fringe on her blanket, the blanket made with love. Only three more weeks and she'd be home, Lord willing. For her health's sake, and for the family business. She looked over at Rueben, ever at the recliner, reading letters and cards that just arrived. "You'll need to tap the trees soon, *jah*? Maple syrup season's coming on…"

"My favorite time of year and with a hard winter, the sap will be flowing mighty fine." He walked over to take her hand. "I'm not leaving you, if you're concerned."

"Reuben, I know," she said.

"So thankful, too. I'm sure Joshua and Eb can handle a lot of the work…"

"Eb?" Susanna narrowed her eyes. "You wouldn't let him help last year because of the shunning."

"Just got this letter from Eb. He's feeling the need to repent for turning his back on God…"

"Praise be. But why the change of heart?"

Rueben pulled at his beard. "It's so unbelievable, but he found out some good news. Raven is his daughter."

Susanna gasped. She remembered Raven telling her on the first day they met that she never knew her parents. How painful that was for her. Their talks had deepened and Susanna prayed she'd somehow be reconciled with her family in Salamanca. But Eb was her *daed*? She looked at Rueben. "How is he her *daed*?"

"Remember I confessed about my *rumspringa*? How Eb and I had English girlfriends? Since Raven's been living with him, lots of clues popped up, and Eb got suspicious. Long story, and it's all in the letter for you to read…."

Susanna pursed her lips. "Did Eb know he left Raven's *mamm* pregnant?"

"*Jah*, I remember as if it were yesterday. He was going to run away with her and get married, but said she needed time to think. Eb never heard from her again…"

Susanna thought of Raven knowing her *daed* was Amish. "Maybe Raven will be Amish, too."

"Why would she do that?"

"Eb, she has a *daed* who's Amish, and the man she loves is Amish."

Rueben cocked an eyebrow. "Who?"

"Can't you see it? Joshua and Raven love each other."

Reuben slowly went to the recliner and sat down. "And you encourage this?"

"If Raven converts, *jah*. I would."

"I just. I don't know. Always figured he'd marry a girl from a *goot* Amish home. Someone who knows our ways."

"And you think Lottie does? *Nee*, what I see in Raven is a Christian woman. Isn't that what we want more than anything for Joshua?"

Rueben looked out the hospital window. "I've been pressuring Joshua to marry Lottie, you know that? People will always say he's the *daed*…"

Susanna pulled the blanket up closer to her neck. "I'm trusting God to reveal the truth…"

~*~

Raven heard Eb come in the back door. She felt the cold chill wisp through the house. When Eb came into view, he held out a big, red, heart-shaped box of chocolates. He planted a kiss on her cheek. "Happy Valentine's Day, Daughter."

Raven put her head down, trying to hide the tears. She heard sniffling and looked up at Eb. "You too?"

"*Jah*. I'm still breaking down. To know you're my daughter has made me a happy man. A restored man."

Raven got up to get a tissue. "To know I was wanted…that my parents wanted to get married…that I wasn't a mistake. It's overwhelming at times. I always felt deep down I wasn't supposed to be born."

Eb embraced her. "I have nothing against your grandparents, but I wish they would have told me the truth."

Raven nodded. "Me too. They shouldn't have told you my mom took me when she ran off."

"Even if Flo was gone, I wanted to be your *daed*."

"Because you wanted to do the right thing? The honorable thing?"

"Nee, I loved your *mamm* and I loved you. I never saw you as a *boppli* because…"

"Why?"

"Well, you know the Amish are pacifist and won't fight. Some friends went with me when you were born so I could see you. We were met with some resistance. Got beat up real bad."

"What?" Raven remembered her grandfather's distain for the Amish because he said they weren't real men, not defending themselves. Was he referring to Eb? "Were you badly hurt?"

"*Jah*, and my *mamm* and *daed* got afraid. Some broken ribs and all and had to be bandaged up. So I sent a letter to Flo asking her to meet me and she came, but like I said, needed more time to think…"

Eb seemed to fall into a trance, thinking of something so long ago, but with such deep emotion. That he loved her mom Raven had no doubt. "Would you like to find her?"

He put up his hand in protest. "I'm going to be reinstated into the Amish, having repented of my turning to the bottle instead of God. I never stopped being Amish, and the last thing I need is to be drawn backwards." He paused and narrowed his eyes. "Do you want to find her?"

"Since I knitted that scarf for Aunt Brook, I can't explain it, but I'm not afraid to go down and see her and ask questions about my mom. Lawrence wants me to meet someone who knows my Aunt Brook and wants to talk to me first. Not just go surprise her."

"Benny Kettle?"

"Yes. I guess he runs the Indian museum in Salamanca."

"I met Benny years ago. He's a *goot* man who's trying to share Christ with his People. Lawrence has helped him for years." He grinned. "I think Lawrence has his eye on Benny's daughter. Has for a while, but was taken with you for a spell. He's taking Heather out on a Valentine's date tonight."

Raven was relieved Lawrence was seeing someone. He'd be the last person she'd want to hurt. No wonder he suggested such casual dating. He was weighing his feelings for Heather and her. She thought of the forecast. "Eb, is Lawrence driving to Salamanca tonight?"

"*Jah*, all dressed up and all."

"But there's a blizzard warning. Hope he plays it safe."

"I think if he gets stuck at Benny's house, he'll be glad." He rubbed his hands together. "Want to put together a puzzle?"

"Joshua made me a Valentine's meal. You know about us, right?"

"I'm not blind or daft. But you need to be Amish."

"And I'm reading all the books you gave me to study and talked to the bishop. He doesn't bite like I supposed. Really a humble man, I now see cares so deeply for those in his church. I was impressed."

Eb took her hand. "Listen Raven, if there is a blizzard warning, you need to stay here."

Raven cocked her head. "Why? I'd be next door."

"You can't see the nose in front of you in a blizzard. People have gotten trapped in places for days."

"I'll come home if I see any snow. How does that sound?"

~*~

Bud and Chuckey looked through their binoculars to see Lottie walk down the road on her usual trip to see a "sick person". They soon saw Bruce's car and Lottie get in. Chuckey grabbed his walkie-talkie. "Miss Meadow, come in. S.O.S."

When there was no response after several attempts, he called Timmy and Cliffy. "Timmy, Cliffy, Skyhawk. Do you read me? S-K-Y-H-A-W-K!"

"This is Timmy. Miss Meadows is here. Now we'll nail those two. Here she is."

"Chuckey. This is Miss Meadows. Are you alright? And what is Skyhawk all about?"

"Well, Bud and I made it our code word. We watch Lottie like a hawk. Get it? Anyhow, she just got in the car with Bruce."

"Now? Are you sure?"

"*Jah*, I mean yes! Will you follow?"

"I suppose, but there's a blizzard warning, right?"

"Mr. Miller said he smells snow, is watching his barometer and looking at clouds. No TV, remember?"

"Chuckey, this is Joshua. Raven told me about your plan and it's *goot*, but I don't want Raven driving tonight. It could be dangerous. If those two are going out, it'll happen again, when the roads are better."

"Alright. Don't really feel like I'm on a mission if my orders aren't carried out."

"Chuckey, this is Miss Meadows. Can you see if they're still in the car? Is it parked?"

"Bud gave me a thumbs up. They're still there."

"Exactly where?"

"Corner of Willow and Stotler."

"I'm coming."

~*~

Raven felt her hands shake as she drove. She didn't mind the winter weather, but when a warning came out, she figured there was good reason. Since the Millers lived so close, she was sure she could get Joshua's name cleared tonight.

She gripped the steering wheel tighter as snow slowly started to come down. She'd promised Eb to come straight home. Since the roads were still clear, she accelerated faster, hoping to complete her mission and get home. She passed the Millers' house and soon saw Bruce's car but it was pulling out. Oh no! Should I turn back or follow them? I'll follow them. Raven thought of Joshua and the constant undercurrent of disapproval he was feeling from the Millers and even his Aunt Hannah and Uncle David. Like he was hiding something...Susanna would be home in two weeks and she wanted the whole bizarre situation resolved.

As she followed Bruce, she thought of what it would be like to be part of the Yoder family. Being Joshua's wife was the greatest joy, but having Susanna for a mom would be too good to be true. And the many Amish women she'd met who'd been coming in and out of the Yoder house having their work frolics, washing down walls and painting. Making the house sparkle as a surprise for Susanna. She was growing fonder of these dear women.

Raven noticed Bruce was slowing down as the Grainery appeared. Many sweethearts would be having dinner tonight there. But how could Lottie go out somewhere in Cherry Creek with an *Englisher*? She thought back to when she saw her with Joshua when she was there with Lawrence. No other Amish in the restaurant but them and they looked so uncomfortable.

She saw through the falling snow Bruce get out of the car, and a girl that didn't have Amish clothes on. Bud!

Chuckey! This wasn't Lottie. How could they get this mixed up? But when the girl turned, she looked like Lottie. Surely not!

Raven got out her camera and got out of the car, praying she was doing the right thing. She felt like a spy and it wasn't a good feeling. She felt immature, but so much was at stake. Raven put her scarf around her mouth, and her hat covered much of her face. Only her eyes could be seen. She decided to keep it that way when she got into the restaurant. If Lottie saw her she might panic and run, and she needed proof.

When she opened the oak doors to the Grainery she saw Bruce and Lottie ahead of her, and a hostess seating them. So far so good. When the hostess came back to seat her, Raven said she was coming in from out of the storm, but said she'd like a hot chocolate. Raven noticed wooden lattice could make a barrier between her and Lottie, and asked for a table on the other side of them. When seated, she still kept her wool hat on and her gloved hands to her face.

She peered through the lattice. Lottie was indeed in English clothes, and so immodest. She had on make-up, too. She and Bruce held hands and talked, playing footsies under the table. Raven felt the urge to just go over and tell Lottie off. How dare her try to trap Joshua into a marriage? No. She needed to calm down, take the picture and leave. Raven got her camera, focused through the hole in the lattice, and got a few pictures. One with Lottie looking right into the camera.

Chapter 18

*W*hen Raven pulled into the Yoder's driveway she could barely see an inch in front of her. She couldn't even really see the house. Raven pulled into what she assumed was the driveway and grabbed her camera, and got out of the car. But when she did she lost her orientation, not knowing which way to walk. Surely she would reach the house, even if she walked into it. So she walked forward, for what seemed like an eternity, not knowing where she was. Then she ran into a wall. The house! She wouldn't let go of the wooden structure until she found the door, but when she did, she realized she was in the barn.

Raven walked over to a chair and plunked herself down out of sheer exhaustion. Driving in what turned so quickly into a blizzard and seeing Lottie with Bruce was too much. She thought of Eb and how worried he must be. She always wanted a dad who would worry about her, and now she had one, and was thankful. She pulled out her cell phone to call him, but he didn't pick up. The phone was disconnected? He must have turned it off as one more step to returning to the Amish. Raven searched through her purse for a walkie-talkie, but didn't find it. She must have left it at the Yoder's.

As the temperatures dipped she felt the chill through her. She remembered as a little girl having to milk the cow in freezing weather, and nestling up against the cow for warmth. But the last time she was near that cow too many flashbacks came rushing in. Stiffening her arms in resolve, she made her way over to the large black and white animal and hugged it, and only memories of Eb finding her and helping her flooded her mind. How awesome God was, to orchestrate such a plan, to find her father.

Thank you Lord for bringing me to my wonderful dad. I'm finding a home, the home I've always dreamed of. The next logical step is to live among my family...my Amish family....and be Amish.

When she felt warm enough, Raven got one of the lanterns and hung it by the window. If Joshua could see it, he'd know she was alright. She lit another lantern as the darkness of night set in, and looked around at all the animals. She'd always wanted to live on a farm again. It was her secret dream. If she turned Amish, she'd have a rural life like she had on the reservation. She'd always found peace among farm animals.

Why was she feeling like she was coming back to her true self? Was it genetic? Was this the Amish blood in her crying out? She'd gone through life so aimlessly, taking the next logical step. Needing an income at eighteen, she enlisted in the army. But it was against her grain, shooting at targets, being told she'd have to possibly kill someone someday. She never fit in. But she did among the Amish...

But could she live with the same outfits every day? No jewelry? Were these things the most important things in life though? No, love was. Too many years of feeling like a pearl locked up in a clam had to come to an end. Who cared if you had what society said was important, if you didn't have someone to love?

Her grandparents had love in their marriage, even though poor. They were rural farmers and had a dress code of sorts, out of necessity, usually clad in denim for durability. Was it any different with the Amish? They wore their traditional garb to be self-sufficient, making their own clothes out of simple patterns. Susanna Yoder was a gorgeous woman, no matter what she wore, but it was her inner beauty that first struck Raven. A beauty that was evident even though pale and sickly.

She looked out as some of the ice melted on the window where the lantern was hung. Her resistance to becoming Amish was all but melted away too. She heard someone pull the barn door open.

"Raven! Are you in here?" Joshua yelled.

She took the lantern down near the window and made her way to Joshua. "You found me."

He took her hand. "I have a rope attached to the house. There's a break in the storm so we need to get over there now."

Grasping his hand, she closed the barn door and they started for the house. So much snow had fallen in such a short time. Midway, the wind picked up fiercely and she could barely see Joshua in front of her, but she held on to his hand and the rope. The wind threatened to blow her over, but Joshua gripped her tighter and steadied her. He yelled that they reached the house and soon heard Cliffy and Timmy, worry in their voices.

"I'm fine boys," she yelled as she was almost into the house.

Cliffy and Timmy hugged her as soon as she stepped inside. "We thought you had an accident and died," Cliffy said, face red.

Timmy clung to her arm. "Glad you're safe."

Raven didn't realize the concern she caused, but couldn't deny that her heart was warmed when all three kept saying the same thing. "We were worried." It was nice to be worried about. For a moment the image of the four of them being a family, Joshua's dream, flashed before her. Was this God's plan?

So much concern was etched on their faces, that she unzipped her ski jacket pocket to reveal a camera. "I think it was all worth it." She turned to Joshua. "I have the evidence you need to clear your name…"

~*~

Raven sat knitting a shawl she thought was for her aunt, but the more she knew what love was, the more she grieved for the little girl whose aunt was so cruel. Through the morning light, the colors of mint and red played well off each other. No, she would be making this shawl for Marilyn Rowe. Jim told her Marilyn blamed herself for Appleton burning down, and along with the cloud coverage in February, was feeling depressed. The group meeting she had with all the boys over at the Yoders, a couple days after the blizzard, went well and they were all making something for Marilyn as well.

The more she thought of what lay ahead of her this day, the faster she knit. Together with Joshua, they would be having lunch with the bishop, and showing him the picture of Lottie in English clothes together with Bruce. Joshua was so shocked when he saw her picture, and calculated the time when she broke off their engagement; when Bruce had become a regular driver for the Amish. It appeared she didn't break off the courtship because of Susanna's health, but she'd fallen for someone else.

When she heard Eb mosey down the step, she looked up. "Morning, Dad."

"Morning, dear one."

"Lots of pancakes on the griddle. Help yourself. Coffee's warm, too."

Eb yawned. "What's the occasion? I usually make breakfast since you English get up so late."

"I have a lot on my mind…"

"Want to talk?"

"Joshua and I will be showing the bishop the picture of Lottie and Bruce today. I don't know. I feel really sad about it and don't know why."

Eb poured coffee from the blue speckle ware pot. "It needs to be done, though. Look at it like justice is being done. The truth has come out and you just helped a little." He cocked his head down to meet her eyes. "It's something else, too. What?"

Raven started to knit again. "Well, it's a secret but I can trust you. Joshua wants me to take baptismal classes. He's going to ask the bishop to give me one-on-one instruction."

Eb clapped his hands. "Ach, Joshua wants to marry you, and my daughter will be Amish?"

Raven put the knitting down. "I love Joshua and you, but some of the Amish ways seem so hard."

"Don't like living with no electricity? Is that it?"

"It even surprises me, but no. I don't mind it. It's being so confined to a small place, living so close to everyone in your church. I mean, we all make mistakes, but here everyone knows."

"So they can help you out. You have it backwards. We Amish don't condemn someone for sinning or making mistakes. We're human, made from the dust. It's when we refuse help and turn on God is where you'll get in trouble, like I did."

Raven sighed. "But it looked too harsh."

Eb took a swig of coffee. "The English want things done fast-like. We move in pace with nature, more slowly. I was shunned for two years, but all along the People were praying and sending notes of encouragement."

"But you were shunned…"

"I refused any help or counsel. I went to the bottle and cursed God. It was a dangerous path to be on, and I knew it. Every day I'd compare my life to the Amish around me, knowing I was off track. It was their steadfastness that brought me back."

"I thought it was finding me and realizing God wasn't mad at you."

Eb smiled. "Finding you was like getting an extra scoop of ice cream. Lawrence helped me understand God, and AA did help with my addiction, but all along I yearned for my Amish life. Problem was, I had no wife and daughter anymore to share it with. Now I have you."

Raven looked at Eb's misty green eyes. "Pray for me, okay? I want to do the right thing."

"Like I said. The English want things done too fast. Why not take the baptismal classes and as you do, over the next few months, ask God to show you his path. You act like you're going to get all your answers today."

Raven looked out the window and remembered how dark it was an hour ago. Now she could clearly see the blue birds at the bird feeder. That all took time, and maybe a lot could be learned from nature. The sun slowly comes up, and slowly reveals the landscape. "Eb, in my Native American upbringing, there was lots of talk about learning from nature. When did I forget it all?"

"That's something you'll have to figure out. I don't know how fast paced you really lived as an *Englisher*." He got up and stacked pancakes high on his plate and drizzled them with maple syrup. "Got a letter from Rueben. He's so happy I'm back with the Amish and can help him make maple syrup. I've missed that."

"The boys can't believe they're allowed to help. Did he say anything about when Susanna will be home?"

"She's coming home with him. Everything's set. Her sister, Hannah, has people lined up to help her in recovery. So, in a week, she'll be home. Praise be."

"Yes...I can't wait to see her."

~*~

Joshua squeezed Raven's hand as he knocked on the bishop's door. "He's a *goot* man. Don't worry."

But she couldn't help it. So much was at stake. How could Joshua not be unnerved? When a man with a long black beard, speckled with gray, came to the door, his eyes seemed to look beady when they fell on her and narrowed when they landed on her and Joshua holding hands. "Come in."

He escorted them into the kitchen, where his wife had lunch spread out on the long oak table. "This is Elma. Elma, this is Raven, the one who brought all the foster *kinner* up here from Appleton."

Elma nodded and a warm smile spread across her face. "I think it's nice you care so much for orphans. Nice to meet you."

Raven was immediately drawn to Elma. She was as loving as Susanna.

Elma named all the items on the table as if Raven didn't know the names of their foods. "Cold ham, homemade bread, mustard, mayonnaise, pickled eggs and chow chow."

Well chow chow was new to her, but it appeared to be a mixture of vegetables. "Thank you so much, Elma."

She nodded and met Raven's eyes. "I'm so glad to have you come."

They each made a sandwich and filled their plates. Elma brought a teapot full of tea over. "I even sat out my good China tea cups."

Raven put her hand on her heart. "Elma, I feel like the Queen of England. Thank you."

They all took their seats at the table and everyone bowed their heads. Raven assumed this was the silent grace. She thanked God for Elma. What a pleasant surprise. She expected the bishop's wife to be always hovering under her husband's stern hand, but she saw a woman who appeared to admire her husband.

The bishop took the teapot and poured some into his cup. "Joshua, you said you have something to show me. Let me see."

Raven got the picture out of her purse and gave it to Joshua, who handed it to the bishop. "Moses, this is very sad, and I want you to know I take no pleasure in showing you this."

Joshua called the bishop by his first name? And his name was Moses? She noticed the bishop look closely at the picture. "Who took this?"

"I did. I was in the same restaurant."

Moses looked at her sternly. "Do you always carry a camera with you?"

Joshua put his hand on Raven's back. "The boys who live with Lottie, Bud and Chuckey, have seen Bruce with Lottie. They used their walkie-talkies to contact Raven when they saw Lottie and Bruce together so she could take a picture. She was trying to clear my name."

The bishop bowed his head and was silent for an uncomfortable time. Elma looked at the picture, sadness pulling her whole countenance down. Moses looked up. "So you think Bruce is the *daed*?"

"*Jah*, I do. She broke off our engagement when he became a driver. She obviously was led astray by him."

The bishop took a deep breath. "Well, Joshua, I never really believed you were the *daed*. But you insisted on having a good name and that's to be admired. But I've been hearing reports that you're attached to an *Englisher* and I'm supposing that it's Raven?"

"*Jah*, and she's willing to take the baptismal classes and become Amish."

Elma's smile returned. "That's *wunderbar*. Susanna will be so happy."

Moses looked at his wife, baffled. "Why would Susanna be happy about her son being attached to an *Englisher*?

"Well, she hoped someday Raven would be her daughter and prayed and prayed this would happen."

Raven felt her eyes mist. Susanna wanted her as a daughter-in-law? Over all the Amish girls that still made their presence known to Joshua, Susanna preferred her? Why?

"Susanna is a wise woman. Being through so much sickness has tested her faith and refined her like fire does gold," Moses said. "Raven, do you want to be Amish?"

"Eb, I mean, Dad, loaned me many books he had to use during his baptismal classes. I agree with everything. I love Rules of a Godly Life."

"Could you give up modern conveniences and your job? Live more simply?"

Raven was relieved that the bishop softened toward her. "I grew up rural, milking cows and not having fancy clothes. I think today, people have too many choices and with that comes more clutter, in the house and in the heart." Raven saw out of the corner Joshua was beaming, obviously happy with her answer.

Moses scratched his chin as if deep in thought and then grinned. "Had a visit an hour ago from someone else who wants to take baptismal classes again for spiritual growth. Can you and Eb come over on Monday nights for classes?"

Raven couldn't help but laugh. "He knew I was really nervous to come."

"And why's that?" Elma asked.

"So much at stake…"

She reached for Raven's hand. "Because you're so much in love." She turned to Joshua. "But be careful. You know Raven has to accept from her heart the Amish way of life. You can't force her. And if she can't embrace our doctrine and ways, you can't propose. Understand?"

"And no courting until she is Amish," Moses warned. "I don't want to see you two out and about in a courting buggy."

Joshua grinned at the bishop. "Can you meet twice a week so the classes end in nine weeks?"

"*Jah*, I can. We can have her ready for New Birth Sunday. Raven, are you willing to speed up the classes?"

"Yes, I am. Absolutely."

Chapter 19

$\mathcal{L}$ater that night, Raven was still marveling at the love in the home of Moses Byler. Why did she think he'd be some kind of dictator? He was humble and took the opinion of Susanna in such high regard. He also hung on Elma's words, looking to her for advice. She opened one of the many books the bishop gave her and was jolted when a loud knock almost broke down the side door. She ran downstairs and saw Eb letting in Chuckey and Bud, followed by Eli Miller.

No one said hello, but Eli snarled at her. "These boys have brought havoc down on my house."

Eb put one hand on Bud's shoulder and the other on Chuckey's. "That's a pretty hard accusation, Eli. Now you watch what you say. Words can hurt."

"These boys were spying on Lottie and –"

"Raven found Lottie with Bruce together and your daughter was wearing English clothes. We know, and are awfully sorry. Your pain must be great."

Eli fought tears. "Lottie is under a temporary ban."

"And we know the ban makes us come to our senses, even though it took me two years," Eb said. "What do the boys have to do with this?"

"Lottie wants them out of my house."

"It's your house. Why not have Lottie leave? Stay with an aunt. These boys have done nothing."

"She's pregnant, Eb. And she's my daughter."

Raven held on to the arm rest of a nearby Amish rocker. How many times had the natural child not been happy she was in their home and she was suddenly taken out, put in emergency foster care? It was the ultimate feeling of rejection. Of not being wanted…

Eb came over to her. "Dear one, you okay? You look so pale."

Raven sat in the rocker and clasped her hands in front of her. "I'm fine, Dad." She turned up at Eli in pity. "You've missed out on the opportunity, the privilege of raising these two fine boys. I already know of a place where they're loved and wanted. You can leave now and we'll get all the boys' things tomorrow."

Eli bowed his head in shame and walked out the door, into the bitter cold. Chuckey and Bud looked wide-eyed at her. "Who wants us?" Bud asked.

"Well, I do and so do Mr. and Mrs. Rowe. We'll all just be one happy family, but live in different houses."

Bud and Chuckey fist bumped. "We can go back to Appleton?"

"In April, in five weeks. Until then, I'll need to find you a place to stay."

"Why not here?" Eb asked.

"Eb, I'll need you to be approved to be a foster parent." Not wanting to cause any more stress to the boys, she forced a smile. "But I can get it all done in no time at all. For now, how would you boys like to stay with Joshua, Cliffy and Timmy?"

Bud and Chuckey both gawked at her and said in unison, "Sure."

~*~

Joshua ran his hands through his hair. "My *mamm's* coming home next week. She's still in recovery and needs lots of care."

"How about one boy?" Raven asked. "Maybe put one here and another with your Aunt Hannah. They've been excellent foster parents. I guess I wasn't thinking."

Joshua collapsed on the bench. "I'm sorry. I'm just overwhelmed. Maple syrup season is a busy time. I'm working sixteen hours a day. With *mamm's* care…"

"But there's women lined up to care for Susanna. You won't be doing it. I'll be helping, too."

"Who told you that?"

"Elma."

Joshua motioned for her to come and sit next to him. "She took a real shine to you. So now you're going to do work frolics, too, like a *goot* Amish woman?"

Raven slapped his shoulder and laughed. "I want to help. And word has it you'll be getting help with the maple syrup."

Joshua bit his lower lip to hide a grin. "And let me guess who told you that. The bishop, because he too can't help but love you, *jah*?"

"No, he told Eb, I mean Dad, and Dad told me."

Joshua sighed. "Well I'm glad. The men have helped over the years with the maple syrup, but *mamm* need extra special care this year. You say it's all been arranged?"

"*Jah*," Raven said. "Elma and your Aunt Hannah know the special needs your mom will have during recovery and are preparing. Isn't it *wunderbar goot*?"

Joshua encircled her with both arms. "Your German needs help. You'll need to be fluent. Amish husband and wives talk German in the house. It's the Amish way." He bent down to kiss her on the cheek. "I can't wait until we can wed."

"Me too." Raven looked up at him. "Me too."

Joshua cupped her cheeks in his hands and kissed her tenderly. "I love you so much. And I want to have a house full of *kinner* with you. But for now, I'll have to settle for four."

Raven kissed him back. "Four?"

"The two upstairs, and Bud and Chuckey."

Raven couldn't believe the kindness of Joshua Yoder. She wrapped her arms around him. "*Danki.*"

~*~

Raven's first baptismal lesson wasn't anything unusual. She'd already read Dordrecht Confession of Faith and found it similar to what Lawrence's church believed. Both were Anabaptist, believing in adult baptism. But the Bishop asked if she held any sin in her heart and when he asked about unforgiveness, she knew God was speaking through him.

She thought of the radical forgiveness of the Amish after the Nickel Back School shooting. But it did seem extreme to forgive the one who killed innocent children while in school. But the bishop pointed to a little booklet he'd given her, Rules of a Godly Life. His finger laid on Rule 13:

Permit not envy or hatred in your heart, nor carry a grudge against anyone. God loved us when we were His enemies and therefore He expects us to love our enemies for His sake. It is but a small thing for us to forgive our enemies, in comparison to what God has forgiven us. Even though you may think your enemy unworthy of your forgiveness, it is well worth doing it for Christ's sake.

She'd read this before, but Moses showed her that in this rule it's for someone else's sake: Christ's. Then he opened his Bible and showed all the commandments to forgive. When she told him of Aunt Brook's behavior, he didn't flinch. She needed to forgive her, and he would go with her to Salamanca if she wanted. Raven thought of how Joshua sacrificed so much for Susanna's sake; so his mom would live. If she forgave for Christ's sake, would that make Christ able to live in her more fully, or make Him seem more alive to others?

Being at Moses and Elma's over the past week, along with her dad, pretending to learn so she didn't feel so uncomfortable, was transforming her. Could love really change someone as hard as Aunt Brook?

~*~

Raven picked up the mint and red shawl she finished for Marilyn and put it in a gift bag. She and the boys would be visiting Marilyn and Jim today, and hopefully cheer them up.

She looked out the window to see Lawrence's car pull into the Yoder's. The four boys all bounded down the side stairs and got into the van. She noticed Joshua talked with ease to Lawrence now, secure that she loved him. And it seemed like Lawrence was spending a lot of time on the reservation in Salamanca with Benny Kettle and his daughter, when upon mentioning her name, Heather, he couldn't wipe the smirk on his face. Raven hoped he found someone to love, too. And she prayed for Chuckey and Bud, that they'd find love outside the Yoder house.

~*~

Seeing Marilyn hunched over in a rocker startled Raven. The woman was rapidly aging and needed a good dose of medicine, encouragement. Her eyes widened as the boys one by one went over and hugged her, leaving presents at her feet. Raven went over to plant a kiss on her wrinkled face and Lawrence did as well. But Jim watched in the corner, hand on his chin, face etched with concern. She saw Larry come around the corner with the same look of dismay. Raven told the boys to fill Marilyn in on all their adventures in living in Amish country and let her open the presents. She walked out of the room and motioned for Jim and Larry to follow her into the kitchen.

"What's wrong with Marilyn?" Raven asked in hushed tones.

"Depressed," Jim said. "Feels like it's her fault Appleton burnt down."

Larry spoke up. "Dad, that's not what the doctor said."

Jim dismissed what Larry said as if shooing a fly.

Raven looked at Larry. "It's not my business, but you can tell me, right?"

Larry looked at his dad and then evenly at Raven. "She's showing signs of brain deterioration."

Jim put his hand up in protest. "Everyone in their eighties has some form of it, Larry. You heard the doctor as well as I did. She's not losing her mind."

"I know, Dad. Just a little memory loss…"

Raven only heard one thing over and over in her mind. Eighties? Marilyn and Jim were in their eighties? They looked like they were in their late sixties. "Jim, if you don't mind me asking, how old are you?"

"Eighty-two. Marilyn's eighty-one. Surprised?" He winked and tried to make his eyes twinkle. "Marilyn and I eat right, exercise and have the boys to keep us young."

Raven nodded. "I can see that. I guess I just didn't put one and one together when you said you sold apples during the Great Depression…"

"I dropped into this world the same year as the stock market crashed: 1929. As you know, the Depression hit rock bottom in 1933 and I was out the next year at five selling apples. Marilyn thinks I exaggerate, but it's true."

Larry put his hand on Jim's shoulder. "I'm proud of Dad and everything he's done at Appleton, giving back to boys who have a rough start. My parents took that dilapidated house and turned it into a place where boys could be proud to live."

"It is inspirational, really," Raven said. "But what did your father do, Jim? I mean, didn't he have a job so that you didn't have to peddle apples?"

Jim's eyes seemed to glaze over. "My dad was a drunk. Made moonshine and drank it away. Mom took in sewing and did what she could to feed us. Life was hard…."

"But one man's pain is another man's gain, or something like that," Larry said. "Don't know how many men write or try to stop by to visit and tell my parents what they're up to: doctors, lawyers, singers, actors, you name it."

Raven noticed the Rowes' got an unusual amount of mail. They didn't use the internet, so seeing a handwritten letter seemed so old-fashion, yet refreshing.

"I wouldn't change anything about my life. Not a thing. Just don't want to see Marilyn go downhill…"

"Do you think she has the winter blues?" Raven asked. "I brought her yarn into the hospital. Has she done any knitting?"

Larry shook his head. "Hasn't touched it."

"Well, she needs to join the knitting circle Susanna Yoder's starting in a few weeks."

Jim smiled broadly. "Now that's a good idea. So glad Susanna will be back with a new kidney, and it appears she'll be like her old self. Always finding ways to gather women together in one of those bees she has."

"A bee? What's a bee?"

"Oh, the Amish women do all kinds of things to get a job done and have fun, too. Did you notice in the fall any women stirring big copper kettles outside? They were making apple butter."

"I didn't know that. Who gets all the apple butter, though? Everyone has apple trees around here."

"They share it. 'Many hands make light work', they always say. Our church does the same thing, though, like when we clean or do the landscaping."

Larry patted his dad's back. "Are you going to tell Raven, or should I?"

"What?"

Jim playfully shoved Larry. "The apple doesn't fall far from the tree." He winked. "Larry and his wife will be taking over Appleton when it reopens."

Larry pursed his lips. "My kids are grown and all out of state. Renee and I plan to move in along with my parents and care for boys. I understand Bud and Chuckey want to come and stay permanently?"

"I marked them down as residents in April, and five others will arrive, too." She nodded and turned to go into the living room. Marilyn's eyes were bright and aglow with love for the boys. At her feet lay clay pots the boys filled with seeds so she could start her flower garden early. A wooden checkers set Joshua helped Timmy and Cliffy make sat on her lap. A red and blue nylon kite that Hannah and David helped Toby and Ethan make made Raven snicker. Being Buffalo Bill fans, the boys picked the team colors, and the Bylers had no idea why.

She grabbed her gift bag and asked Marilyn to close her eyes. She took out the shawl and wrapped it around her. When she told her she could look, Raven was not prepared for Marilyn's response. She grabbed Raven by the wrists and broke down and cried. "Thank you. Thank you."

Bud stood up and went over to put his hand on Marilyn's shoulder. "Don't cry, Mrs. Rowe. We all know you didn't mean to burn down Appleton."

Chuckey got up and stood behind her rocker, then planted both hands on her shoulders. "I'm glad it was you who started the fire and not one of us."

Marilyn grabbed for the boys hands. "I'm not crying because of that...I'm just so happy to see you all. Little overwhelming."

Lawrence came over and asked the boys to say good-bye. It was snowing and they needed to get back to Cherry Creek, but Raven knew he was only trying to give Marilyn time to absorb it all. It wasn't her fault. She wasn't losing her mind. Raven wondered if she needed the boys now more than ever.

~*~

Joshua ran out to the van as soon as it pulled into the driveway. Although so many friends and family wanted to be there to welcome Susanna home, she was still so susceptible to germs, and couldn't be in crowds. But she asked that Raven be there. She felt honored, but out of everyone, why her?

When Joshua hovered over his mom, a fire burned in Raven to marry this man. He was selfless and strong enough to truly cherish someone, not a selfish bone in him. She'd never seen this in any man she'd ever dated, it was always what they could take.

When Susanna's eyes met hers, a smile despite the pain spread across her face. "Raven. So *goot* to see you. To be home." She walked with the support of Joshua and Rueben and wasn't free to give her special hugs, but her eyes said it all. She was glad to see her, and knew about her son's attachment to her. Their plans to marry if she was baptized and the church district was all in agreement.

Joshua told Susanna to look around and she gasped at the fresh white walls, polished oak cabinets and china closet, and waxed floors. "The whole house is like new. Lots of women had a frolic here," Joshua said.

Susanna's eyes lit up as she surveyed the kitchen and looked over into the living room. "Praise be."

Joshua led her to her rocker, and after having someone one-on-one time with her, she motioned for Raven to come over, asking everyone else to leave. Susanna laid her head back on her rocker and looked at Raven. "How are you, dear one?"

"How are you?" Raven asked. "Are you in much pain?"

"It'll be an upward climb, but I won't complain. But to be honest, I wish I could throw all those pills out the window."

"What pills? I thought you were better."

"Ach, my body sees this kidney as an intrusion, so I take lots of anti-rejection medicine, or my immune system will attack my kidney."

Raven pulled up a spare chair. "I didn't know that. How long will you be on the medicine?"

"My whole life." She closed her eyes as if what she said was painful. "I hear Eb's your *daed*. God works in mysterious ways, to bring you two together *jah*?"

"Did you hear the story, about how EB was on my doll's foot?"

"*Jah*. Eb wrote to me often." She looked at Raven in a curious way. "Now, how is my son doing? I hear he wants to get married."

Raven couldn't hide her smile. "I love Joshua, Susanna. He's the best man I know."

"And how are baptismal classes coming along? Eb told me all about that, too."

Raven clasped her hands. "I'm learning a lot, not just about Amish spirituality, but myself. The bishop wants me to visit my aunt in Salamanca...to forgive her. It was her fault I was put in foster care. But I'm struggling."

"How so?" Susanna asked.

"Not feeling any forgiveness toward her, only resentment."

Susanna's eyebrows shot up. "Forgiveness and feelings are separate. We forgive because Christ commanded us. I'm sure Moses and Elma explained that."

Raven lowered her head. "Yes, they did. But it seems...like being a hypocrite. It's like saying something you don't mean."

Susanna nodded. "I see ...Let me explain it how it was taught to me years ago. When a seed is put in the ground, you can't see it, *jah*? But in time you will and the plant will grow. That's what forgiveness is like. Do you feel a seed, a little mustard seed, of forgiveness in your heart toward your aunt?"

"Yes, at times I feel more than a seed, maybe a whole flower, and then I'm back to wondering if I have a seed at all."

Love shone from Susanna's eyes. "Raven, I've loved you since the day I met you. You talk Amish-like. Real honest and straight forward."

Raven squeezed her hand. "I felt the same about you."

"Raven, I know you can forgive. You know why?"

"No."

"Because you have Christ in you to water that little seed of forgiveness. And He'll continue to water it and make something beautiful out of it. Trust me. I've had to forgive before…"

Joshua was so much like his mom. Wise and so loving. She'd forgive Aunt Brook for God's sake, Joshua's sake….and Susanna's sake. Lawrence said he found her aunt with the help of Heather. She knew what needed to be done. "Thank you, Susanna. This talk really helped me," she said, to the lovely woman she hoped someday would be her mother-in-law.

Chapter 20

Lottie was never pregnant? Raven had suspected it, but couldn't believe it.

Joshua shook his head and looked over at Eb, sound asleep in his rocker. "She apologized. Said she knew she was falling away from the Amish life, and felt if she married me, I'd keep her on the straight and narrow."

"And so now she'll confess her sin before the Amish after church and all is forgiven? Just like that?"

"*Jah*. Of course, but sin leaves scars."

"What do you mean?"

"Well, we'll all forgive, but her reputation will take time to recover. It'll be blemished for a long while. No Amish man will want to marry her until she shows she acts…Amish."

Raven looked at their locked hands. "I'm glad the truth came out and your name isn't blemished."

Joshua kissed her hand. "I have you to thank. And you got caught in that blizzard because of me."

"But you rescued me, my knight in shining armor."

Joshua narrowed his eyes. "The bishop did explain that the Amish are pacifist, *jah*?"

"Yes. Why?"

"Well, knights go to war. So when you call me a knight I…get confused."

Raven snickered. "It's just an expression. It means someone who saves you, I suppose."

"How did I save you? From the fire? You called me a shining knight then…."

Raven kissed Joshua on the cheek. "When you listened when we first met. It was like you were pulling poison out of me. Such bitterness. But I'm not done yet. I need to go to Salamanca and face Aunt Brook."

"Want me to come with you?"

Raven leaned her head on his shoulder. "Would you? I don't understand this Amish forgiveness and I'm scared."

~*~

When the sky blue station wagon pulled into the Yoder's, Raven knew Marilyn had arrived at their new knitting circle. Susanna was still much too weak to knit more than a few rows, but this group gave her purpose. Knitting shawls for patients on transplant lists was her new calling, along with giving lots of love to Timmy and Cliffy. But Raven agreed with Joshua: she was pushing herself too much. She had to get her blood checked daily at the clinic, and it wore her out.

Jim walked Marilyn to the side door and quickly said hello and then rubbed his hands together, saying he was eager to join the large group of men working at the sugar shack. Raven looked out the back window to see Joshua patiently show all six boys how to tap a maple tree. What a good father he'll be someday….

Marilyn chatted with Susanna while Raven cut the raisin bars into squares and then she took a seat.

"Marilyn, how are you?" Raven asked.

"Oh, cold. It's so cold all the time."

Susanna slowly got up to get a raisin square, obviously in pain. "I could have gotten that for you," Raven said.

"Need to move my legs more. Don't want any blood clots. Anyhow, I've laid around for three years and it feels good to walk. Just a painful incision."

"Marilyn, do you want a raisin square?" Raven asked.

Marilyn looked up. "I made pies this morning and need to watch my figure. Brought a few for the boys."

Raven felt her heart swell. The boys' visit was like medicine. Marilyn's depression seemed to be lifting, gaining some old interests back. Raven looked up when Hannah, Mary, and Lottie filed into the kitchen from the side door. She quickly turned to get plates and cups to put on the table. She didn't know Lottie was coming and wasn't able to look at the girl who almost ruined Joshua's life.

The women talked about all they did to spruce up the house, and Susanna marveled at how many women came to help. Raven reminded herself that this knitting circle was for Susanna and turned around with a pot of hot tea. "Anyone want something hot to drink?"

Hannah blew air into her cupped hands. "I'll take some. *Danki*, Raven."

"I'll have some too," Mary said.

Lottie took her knitting needles and yarn and sat in a chair, not meeting Raven's gaze.

"Lottie, do you want some?" Raven asked.

"*Nee*," she said, smugly.

Mary sat next to her daughter and whispered something in her ear.

"*Danki* for asking, Raven," Lottie said evenly.

Raven looked over at Susanna, who shrugged her shoulders. Lottie supposedly repented before the people of lying and making a false accusation. Was she really sorry?

Marilyn looked at all the women. "So, how are my boys doing up here in Amish country?"

Hannah took a seat and started to knit. "David and I love Toby and Ethan so much that...we're hoping to adopt them." She looked up at Raven. "Is that possible, being Amish?"

"Yes. It's a lot of paperwork but absolutely."

"Can you handle this paperwork?"

"I can point you in the right direction," Raven said.

"I think Eli and I overreacted," Mary said. "And I'm asking your forgiveness. What happened concerning Lottie is water under the bridge?"

Lottie looked up, eyes glaring at her mom. "I don't want those little spies back."

Marilyn laughed. "They spied on Raven at Appleton. Remember Raven? How they listened to you talk on the phone? Watching you and Lawrence with binoculars out the windows?"

Raven couldn't help but smile. "I remember. And the rumors they spread..."

"So they're brats if you ask me," Lottie snapped.

"They're boys," Marilyn said, defensively.

Mary cleared her throat and looked over at Susanna. "How are you feeling? Your eyes are half shut."

"Doing some 'casting off prayers'. Learned it from Deborah Weaver from Smicksburg. It's a knitting term but Deborah said one night while casting off, she thought of the scripture that says to cast your cares upon the Lord because He cares for you…Got the idea for this knitting circle from her."

"Well, I think you need to lie down. You look pale." Hannah went over to her sister and placed her hand on her forehead. "You have a fever."

Susanna sighed. "I will for a while. Road to recovery is hard."

Hannah got a pitcher out of the icebox. "You need something cool to drink. And then just rest there while we knit." She turned to Raven. "Do you think she's up to having the knitting circle here? We can have it at my place."

"What would Raven know?" Lottie blurted. "She doesn't live here."

Marilyn chuckled. "Not yet."

"And what does that mean?" Mary asked.

Marilyn cocked one eyebrow. "A little bird told me something…but it's a secret."

Raven put her index finger to her lip, hoping Marilyn would say no more. Marilyn nodded and looked down and knit. Raven turned in her two weeks' notice since she couldn't work at Appleton once she was Amish. It might have been premature, because the *Gmay* or church had to vote her in, and she had to forgive her Aunt Brook. If she wasn't allowed in, she'd wait until the vote in the fall, when baptisms were held again. She knew she'd found a home among the Amish…and with Joshua.

The side door opened and Bud and Chuckey barged in. They went over to Marilyn and hugged her. "Thanks for making us pies. And you made my favorite!" Bud said "Chocolate cream!" A grin lifted his face. "Mr. Rowe said the piece I took was too big, since we're on a diet."

"*Ya*," Chuckey laughed. "He made our pieces smaller, but you know what? He was hiding behind a big old tree eating an extra piece, and we caught him."

Marilyn acted surprised. "No, Mr. Rowe would never do such a thing."

Raven knew that love healed, and she was witnessing a miracle. Bud and Chuckey adored Marilyn and she needed them, just like she did, and she was just beginning to realize it. Raven got up and looked out the back window and noticed that Cliffy and Timmy were near Joshua, and that Toby and Ethan hovered around David. These two men would be their fathers, the thing they wanted more than anything in life. She looked over to the right and saw Eb…her father…the man she'd come to cherish. She noticed the sun peeking through the clouds and thanked God for bringing people together, like yarn knit together to make something beautiful.

~*~

Raven clung to Joshua as they walked the muddy dirt road to her Aunt Brook's little log house. Benny Kettle had shown them the way, and waited in the car with Lawrence and Eb, all praying for her. If she went by her feelings, she'd be running back to the car, but she'd learned from the Amish, forgiveness was an act of obedience. Joshua said encouraging words but memories of this place filled her mind and crowded them out. She stopped when she saw the cherry tree. The tree that she planted with her grandmother. Tiny buds were forming, which was unusual for Mid-March. Was this a sign that her grandmother was with her?

She squeezed Joshua's arm harder. She had living people who cared for her. To lend her strength. Raven stopped and turned to Joshua. "Thank you for coming with me. It means so much."

Joshua took both her hands. "Just remember all the scriptures we wrote down. If she says something nasty, remember to think on them. Okay?"

Raven looked at the man she hoped to marry. "I will. And I'm a pacifist now that I'm learning to be Amish, so I walk away from an argument if it doesn't stop?"

"*Jah*, or run if someone comes after you." Joshua winked. "I've run before. No shame in it."

They continued down the muddy road and were soon greeted by two coon dogs. Their deep bark was deafening, but soon they ran back into the house, as if by command. Raven looked and saw a short woman with black hair in the doorway. She walked out onto her porch and looked suspiciously at them.

"What do you want?"

As Raven got closer, she couldn't believe what a little woman her aunt was. Being nine when she left, her aunt was a formidable foe, but now she saw a woman with hollow eyes. "Aunt Brook. It's me. Raven."

Her aunt walked down the steps to get a better look. "I asked before. What do you want?"

"I just came to say I remember all those nights in the attic. The hunger and bruises." Nausea washed over her and she held her middle. "I want you to know I forgive you."

Her aunt came closer to her and suddenly slapped her in the face. "Forgive me? You've killed so many people. My mom and dad and your own mom. I should be forgiving you."

The sting on her cheek made it hard to think of any scripture. "What are you talking about? I didn't kill anyone."

"Oh, you would say that. Your grandparents died young because you were a burden and my sister, your mom, wandered off after you were born, so depressed she was. Police never found her body."

She couldn't think. Was she such a burden it killed her grandparents? Was her mom dead? She heard someone yell from behind her. It was Eb…her dad.

"Flo ran off to be with me. We had plans…"

Aunt Brook grew pale and stepped back. "I remember you," she hissed. "Then my sister's alive. And you never bothered to come tell us."

Eb scrunched his face, confusion distorting his appearance. "I haven't seen Flo since the day we met to run off. She got cold feet. Never saw her again."

Aunt Brook clasped both hands over her mouth in disbelief. "Are you telling the truth? Maybe she's alive?"

"Said she needed time to think, and was headed towards Buffalo," Eb said.

"She did? We thought she drowned in the Allegheny. Talked about it… She got so depressed after giving birth to you." She eyed Raven sharply.

Joshua put his arm around Raven. "You are fearfully and wonderfully made. Remember?" He turned to Raven. "He planned you, *jah*?"

Aunt Brook rolled her eyes. "You Amish and your talk about religion." She pointed at Eb. "He got my sister pregnant."

"Christians aren't perfect. We need the Lord's forgiveness every day," Joshua said.

"I'm sure you do, Handsome. Going to get Raven pregnant, too?" She laughed a bitter laugh. "Make it a family tradition."

Raven stomped a foot and charged at her aunt, but Joshua and Eb held her back. "You are so spiteful!"

Eb and Joshua turned her around and looked at her evenly. "Raven, you need set free. Forgive her," Joshua pleaded.

Raven put her head down and said a silent prayer.

Lord,

I can't forgive this woman. Help me. I need your help. Now.

She stared at the mud under her feet. An image came to her mind of her making mud pies and her grandparents pretending to eat them. How they'd laughed. She looked back at the cherry tree. She collected blossoms and her grandmother wove them into a crown, calling her the Cherry Blossom Queen. Her eyes misted at the thought.

Raven turned and looked at her aunt. "I'm sorry Aunt Brook. I shouldn't have called you spiteful. I think you're just a really sad person. I forgive you for everything, and I hope you'll forgive me for being so angry with you over the years."

"Go away. You've done enough damage to this family."

"I will, but is Uncle Ram home? I'd like to see him."

She swatted at the air. "He ran off after you left. Blamed it all on me."

Raven had to choke back tears. So her Uncle Ram did care for her. Maybe she'd remember more of his kindness when more good memories surfaced. "Do you know where he is?" she asked.

"I don't know. Now get off my land." She spun around and charged up the steps, banging the front door shut.

Eb rubbed Raven's back. "Are you alright, dear one?"

Raven looked up at the clouds as tears streamed down her cheeks. "Free…"

Chapter 21

*R*aven knit that night out of sheer delight. A sense of well-being enveloped her. Her knitting through the years gave her a sense of control and comfort, but tonight she felt something else pour from her. Creativity. Every time she'd thought of a new design or color combination, like Marilyn's mint and red shawl, she'd inwardly cringed, wondering if it was a mistake. Was it because she thought she was a mistake?

Well, she knew better now. She was created by God. He actually thought her up. The idea amused her. She imagined God molding clay and designing her. The thought was too big for her to comprehend, so she thought of Susanna's favorite Psalm...131...I don't concern myself with great matters, Nor with things too profound for me.

Raven looked in her basket of yarn and felt peace. How many times had she stared at it, feeling condemned that she couldn't make her aunt a shawl? But she just couldn't and told the bishop, and he said move with the pace of nature. Slowly. Maybe she was supposed to make the shawl years down the road. Who knew? But for now, after such a stressful day, she decided to make something fun. Since Bud and Chuckey were Buffalo Bill fans, and they'd be returning to Appleton soon, she'd make them red and blue hats. She'd miss seeing them over at the Yoder's but they were needed at Appleton.

Raven heard a knock on her bedroom door. "Come in, Dad."

Eb came in with a mug in his hand. "Thought we'd have our last hot chocolate for the winter. Spring's coming on mighty fast and we'll soon be making root beer."

Raven set down her needles and took the mug. "Thank you. How do you make root beer?"

Eb grinned. "It's an Amish secret recipe. And you're not Amish yet. After your baptism, I'll share it with you."

Raven smirked. "Very funny. You know I'm worried. With trying to tie up loose ends at work, I haven't had time to practice any German. And I'm supposed to have a trial period of living without a car. When will that happen?"

"Have you asked the bishop?"

"I will tomorrow." She picked up some yarn and fidgeted. "What if I don't make it in?"

"You'll stay with me, have no car, practice German, and try again in the fall. There's no hurry."

Raven looked at Eb as if never really seeing him before. "You're right. When I kneel and take the vow, I need to make sure I mean everything. It's as serious as a wedding vow."

"*Jah*, it is. Maybe you need the summer to really absorb it all and plan your wedding."

"And if I don't get accepted in by fall? There will be no wedding."

Eb scratched his bearded chin. "You're thinking English-like. Always in a hurry. Are you afraid Joshua won't wait for you to be accepted into the flock?"

"Well, we can't court until I'm Amish. It's hard."

"Well, you can talk to the bishop tomorrow about all this. For now, let's enjoy our hot chocolate."

~*~

There was a peace in the bishop's house Raven still marveled at. Was it here where so many Amish made peace with each other, working out differences instead of running away from them?

"Have you ever tried meadow tea, Raven Meadows?" Elma asked, warmly.

Raven took the delicate tea cup filled with the mixtures and took in the aroma. "No, but I like its name." She took a sip. "We had something similar on the reservation. We grew our own spearmint." Aunt Brook helped her plant her spearmint patch. Raven remembered it as if it were yesterday. She slowly lowered the delicate tea cup, afraid she'd drop it.

Joshua turned to her and put a hand on her shoulder. "Raven, are you alright?"

She didn't know what to say. This was a serious meeting concerning the timing of her baptism, and Moses was sitting right across from her. A man she really wanted to be liked by, but this image of Aunt Brook startled her. She wiped sweat beads forming above her lips. Is this what a panic attack is? "I'm sorry. The meadow tea just brought back a childhood memory."

"Another bad one?" Moses asked, deeply concerned.

Raven remembered stories of Amish forgiveness. She'd read they were some of the happiest people in America, because they forgave, not carrying loads of anger and resentment. No, they had little baggage. Was this a part of unpacking the baggage of her childhood? "It was a good memory. Aunt Brook helped me plant my spearmint patch. She laughed and hugged me."

"How old were you?" Joshua asked.

Raven looked up. "A preschooler, maybe. Don't really know…"

Moses tapped his fingers on his well-worn Bible that was sitting on the oak table. "Have you had other *goot* memories since you forgave her?"

"No, just now was the first. Am I supposed to go down and visit her again?"

The bishop shook his head. "You did your part. You released her unto God. Maybe you're to pray for her."

"*Jah*, Raven, pray for her. Maybe even make her one of those prayer shawls my *mamm's* making." Joshua said.

Elma sat next to her husband and reached for Raven's hand. "Now let's just slow down. God will make it clear if you're to not look back, like Lot's wife, or go back and talk more with your aunt."

Moses smiled at his wife. "He who finds a wife finds a *goot* thing, just like this book says." He picked up his Bible, and looked at Elma, whose face was slowly turning pink. "And we're here to talk about your wedding plans, *jah*?"

"My baptism," Raven said.

"You're looking to convert to be married to Joshua, so they're tied together." He took a sip of tea. "Now, we've gone over all the book learning, but Raven you'll need to live without a car. It's the car that makes life go so fast. Makes it so you don't travel too far from your church and everyone sees your Christian walk daily."

Raven always felt she could live in a cabin in the woods with no neighbors, being close to nature, like when growing up. The thought of not driving though seemed to suffocate her even by talking about it. Maybe she had to go through withdrawal from modern conveniences, like Eb did from alcohol. She turned to Joshua, and reminded herself he was worth it. "I quit my job and am living with my dad without a car, starting next week. Need to wrap things up at Appleton. Is that okay?"

Moses sighed. "And you plan to get baptized on New Birth Sunday? It's not far off." He bit his lower lip and stared into his tea. "I'm thinking that's not possible. You'll need to wait until fall. Like I said, the car's the hard part."

"What are we supposed to do about our relationship?" Joshua asked. "You said we couldn't court until she was baptized."

"*Jah.*"

"Can we spend time alone together, like in a dating way?"

"Joshua, like in a *rumspringa* way? *Jah*, if you weren't baptized, but you made an oath to the *Gmay* not to court or 'date' an *Outsider.*"

Elma got up and replenished their empty tea cups. "Do you love Raven?" she asked Joshua.

"*Jah*. Want to marry her."

"And the Bible says love is long suffering. You know that. Sometimes we suffer when we wait for a *goot* thing. Animals are giving birth now, being spring, but they've been mighty uncomfortable for a while, carrying their young. You only need to wait six months."

"She's right," Raven said. "Good things come to those who wait."

"Is that an English proverb?" Elma asked. "I like it."

"Just something I've heard, and believe to be true."

Elma grinned. "Raven, do you know how to cook?"

Raven shook her head.

"How about we take the next six months and I teach you all I know about gardening, preserving. Ach, we can go berry picking together. So many *wunderbar goot* work frolics to look forward to. Making apple butter in a big copper pot in the fall."

"And maybe when time starts to stand still without a car, you'll have time to think clearly on what to do about your aunt. Susanna has that knitting circle and maybe you should knit her a prayer shawl." Moses pulled at his beard. "Susanna needs lots of healing on her road to recovery and you can be a great help."

"But being around Raven so much would be a temptation," Joshua said. "She'd be next door and in and out of the house. It's hard for me not to want to kiss her."

Raven slapped Joshua's arm. "How can you talk like that?"

"It's the honest truth."

Elma let out a laugh. "Raven, we Amish don't beat around the bush like so many English. We're honest and frank."

Raven looked over at Joshua. "No more kisses until the day of our wedding."

Joshua threw his napkin up in the air with a sigh. "Bishop, this will be too hard."

"I won't change my mind. Look at this as a test. Do you love Raven for her inner or outer beauty."

"Both," Joshua said. "How can I promise to do something I might not be able to do?"

Raven started to snicker, not ever seeing Joshua so animated. "Because, Joshua Yoder, I won't kiss you." She turned toward the bishop. "Moses, you have my word. Until I'm baptized, I won't kiss this man again." She put her arm on Joshua's shoulder. "We'll be good friends for six months."

Elma clasped her hands on the table. "Raven, I'm amazed. You act so Amish…"

"I hope I'm always a Christian before anything else. But thanks. That's a compliment."

Moses took in a deep breath. "Raven Meadows, I have high hopes for you. Very high hopes."

Epilogue

*R*aven and Joshua planted a field of celery for their wedding, and sometimes looked with longing at each other, as they passed by the garden rows, but Raven always pushed him away, saying she was the one who made the vow to not have any physical contact.

Raven helped Susanna recover. There were a few setbacks on her road to recovery, but every day she made more progress. Raven took her in the buggy Eb bought to the doctor in town. Sometimes, she even had the nerve to drive the buggy to visit Appleton, and when she did, she took Chuckey and Bud out on rides.

Hannah and David went through the process to adopt Ethan and Toby. Joshua filed the necessary papers to adopt Timmy and Cliffy as a single man, shocked that he could adopt without a wife. But he knew Raven would soon be his bride.

Eb started up his furniture business again, and Raven loved to rub down the oak wood with linseed oil. But Eb would only talk to her in German, which she found maddening at first, but was glad Eb didn't give in, learning the language faster by constantly hearing German. Every now and then, she'd look at Eb, and thought of her mother. Was she alright? Was she alive? Such thoughts prompted her to ask Lawrence to take her to Salamanca again. She'd only had one good memory of Aunt Brook, but it was enough to give her strength to face her again.

Joshua went with her and together with Lawrence, they knocked on Aunt Brook's door again. Her aunt hugged her neck. When Raven visited the first time, her aunt thought her sister was dead. Aunt Brook found Flower Meadows after inquiring at several reservations. She was given information that led her to a reservation in Canada. Flower was married and had three children. She apologized for not writing and said the longer she put it off the harder the task was. Flower didn't want her husband to know about Raven, and wanted a clean break from her past. Raven's natural mother had no desire to see her…ever.

Raven cried many tears when she heard this. Tears that fell on the shoulder of her soon to be new mother-in-law, Susanna. Elma helped her, too, and became like another mother. Susanna encouraged Raven to knit a prayer shawl for her aunt, which she did. Her Aunt Brook gladly accepted it, and apologized for being so harsh toward her as a child. Thinking her sister was death, she'd taken her anger out on her. It took Raven a few more visits to be able to embrace her aunt, but when she did, she felt the grace of God in her heart to truly forgive her.

In late October, Raven was baptized into the Amish church, Eb standing by her, tears flowing down his cheeks. After the service, Joshua took her hand and they ran through the fall leaves and hid behind an oak tree. He drew her to himself and kissed her for what seemed like an eternity. Now that Raven was a member of the church, they were now free to court. Joshua asked her to marry him, and they did, two weeks later.

Aunt Brook came to the wedding wearing the shawl Raven made her, and sat beside Susanna. Raven wore her new navy blue dress with a white apron and *kapp* that she sewed on Elma's sewing machine. When she said her vows, she looked into Joshua's blue eyes and marveled at the power of pure love.

Raven embroidered a pillow to put on their bed. On it was the Amish proverb, *Kindness is a language which the deaf can hear and the blind can see.* The pillow was a constant reminder to be thankful for her husband whose kindness caused her to see the love of God and hear Him gently whisper, I love you, dear one, my child.

DISCUSSION GUIDE

1. When Raven first comes to Appeton, we discover she's prejudiced against Christians. What were some of the preconceived ideas about Christianity that tainted her judgment?

2. When Raven meets Susanna, her hard heart is slightly cracked by the love of God. Many times we think we need to do say the right words, but an Amish proverb says, People don't care about how much you know until they know how much you care. Do you agree with this proverb? Was there a time in your life when actions spoke louder than words?

3. Raven is suspicious of Bible Club and attends with the boys. She hears John 14: 16-18:
"I will ask the Father, and he will give you another Advocate, who will never leave you. He is the Holy Spirit, who leads into all truth. The world cannot receive him, because it isn't looking for him and doesn't recognize him. But you know him, because he lives with you now and later will be in you. No, I will not abandon you as orphans—I will come to you."

Feeling of abandonment surfaced in Raven. According to Merriam –Webster Dictionary, abandonment means "to withdraw protection, support, or help from". Feelings of abandonment can plague us all at times. What does the scripture above tell us to do in these times? Read

John 14, the whole chapter, like Raven did, and see if you too find comfort.

4. James Rowe had a sad childhood like Raven, and through his father alcoholism he had to deal with of abandonment too. He handled his pain differently with God's help. In giving to the boys at Appeton, he was a blessed and happy man. 2 Corinthians 1:4 says,

   "He comforts us in all our troubles so that we can comfort others. When they are troubled, we will be able to give them the same comfort God has given us." (NLT)

   Take inventory of hardships in your own life. Have you received God's healing and comfort? If so, do you think He wants you to help others who are experiencing the same problems?

5. Joshua was drawn toward Raven for what reasons? What does this tell you about his character?

6. When Suzanne is rushed to the hospital, Joshua looks up at the stars and thinks. Christ's light shines brightest when all is dark around us. Corrie Ten Boom, who recounts her time spent in Nazi Concentration Camps in *The Hiding Place* said a profound thing. "In darkness God's truth shines most clear." Can you think of a dark time in your life when Christ's light shone like the stars? Was the dark valley you went through worth it to see Christ's light brighter?

7. Milking a cow brought back memories of abuse inflicted by her aunt. She cries out "Why God?" Do you think this is scriptural? Read Jonah 2:2 and Isaiah 1:18 and discuss.

8. Raven is embarrassed that Eb found her crying in the barn. He says to her, "It's good to cry. I go to the bottle." Studies show crying has many benefits, such as cleansing the body of harmful toxins and helping the body relax. Do you think it's good to cry? Read Luke 11: 32-36 and Psalm 34:17-18.

9. Raven pretends she's dead after "Amish skiing". When the boys find out she was just kidding, they bombard her with hugs. Do you think the boys had a part in Raven feeling loved?

10. Rueben blames Eb for leading him down a path to immorality. Did Ruben have just cause to feel this way? Can we lead others astray?

11. Lottie seduced Joshua while he was sick and on a buggy ride. Her behavior continues to decline into lying, manipulation, and total lack of self-control. Do you think her company with Bruce caused this change in behavior, or jealousy over Joshua's attention toward Raven? Or both? See Proverbs 27:4 and Psalm 1:1.

12. When we first meet Raven she has very few happy memories of her time in foster care. As the story continues, more happy memories surface. What's changing in Raven?

13. Eb says, "I call a TV a box. Don't' know why people watch other people live. Why not just live yourself? Makes no sense to me." This is how the Amish really feel about television. Do you agree? How can you change viewing habits?

14. After Brandon's visit, Raven can't believe she'd dated someone like him. What made her see she was in an abusive relationship?

15. Raven realized why she didn't like Ellington at first. It was like a Thomas Kinkade painting with houses full of warmth and happy families. Raven desired to be in a family, as did the boys at Appleton. What does the Bible say about desires in Psalm 37:4?

16. Granny Weaver and her knitting circle from Smicksburg visit Susanna in the hospital after her transplant. They knit her a blanket and love seemed to pour from the blanket, making such a difference to her aching body. Do you think gifts can really make a difference? See testimonies at Prayer Shawl Ministry at http://www.shawlministry.com/stories.html

17. The Amish church council wait on God to see if he clears Joshua's name after being the father of Lottie's baby.

Psalm 37:5-6 says:
Commit everything you do to the LORD.
Trust him, and he will help you. He will

make your innocence radiate like the dawn,
and the justice of your cause will shine like the
noonday sun. (NLT)
Can you recall a time when the Lord cleared
your name or defended you?

18. Raven had a hard time forgiving her aunt because she doesn't feel forgiveness. Susanna tells her forgiveness is like a seed planted. You don't see any signs of life for a while. What she's saying is forgiveness is not based on feeling, but faith. As a gardener, I know it takes faith to believe a tiny seed can become a plant. Is there someone you need to plant a seed of forgiveness toward, even if feelings don't follow?

19. Susanne has a favorite Bible verse. Psalm 131:1-2. When my mother was declining I'd go over to my sister-in-laws and cry. She'd hold me, just like Raven, and say….Psalm 131. In other words, don't try to figure it all out, but rest in God.

    Read Psalm 131:1-2 several times. What do you need to   stop trying to figure out, and simple trust God that He's in control?

    Lord, my heart is not haughty, Nor my eyes lofty.
    Neither do I concern myself with great matters, Nor with
    things too profound for me.
    Surely I have calmed and quieted my soul, Like a weaned
    child with his mother;
    Like a weaned child is my soul within me. (NKJV)

AMISH RECIPES
Oatmeal Whoopie Pies

4 c. brown sugar
1 ½ c. Oleo (Crisco)
4 eggs
4 c. flour
4 c. oatmeal
2 t. cinnamon
2 t. baking powder
2 t. baking soda dissolved in 6 T boiling water

Cream together sugar, Oleo, and eggs. Add pinch of salt, flour, oatmeal, cinnamon, baking powder. Add soda water last. Beat and drop by teaspoon full on greased cookie sheet. Bake at 350 degrees. Take two cookies and spread with filling, holding them together.

Whoopie Pie Filling

2 egg whites
2 t vanilla
4 T flour
4 T milk
4 c. powdered sugar
1 c. Crisco
Beat egg whites until stiff. Add other ingredients. Spread between cookies and enjoy.

Homemade Hot Chocolate Mix

2 c. powdered milk
1 ¼ c white sugar
½ c unsweetened cocoa (bakers cocoa)
Stir all ingredients together and put in airtight container. Can use for up to 2 months. To use, mix 2-3 Tbsp. (heaping) of mix into a cup and fill with boiling water. Enjoy!

RECOMMENDED READING

Books mentioned in *The Amish Doll*

The following Amish books can be found at Scroll Publishing: **www.scrollpublishing.com**

Pathway: Devoted Christian's Prayer Book

This small book is a collection of prayers from an Amish and Mennonite prayer book that dates back to 1708 or earlier. It can be used in daily devotions or on special occasions. The book also includes the Dortrecht Confession of Faith and "Rules of a Godly Life." 124 pp. Hardback.

Family Life Magazine, a monthly magazine designed for adults and families. It contains articles on Christian living, parenting, and homemaking. It also contains editorials, letters from readers, medical advice, poems, recipes, and children's stories.

Devoted Christian's Prayer Book. A collection of prayers from an Amish and Mennonite prayer book.

1001 Questions and Answers on the Christian Life; This book covers virtually every aspect of the Christian life: salvation, baptism, the new birth, faith, prayer, discipleship, non-conformity to the world, child training, courtship, dress, nonresistance, swearing oaths, worship, and numerous other topics. The answers are from an Old Order Amish viewpoint, and so this book serves as a handy reference book on Amish beliefs.

The Martyr's Mirror Classic accounts of more than 4,000 Christians who endured suffering, torture, and a martyr's death because of their simple faith in the gospel of Christ. Songs, letters, prayers, and confessions appear with the stories of many nonresistant Christians who were able to love their enemies and return good for evil.

Books about Jesus.

More Than a Carpenter: Josh McDowell, Sean McDowell Tyndale House (2009)

Jesus Among Other Gods: The Absolute Claims of the Christian Message, Ravi Zacharias, W Publishing Group (February 8, 2002)

The Case for Christ, Lee Strobel, Zondervan; 1 edition (September 1, 1998)

The Jesus I Never Knew, Phillip Yancey, Zondervan (February 1, 2002)

Recommended Reading about the Amish

The Amish Way: Patient Faith in a Perilous World, Donald B. Kraybill, Steven M. Nolt, David L. Weaver-Zercher - John Wiley & Sons (2010)

The Riddle of Amish Culture: Donald B. Kraybill, The Johns Hopkins University Press; Revised edition (September 27, 2001)

The Amish in Their Own Words, Brad Igou, Herald Press (VA) (October 1999)

Think No Evil: Inside the Story of the Amish Schoolhouse Shooting...and Beyond, Jonas Bieler, Howard Books (September 22, 2009)

Books that Properly Portray the Seneca Indians of Western New York

A Friend Among the Seneca's: The Quaker Mission to Cornplanter's People. David Swatzler, Stackpole Books; 1st ed edition (November 1, 2000)

Light and the Glory: 1492-1793, Peter Marshall, David Manuel, Revell; (June 15, 2009)

A Narrative of the Life of Mrs. Mary Jemison, James E. Seaver, University of Oklahoma Press (March 15, 1995)

ACKNOWLEDGEMENTS

Jesus Christ, who keeps me knit together in His love.
(Psalm 139:13)

My husband, Tim Vogel, for coming up with the idea for the mystery of the Amish doll, and how the answer was under the black boot. You mysterious man, you. Love you much.

First Readers Betty Berkey, Karen Berkey, Bette Fisher & Karen Malena, Your encouragement gives me wings, and you corrections make me look better than I am.

Grace "Hawkeye" Yee, my gentle editor and friend. Someone who can say it like it is, but never leaving me discouraged. You're a gem.

Pittsburgh East Scribes writing group. I learn so much from you all.

My agent, Joyce Hart, who continues to believe I am a writer....

My readers...I keep writing by your encouragement.

CONTACT THE AUTHOR

Best-selling author Karen Anna Vogel is a trusted English friend among Amish in Western PA and NY. She strives to realistically portray these wonderful people she admires, most stories being based on true stories. Karen writes full-length novels, novellas and short story serials. She hopes readers will learn more about Amish culture and traditions, and realize you don't have to be Amish to live a simple life. Visit her popular blog, Amish Crossings at karenannavogel.blogspot.com

Karem is an empty nester, having four grown kids who flew the coop. Karen and her husband, Tim, enjoy homesteading in rural Pennsylvania. They run a family business, Thrifty Christian Shopper, an online business Karen created ten years ago

.Karen would love to get to know you better on her author page on Facebook, where all things Amish, knitting, gardening, simple living, recipes…..all things downhome goodness are shared amongst Karen's readers. https://www.facebook.com/VogelReaders

HOW TO KNOW GOD

God so loved the world, that He gave His only Son, that whoever believes in Him should not perish but have eternal life. John 3:16

God so loved the world

God loves you!

"I have loved you with an everlasting love." — Jeremiah 31:3

"Indeed the very hairs of your head are numbered." — Luke 12:7

That He gave His only Son

Who is God's son?

"Jesus answered, 'I am the way and the truth and the life. No one comes to the Father except through me.'" — John 14:6

That whoever believes in Him

Whosoever? Even me?

No matter what you've done, God will receive you into His family. He will change you, so come as you are.

"I am the Lord, the God of all mankind. Is anything too hard for me?"

— Jeremiah 32:27

"The Spirit of the Lord will come upon you in power, … and you will be changed into a different person." — 1 Samuel 10:6

Should not perish but have eternal life

Can I have that "blessed hope" of spending eternity with God?

"I write these things to you who believe in the name of Son of God so that you may know that you have eternal life." - 1 John 5:13

To know Jesus, come as you are and humbly admit you're a sinner. A sinner is someone who has missed the target of God's perfect holiness. I think we all qualify to be sinners. Open the door of your heart and let Christ in. He'll cleanse you from all sins. He says he stands at the door of your heart and knocks. Let Him in. Talk to Jesus like a friend…because when you open the door of your heart, you have a friend eager to come inside.

Bless you!

Karen Anna Vogel

If you have any questions, visit me at www.karenannavogel.com and leave a message in the contact form. I'd be happy to help you.

Made in United States
North Haven, CT
09 June 2022

19999406R00166